IMMORTAL CHAOS

Who Let the Gods Out?

About the Author

Mary Evans is quite old, has puddle-water eyes and very disobedient hair. She likes sunflowers, things that rhyme and eating pudding first. She doesn't like rude, getting up in the morning or Wednesdays.

I hope you enjoy my book.

This is where to find me. Or I might be in the park.

info@storystew.org
www.storystew.org
@StoryStew

IMMORTAL CHAOS

Who Let the Gods Out?

Mary Evans

Published by Story Stew, London 2014

First paperback edition printed 2014 in the United Kingdom.

ISBN 978-0-9928868-0-6

Printed and bound in Great Britain by Clays Ltd, St Ives plc
Typeset by Ellipsis Digital, Glasgow
Cover Design by Silent Deer, London

For more copies of this book or to contact the author,
please visit www.storystew.org

For Ian

It's something unpredictable.
But in the end that's right.

Contents

Chapter One

A Not Quite Normal Day

It began on a Friday, as strange things often do. This particular Friday had been stranger than most, although it had started normally enough. Elliot Hooper got up at 7.30am as normal, made his Mum breakfast at 8.15am as normal, went to school at 8.55am as normal and was in the headmaster's office by 9.30am, which was, in fact, slightly later than normal.

'Oh Elliot,' sighed Graham Sopweed, headmaster of Brysmore Grammar School. 'What are we going to do with you?'

He looked into the blue-green eyes of the 13-year-old boy before him, as Elliot scratched his shaggy blond head for an answer. Two years earlier, Graham Sopweed had watched as Elliot was proudly escorted through Brysmore's gates by his Mum, Nan and Grandad. The reports from his primary school had been glowing. 'Elliot Hooper is a wonderful student who is sure to set Brysmore alight,' his previous headmistress promised. There was no doubt that Elliot was a bright boy, but after a promising start, the past year had seen a big change in this young man – and not for the better. Elliot Hooper hadn't set Brysmore alight. But Mr Sopweed was more than a little concerned that he might set the school on fire.

'It's a tricky one, Sir,' Elliot replied after a lengthy pause. 'It's really a question of everyone's best interests. And the simple fact is that I don't want to be at this school, the teachers don't want me to be at this school, the pupils don't want me or the teachers to be at this school, so perhaps it's time we admitted defeat and everyone got home in time for *Deal or No Deal*.'

'Oh Elliot,' Mr Sopweed sighed again, shaking his floppy grey fringe into his eyes, before nervously flicking it out again. 'You know that's not going to happen. And you know you can call me Graham. Let's all use the names our mothers gave us.'

Elliot had many more creative names for his headmaster than the one his mother had given him, but the politest by far was Call Me Graham.

A sudden shout outside the office door nearly made the headmaster fall off his chair. Under other circumstances, Elliot might have felt slightly sorry for the nervous wreck of a man in front of him. The only mystery greater than how Graham Sopweed got the job of headmaster, was how he had managed to keep it. Everything about Call Me Graham was on edge, from his ever-flicked prematurely grey hair that disguised whether he was 25 or 50, to the fingers that fiddled nervously with the buttons on his beloved cardigans, to the awkward wiry body, which always seemed to be curled around itself in an instinctive act of self-preservation. The complete absence of a spine must have helped Call Me Graham to physically contort himself into this position, but the emotional reasons for doing so were less clear.

There were many theories around Brysmore as to why Call Me Graham was such a bag of nerves, not all of them started by Elliot. Some said it was because his wife had left him. Others said it was because she hadn't. There was even a school of thought that believed he was a serial killer on the run, terrified of being returned to the high-security institution for the criminally insane from which he had escaped. Elliot rather liked this last explanation and could imagine the appeals for Call Me Graham's capture on *Crimewatch*: '*So be on your guard against Graham Sopweed, the Cardigan-Clad Killer, and be sure to call this number if he's bored someone you know to death.*'

The ticking grandfather clock in the corner of the office was the only sound to fill Call Me Graham's nervous silence, unconsciously making him twitch every second as he considered his next stammering sentence.

'The thing is, Elliot, everyone at Brysmore wants to help you to achieve your fullest potential,' said Call Me Graham.

'Mmm. Not everyone, Sir,' said Elliot with a raised eyebrow.

'Well, I suppose that the dinner ladies didn't see the funny side of you turning the school canteen into a crime scene.'

'I was doing a public service!' insisted Elliot. 'Their custard is a health and safety hazard!'

'And Mr Britches has had to retrieve his underpants from the school flagpole on three separate occasions now.'

'I can't win!' said Elliot, raising his hands aloft. 'Mr Britches said I wasn't applying myself in PE. Shimmying up that flagpole took strength, stamina and speed. Not to mention a majorly strong stomach. Seriously, that man needs to apply himself to his laundry.'

'Then there's the small matter of all the items that have mysteriously vanished in your presence . . .'

'Where's the proof?!' exclaimed Elliot, holding his empty hands up. 'Innocent until proven guilty, Sir. I learnt that in Mr Fusty's Latin class. And he's guilty of crimes against fashion. Leather elbow patches? Really?'

'And as for Mr Boil—'

'Graham,' said Elliot, looking his headmaster squarely between the twitching eyes. 'If you had to exclude everyone at Brysmore that Mr Boil didn't like, you'd be left with the student teacher from Thailand who thinks Mr Boil's the Prime Minister and Gertrude, the Year 7 class gerbil.'

'The fact remains that you've been sent here again, Elliot. For disrupting assembly. Again,' said Call Me Graham, attempting to be forceful, but wishing he hadn't.

'I have a basic human right to peaceful protest!' exclaimed Elliot.

'Snoring over Mr Dungfold's birdwatching slideshow is hardly a peaceful protest, Elliot.'

'I can't help it if I have a stuffy nose, Graham,' said Elliot. 'Surely you're not going to punish me for my dodgy sinuses?'

'Well, er, of course not Elliot. But that's hardly the point.'

'I mean, we can't help our bodily flaws. You don't give Mr Punge detention for having bodily odour that could wake the dead, do you?'

'That's an entirely different issue.'

'Or make Mrs Halitosis do lines for criminal dental hygiene?'

'Her name is Mrs Haliburton, Elliot.'

'Or suspend Miss Ample for having a bum the size of Belgium?'

'That's enough, Elliot!' said Call Me Graham in a slightly raised voice, making himself jump. 'You have to start treating your teachers with more respect. Please. If you don't mind.'

'Message received and understood, Graham,' said Elliot, rising to his feet and giving Graham a sudden and not entirely welcome hug. 'From now on, I'm a changed man. Thank goodness the teaching profession has mentors like you to keep me on the straight and narrow.'

'Well, that's very kind of you, Elliot, but I'm only—'

'You are truly one of a kind, Sir,' said Elliot, pocketing the confiscation cupboard keys he had just lifted from Call Me Graham's cardigan pocket. 'Oh, and Mr Britches might want to leave it until this afternoon to reclaim his

Birmingham City boxer shorts – looks like it might rain.'

With that, and a quick detour via the confiscation cupboard, Elliot Hooper went about his day. And quite normal it was too – Elliot daydreamed his way through Maths, doodled his way through Geography, was spared French by getting sent outside after five minutes and spent an entire double Chemistry lesson wondering who'd win a fight between King Kong and Miss Braun, his sturdy football coach (Miss Braun on points). Before he knew it, another tiresome day at school was behind him and it was time for Elliot to head home for the weekend, quickly emptying his brain of the little information he had gathered that day.

At precisely three o'clock, Elliot joined the throngs of excited pupils racing down the main corridor, desperate to leave education behind to learn something in the real world. He could see the light shining outside the ornate double doors at the school's entrance. He could feel the warmth of the fresh, clean air that lay beyond the exit. He could taste the freedom of a whole school-free weekend stretching out before him. He could . . .

'Hoo-per!'

He could forget about going anywhere for the next ten minutes.

There was only one person who could make Elliot's surname sound like a dirty word. Only one man who could make Elliot's whole body groan at the sound of his voice.

Only one teacher he could smell from the middle of next week. It was the deputy headmaster, Mr Boil. And he was standing in front of the doors.

Elliot often pondered why someone who loathed children as much as Mr Boil did chose a job that forced him to spend all day around them. Mr Boil looked at anyone under eighteen in much the same way that most people look at used cat litter, with an expression that suggested he had a permanently nasty smell under his nose. And in fairness he did – his own.

Boil was as wide as he was tall, a stumpy, piggy little man who was the only person Elliot had ever seen with fat eyes. He squashed them behind a pair of thick, dark-rimmed glasses, which were sunk into his sneering snout, helping to magnify the hateful looks he bestowed on all his pupils, to whom he begrudgingly taught history. His few remaining strands of dark, greasy hair were pasted over the top of his head, held in place by hope alone in a sorry bid to conceal his growing baldness.

To the naked eye, Mr Boil had three chins, but who knew how many more were lurking beneath his shirt, which was always blue, always too small and always smelled like three-week-old vegetable soup. He truly seemed to hate all children, but reserved a special loathing for Elliot, who had been getting up his pudgy nose ever since he set foot in Brysmore. And who still hadn't returned his best underpants from the school flagpole.

'Where do you think you're going, Hooper?' sneered Mr Boil.

'Home, Sir,' said Elliot quietly. Three o'clock on a Friday was no time to be cheeking a teacher.

'The Brysmore rules forbid running in the school corridor, Hooper,' pronounced Boil like a vicar quoting the Bible on Sunday.

'Sorry, Sir,' mumbled Elliot, desperately hoping that Mr Boil had been given a complete character transplant and was going to let him off.

'And how many times have I warned you about your scruffy uniform?' continued Boil. 'Brysmore rules state that pupils should be presentable at all times. You look like a street urchin.'

'Yes, Sir,' Elliot mumbled hopelessly, feeling his freedom slipping away.

'I really should give you a detention, Hooper,' drooled Boil with a gleeful grimace, like a python toying with a mouse.

'No Sir, please—' Elliot stopped himself short, knowing it was pointless. Most teachers would forgive a moment's excitement at the end of the week. Most teachers wouldn't care about the odd missing button or scuffed shoe. Most teachers would have something better to do on a Friday afternoon. But Mr Boil wasn't most teachers and Elliot had been in this position too many times to waste his breath on begging.

'Arguing with a teacher, eh Hooper! That's it – I'll see you in my classroom in five minutes.' And with a triumphant snort, Boil wobbled off to find a suitably irritating detention for the miserable boy he left standing in the fading sunlight by the school doors.

An hour later, when Elliot had arranged every bookshelf in the history department into alphabetical order, he finally made it outside into the less sunny, but still very welcome evening air. The crowds of proud parents eagerly waiting to drive their children home had long since left, but no-one had been there for Elliot earlier and no-one was there for him now. No-one ever was. With a quick backward glance, Elliot dived off the driveway, hopped over the school fence into the fields beyond and started the long walk home.

The stroll back to Home Farm was Elliot's favourite part of his day. Or it was on sunny days – when it was pouring with rain he didn't feel the love for the mile-long hike. But today was one of those milky warm autumn evenings that made him content simply to walk beneath its honey-coloured sky. He raised his blond head to feel the sun on his face, pushing aside the floppy golden hair that constantly fell across his blue-green eyes.

Elliot squinted into the low autumn sunlight. Was that a star bobbing around in the late afternoon sky? Doubting his tired eyesight – he'd started to go cross-eyed somewhere around 'S' in Boil's book collection – Elliot stopped to have a better look. He was right – there in the middle of the daylight sky was a big, bright star. It struck him as odd, but before he could give it any more thought, his peace was interrupted by a gaggle of Brysmore girls walking in the opposite direction, pointing and staring at Elliot before retreating behind their hands in giggling fits.

Had Elliot listened to these, or any of the other silly girls at school, he would have known that he was considered one of the better-looking boys at Brysmore. But he didn't listen to what anyone said and he didn't care what anyone thought. He went through his school life – most of his life in fact – on his own. There was a time when he'd enjoyed the company of his classmates and might even have been considered quite popular. But things had changed. Right now he didn't have time for friends. And besides, friends had parents. And parents asked too many questions.

Elliot arrived at Home Farm just as the sun was resting on the horizon. He lifted the fraying rope that held the rotting gate in place and paused for a moment on the dusty path that led to the ramshackle farmhouse he called home. He and Grandad had laid that path together and every wonky step reminded Elliot of happier times. He looked at the ramshackle farmhouse that had been his family's home for generations. He could see the missing tiles that made the roof look like a mouth missing some teeth, the dirty windows that blocked more light than they let in and the peeling red paint on a door that could barely keep out a draught, let alone a burglar. And Elliot loved every crumbling brick.

He put his key in the lock – a pointless exercise for a door that could be knocked in by a strong cough – but before he could reach the sanctuary of his home, a terrible sound warbled down the path behind him.

'Coo-ee! Have you got a mo, Poppet?' the shrill voice screeched out behind him.

There were so many words in that sentence that irritated Elliot, but nothing as irritating as the person who said them. He raised an eyebrow, slapped on a fake grin and turned to face his tormentor.

'Hello Mrs Porshley-Plum,' he called in his least sincere voice.

'Hello Pickle!' Patricia Porshley-Plum shrieked in return, using one of the countless stupid nicknames she used in place of anyone's real name. 'Have you got a seccy?'

'I'll have to be quick – I need to—'

'Gre-eat!' squealed Patricia as she approached the house, tottering slightly as the heels on her shoes struggled with the uneven path and the knobbly knees they were supporting. 'Shall we go in for a cuppa?'

'I'd love to,' Elliot lied as he shut the door behind him, 'but Mum's not very well again.'

'Oh no! Whatever's the matter this time, Sugar-plum?' Mrs Porshley-Plum pouted dramatically, her dark pink lipstick making her mouth look like a monkey's bottom. 'Perhaps I should come in and see her?'

'It's catching,' said Elliot quickly, running out of imaginary illnesses to keep his mother away from this annoyingly nosy neighbour. 'And warty. And smelly. Seriously, you're better off out here.'

'I see,' said Patricia, her pointy face scanning every inch of her young neighbour, as if she could spot the lie on his trousers. Patricia's mouth always smiled. Her eyes never did. She straightened her jacket over her bony hips.

'Well, when she's feeling better, we must have That Chat,' she added with a ridiculous wink.

Patricia had been trying to have That Chat with Elliot's mum, Josie, for a while. At Nan's funeral the previous year, she had whispered to Josie at the graveside about her new property development business and how the farm was sitting on a valuable piece of land.

When the doctor came to Grandad's bedside six months later, Mrs Porshley-Plum came round the next day to make an offer for the farm to 'cover his nursing home fees'.

The day after Elliot and Josie laid Grandad to rest, Patricia Porshley-Plum called to say that if they fancied moving on now the two of them were all alone in the world, she'd happily take the farm off their hands for a quick sale.

'Patricia Horse's-Bum will never get her hands on this family's home!' Grandad had raged a few months before.

'She can keep her plastic houses for her plastic people. This is a real family home for a real family and if she thinks she can flash her cash and move us out of the place our family has called home for generations, then she can stick her cheque book . . .'

Josie hit him with a spatula.

But Grandad was right. Elliot needed to protect his family's home. He just didn't have a clue how he was going to do it. Yet.

'I'd better go and see to Mum – lovely to see you, Mrs Horse's . . . Mrs Porshley-Plum,' he said, going to open the door again.

'And you, Sweet-cheeks,' trilled Patricia, turning to leave. 'Get Mumsy to call me – aaargh!'

It wasn't clear whether it was because of the wonky paving stones, the ridiculous heels or her nose being due North in the air, but Patricia Porshley-Plum crashed down on the path like a hippo on a trampoline, spilling herself and the contents of her handbag all over it.

'Here, let me help you,' Elliot offered, bringing his neighbour to her feet. 'Let me get these for you.'

Elliot picked up the mysterious items that fill a lady's handbag and replaced nearly all of them. 'Here you go,' he said, giving the overflowing bag back to the world's most irritating neighbour.

'Thank you. I'll see you soon,' said Patricia, her eyes smiling even less than usual as she turned and staggered up the rest of the path, leaving Elliot to finally make it into his house. His front door closed on the world and Elliot took a moment to rest against it. Home. At last.

Elliot put his school bag down next to the usual pile of post on the mat. He picked the letters up. All were reminders about unpaid bills. As if he needed reminding.

'Mum,' he called softly in case she was enjoying an afternoon nap, 'I'm home.' He peered round the doorway into the cosy lounge, but Mum wasn't in her usual battered armchair by the fireplace. Elliot checked the kitchen, Mum's bedroom and tentatively knocked on all the bathroom doors, but there was no reply to his gentle calls.

Walking past the kitchen for a second time, Elliot noticed that the back door was slightly ajar. His stomach tightened into a familiar knot and he walked more urgently out into the farm's back garden.

He breathed a relieved sigh. There was Mum, kneeling on the grass, happily tending to her vegetable patch. Elliot watched her for a moment, chatting away to the empty garden, occasionally breaking into her own cheery song. He remembered a time when Mum had seemed so much bigger than him, when one of her hugs could smother him in a warm embrace of rose-scented love. But these days she seemed so small, so fragile, so . . . old.

Elliot and his Mum had lived with his grandparents since before he could remember. Elliot only knew two things about his Dad: he'd been very young when Elliot was born and he wasn't there now. Elliot never knew where he had gone, nor why, and whenever he asked Nan and Grandad about their only son, they simply looked sad and said he was too young to understand. Elliot thought his Dad had come to the farm once when he was very young. But he also remembered the Loch Ness Monster living in the bathtub around the same time, so didn't give much credit to his childish memory. Besides, his grandparents had made him happier than any Dad could have done, so Elliot wasn't going to waste energy on a father who obviously didn't care about him, when he'd been blessed with a mum and two grandparents who loved him to bits.

He walked over to where Mum was busily digging. She turned around and her happy face shone in a hundred places as it always did when she saw her beloved son. The blue-green eyes that could have been Elliot's own glistened with delight as she pushed her matching messy blonde hair out of her face with a soil-covered hand. She reached up to give her boy a hug.

'So how was your day, Elly?' she smiled.

'Really great,' Elliot lied. 'Top of the class in history – my teacher was so pleased with me, he didn't want me to come home.'

'You're so clever, Elliot.'

'Must take after you, Mum. So what are you plant—'

He stopped as he realised what his mother was doing. A packet of unopened carrot seeds lay by her side and she was putting the final loving touches to planting a bag of clothes pegs.

Elliot's heart sank. It was happening again.

'Come on Mum, it's getting cold. Let's get you inside.'

He helped his mum up and gently guided her back towards the house. Taking one last look above as the night sky drew in, he thought he saw the same bright star he had noticed in the field. Only this time, it seemed closer and was flitting around the sky, as if . . . Elliot shook his head at his own silly notion. Stars didn't get lost. He was tired and needed to eat. He walked Mum to the lounge, sat her in the chair by the fire and went to the kitchen to prepare their supper.

Elliot couldn't pinpoint exactly when Mum started acting strangely. The last year had passed in such a blur of worrying about Nan and Grandad when they were ill, then grieving for them when they died, that he hadn't really noticed Mum's odd behaviour until a few months ago. Or at least he thought so. Maybe it had always been there.

It started with small things – she'd lose something she'd had two minutes ago, or couldn't remember the name of a person or a place. At first, Elliot thought these were the normal short circuits of a stressed and tired mind. But the memory lapses soon became more serious – forgetting there was food in the oven or leaving the bath running. Then one day, Elliot came home from school and Mum was nowhere to be found. He ran down the path to the village and found

Mum in the middle of the road in her nightdress, lost and confused with no idea where she lived. He couldn't ignore it any longer, Mum needed his help. By doing all the shopping, cooking and housework, Elliot had convinced himself that everything was going to be okay. But deep down he knew that Mum needed a doctor.

But it wasn't that simple. What if the doctor said Mum couldn't look after him? What if they took her away? Nan and Grandad had dreaded being put in 'heaven's waiting room' as they called the old people's home and even when Grandad became really ill and the doctor wanted him in hospital, Mum was adamant she could look after him better at home.

'He was born in this bed and he'll die in it,' she stubbornly insisted and cared round the clock for her beloved father-in-law, right until the moment he died in his sleep six months ago.

And what would happen to Elliot if Mum was taken away? He didn't even know if his Dad was alive, much less where he was – and with no other family, where would he go? No, it was better this way. Mum had cared for him all his life and now it was his turn to care for her. If he could just keep everyone else's noses out, they'd be fine. Really.

Elliot opened the kitchen cupboard, even though he knew exactly what it contained. A box of tea-bags, some stale digestives, three small tins of beans and half a loaf of bread. He looked in the chipped cookie jar that guarded their weekly spending money and counted the remaining £3.76 inside. He put the £20 note he had just 'borrowed' from Mrs Porshley-Plum's handbag into the tin and added a note to all the others reminding him he owed money. He'd had to 'borrow' a lot of money lately. There were a lot of notes in the tin.

Nan and Grandad had never trusted banks and the farm used to provide most of their food, so they kept their life savings in a tin under the bed. Elliot was careful to use as little of the money as he could, but he knew it was running out. The farm had long since stopped running and there were only so many vegetables he and Mum could grow. Over time, the workers had left and the animals were sold – all except Bessie, the lame cow Elliot had raised from a calf.

Elliot's early morning paper round brought in a bit of money, but there was barely enough for the basics, let alone the expensive things he needed for school. He remembered Mr Boil's moan about his uniform and made a mental note to try to sew some buttons on his only shirt and polish the shoes that had been too tight since Easter before he returned to school on Monday.

'Beans on toast alright for tea, Mum?' he called through to the lounge.

'Lovely darling, haven't had that for a while,' she replied cheerfully.

Mum's forgetfulness worried Elliot a lot. But if it stopped her from remembering that beans on toast had been their supper every night for the past three weeks, perhaps it wasn't all bad.

He made their meal and sat in front of their small black and white TV to watch a cooking show Mum enjoyed on Friday nights. By nine o'clock Mum was falling asleep in her chair – she slept a lot now – so Elliot gently woke her and helped her upstairs to bed. He laid her nightgown out on the bed, left the room while she changed, then came back to settle her in for the night.

'Do you have everything you need?' he asked as he did every night when he tucked the sheets around her.

'As long as I have you,' she replied as she did every night before she went to sleep. 'You're a miracle, Elliot. Good-night my darling.'

He stayed for a few moments until Mum fell asleep, then crept quietly out of the room and back downstairs.

He returned to the empty lounge, cleared away the supper things and sank down into the comfy armchair. He glanced at the gold watch his Grandad had worn every day of his life, and which he had given to Elliot the day before he died.

'Time is precious,' were his final words to his grandson as his trembling hands put the watch around Elliot's wrist. 'Don't waste a second, my brilliant boy.'

Elliot looked at the time. It was still early, so he flicked the television back on. The elderly set could only receive four channels – three if it was windy – and with nothing on, Elliot picked up the mountain of bills, each one threatening more extreme action if the owner wasn't paid. Water, gas, electricity – the list went on and on.

And then, right at the bottom of the pile, there was The Really Scary Letter.

The Really Scary Letter had arrived three weeks ago and had cost Elliot more sleep than all the others put together. There were no Really Scary Letters mentioned when Mum had seen the advert on the telly promising instant loans if you owned a house. In fact the letter that arrived with the cheque to pay for Grandad's funeral – and the bit extra they'd suggested Mum borrowed on top – was as friendly as the man on the advert, who seemed very happy about the 'hassle-free instant cash' and 'affordable monthly repayments'.

But the monthly repayments weren't that affordable after all. And the cash hadn't been hassle-free. And the man wasn't very friendly when you couldn't pay his money back.

'Dear Mrs Hooper,' Elliot read for the millionth time. 'We act on behalf of EasyMoney Ltd. Your failure to make payments in accordance with your loan obligation of £20,000 has resulted in proceedings to recover possession of Home Farm, Little Motbury, Wiltshire. If the outstanding monies reach us by one calendar month from the date of this letter, no further action will be taken. If you do not take the action required, your home will be repossessed on 24th October . . .'

The letter waffled on for another two pages, but Elliot

understood what it meant in plain English. Unless he found twenty thousand pounds in a week, he and Mum were going to lose their home. And then where would they go?

Elliot picked up another letter from the electricity company. 'We regret to inform you that due to non-payment of your outstanding balance, your service will be terminated on—'

The rest was lost as the house was plunged into darkness.

Elliot pulled out the torch, candles and matches he kept nearby for every time the electricity was cut off and did some rough sums on the back of his maths homework. He could pay the electricity bill tomorrow – thank you Mrs Porshley-Plum – but that would leave them less than five pounds for food next week. But next week would have to take care of itself. Elliot quietly promised that if he was ever rich, he'd never eat a baked bean again.

After a series of gaping yawns told him it was time for bed, Elliot remembered that Bessie needed feeding. He grabbed the torch, pulled on his untied trainers and stepped into the cool evening air to make the short walk to Bessie's cowshed. Looking up at the clear starry night and with no light polluting the sky from his house, Elliot saw the same bright star wandering around the night sky, only this time it was even bigger than before and moving much faster.

He watched the star fly through the air, but rather than shoot across the sky, it was starting to drop. Elliot stopped to take a better look. He was right, the star was falling, and as it came nearer, Elliot could see that it wasn't a single star at all, but a ball of stars, gaining speed and size every second it hurtled towards the ground. The star-ball was out of control and as it plummeted to Earth, Elliot looked around to see what it was going to hit when it landed. His question was quickly answered by an almighty bang a few yards from where he stood.

The stars had come crashing to the ground. Right in the middle of his cowshed.

Chapter Two

A Star is Born

Virgo didn't come down to Earth with a bump – more of a damp, loud, splat. For a moment, the young Goddess lay absolutely still, trying to figure out exactly what had just happened. Surely such a great fall should have shattered her into a million pieces?

But in the darkness she thought she could feel her arms and she thought she could move her legs. Indeed, the fact she was thinking at all was probably a good sign, so she decided to risk some small movements. She slowly wiggled her legs until her feet met with some solid ground. This was good news and, greatly encouraged, Virgo groped around with her hands to see what had broken her fall. She felt the immediate area around her body, but every time she put a hand down, it simply disappeared into the squelchy substance upon which she had landed.

She let out a tired sigh and lay back in the mush. Today had been unusually trying. It had started out well enough back in Elysium, the heavenly home she shared with her fellow members of the Zodiac Council. Her morning began, as it did every day, with a council meeting to discuss the daily issues that arose in the immortal community. Virgo perched upright on her sumptuous purple chair – sofa, really – one of twelve that surrounded the golden table divided into twelve sections, each elaborately engraved with every councillor's Zodiac sign.

Virgo had only ever lived in Elysium, so she'd never really noticed the splendour of the council chamber, a beautiful glass pyramid, which refracted rainbow light from the marble floor and looked out in every direction over the flawless paradise the Zodiac Council called home. The view altered depending on who was looking out on it – everyone's paradise is different. For Virgo, she looked out on a sunny meadow filled with flowers, tame ponies and a golden fountain that dispensed whatever liquid you wished for. As she debated whether a banana milkshake or a hot chocolate best suited her mood today, Virgo plucked a chocolate-covered grape from one of the crystal bowls that overflowed with extravagant delicacies around the table. But then decided she'd prefer a chocolate croissant, which instantly appeared by her side.

She looked out of the window at another perfect day in her perfect home. She knew how lucky she was – after all, who wouldn't want to live in paradise? It was, well, perfect. Once the Council's business was done for the day, perhaps she'd fly a unicorn over the marshmallow meadows? Or swim with the dolphins in the warm waters of Honey River? Or possibly ride the rollercoasters at Wonderland? Or maybe not – she'd done all of those things yesterday. Or was it the day before? Or last week maybe? Virgo couldn't remember and there was no-one to remind her. But that was fine. Her life, like her home, was completely perfect. And if she'd had a friend to tell, she would have told them exactly that.

Virgo was only half-listening as the other eleven members of the Council (twelve if you counted the Gemini twins separately) discussed whether to renew Dionysus's pub licence, or if the Cyclopes were entitled to half-price eyecare. Her mind soon started to wander – not because she was bored, merely thinking. She looked around the table at her follow councillors and wondered if they were as fascinated by debating the same topics every day as she was. Administering the immortal community was, after all, an immense privilege – it had been for thousands of years and would continue to be for thousands more. Yes. Thousands more years doing exactly the same thing. Virgo remembered again how very lucky she was.

'Virgo!' shouted Aries the golden ram, snapping her out of her gratitude. 'So have you done it?'

Virgo tried to look as if she'd been listening, but realised that either of the two possible answers could be wrong. Deciding that no answer was better than the wrong one, she shrugged a bemused apology.

'For goodness' sake, child, pay attention,' snapped Aries, a frustrated bleat escaping his black lips. 'The Muses need that stationery order right away! It's no use being the source of all creativity if you can't find a paperclip.'

'Yes – right – of course,' said Virgo, picking up her golden quill and scratching 'paperclips' on a large piece of parchment. A job. Excellent. That should keep her busy for . . .

'So if we're happy to agree that Orpheus can do another stadium tour – so long as he stops by 11pm so he doesn't upset the Furies – then I think that's everything. Ah. No. One more thing. Thanatos,' Aries announced to a chorus of moans from the chamber as he produced an ornate golden flask with 'Semper Iuvenis' engraved on the front.

Virgo's ears pricked up. She'd heard of the Thanatos job – the only one that required Council members to leave Elysium and deliver a dose of ambrosia to an imprisoned daemon on Earth. It was particularly unpopular amongst the Council, but as the youngest councillor, Virgo had never been allowed to do it. Her mind started to buzz with excitement.

'Any volunteers?' Aries asked.

At that moment, every single pair of eyes in the chamber had somewhere to be that wasn't looking at Aries. Whether it was something fascinating they just wrote down, something had just caught their eye out of the window, or an imaginary speck of dust (although no such thing existed in Elysium) on their robes, not one individual met the golden ram's gaze.

Virgo held her breath. Perhaps it was her turn at last. She raised a tentative hand.

'Uh, Aries? I could always do it,' she piped up.

'Do what?' said Aries impatiently.

'Take the ambrosia to Thanatos,' said Virgo quietly.

As the laughter of her colleagues echoed around the chamber, Virgo remembered how lucky she was that there were such excellent acoustics in her workplace.

'Don't be ridiculous,' snorted the ram. 'You're only a child.'

'I'm nearly fourteen thousand years old,' Virgo challenged, to an outpouring of 'Aw bless' from her colleagues.

'No,' declared Aries finally. 'This is an important job for an *experienced* councillor. You stick to your paperclips.'

'But I—'

'Enough!' snapped Aries. 'My decision is final.'

Virgo accepted this wise and fair decision without question. Curiously, at exactly that same moment, her golden quill snapped in two between her hands.

'Well then, if we have no other offers, I volunteer Taurus,' pronounced Aries towards the bull, who was crocheting a scarf with his horn.

'Me?' whined Taurus, 'it can't be my turn again. Capricorn hasn't done it for millennia.'

'Oh yes I have,' snorted the indignant half-goat Capricorn, spitting out the pencil she had been chewing. 'I had to do it in the middle of a plague. The place stank. If anyone's been shirking, it's fish-features over there.'

'Put a sock in it you old goat!' yelled Cancer the crab, 'I went during the Norman Conquest – I caught so many arrows in my shell I looked like a hedgehog. What about Castor and Pollux? Just because they're only one constellation shouldn't mean they only get one turn.'

'Bog off,' huffed the Gemini twins simultaneously and, before long, as so often happened at council meetings, an all-out fight had broken out around the golden table.

'Take that you big drip,' yelled Scorpio as he hurled Libra's scales at Aquarius, who threw his Aquarian water jug at Pisces, accidentally hitting Cancer and earning himself a very personal nip from her pincers.

'Shut it, Goldilocks!' shouted Sagittarius the centaur, who fired a banana from his bow, splattering squashed fruit all over Leo's flowing mane.

Virgo looked around at the unfolding carnage.

And something happened.

She never knew what inspired her to leave her perfect life in her perfect home. All Virgo knew was that it was the perfect moment to go.

Dodging the flying insults, fruit and body parts, she quietly picked up the flask, slipped it into her white robes and transformed into her glittering Virgo constellation to make the trip to Earth.

Whooshing up into the heavens as a shower of stars, Virgo felt gloriously happy and free. The Earth was so beautiful from up here, like a glassy marble. She flew closer to see the sights of this planet she'd heard so much about. It was extraordinary – one minute she was flying over dense jungle pulsing with every species of creature imaginable, the next, vast deserts with no life in sight for thousands of miles. Everything was just so . . . different. Not perfect – just different.

Indeed, Virgo was so excited by this brave new world that it took her some time to realise that she was missing one useful piece of information.

She had precisely no idea where she was going.

She knew that Thanatos's prison was marked by a stone circle, but from up high, she couldn't make anything out. She decided to drop a little to get a closer look. She had never visited Earth before and, as night started to fall, she became increasingly disorientated. She decided to drop lower still to get her bearings, but suddenly a huge metal bird came charging straight towards her with a deafening roar. Confused in the darkness and knowing she was forbidden to cause any harm to Earth's creatures, Virgo spun out of control, crash-landing here, in this odd squishy mess.

Now that the shock of being in one piece had passed, Virgo's nostrils were hit by a truly disgusting stench. She quickly realised it was coming from her squishy seat and her floundering around had spread it all over her long silver hair and her white robes. Whatever the risks of her new environment, they couldn't be worse than this, so with a great heave, she pulled herself to her feet and took a better look at her crash-site.

She found herself in a large, dark cavern that seemed to

contain nothing but straw. The only light came from the hole her dramatic entrance had made in the roof and, at first sight, that appeared to be her only way out again. As her eyes grew accustomed to the dark, she could make out another figure – to her great relief, she recognised the form as a female Bovinor, the same species as Taurus on the Zodiac Council. This was good news – Bovinors were renowned for their wisdom and Virgo knew that she was in safe hooves. She walked over to make the Bovinor's acquaintance, remembering that Taurus was a stickler for good manners.

'Greetings, Lady Bovinor, my apologies for my abrupt arrival,' whispered Virgo, bending into an awkward curtsey.

Bessie turned slowly to look at the source of the noise and to check if it was holding any food.

'Forgive me interrupting your solitude,' Virgo continued, 'but could you tell me where I might find Thanatos?'

Realising that Virgo wasn't there to feed her, Bessie returned to sniffing her udders, releasing a wholly unimpressed moo as she did.

'I'm so sorry your ladyship, I'm not entirely familiar with your accent,' said Virgo, crouching down to try to catch Bessie's eye. 'Would you mind telling me where I am?'

Bessie once more had nothing to say, although she did release a loud, wet noise from her backside that Virgo didn't understand, but it certainly smelt like the conversation was over.

'Well, er, thanks for your time anyway,' she said, discreetly trying to cover her nose as she backed away from Bessie's parting shot.

Outside the cowshed, Elliot was unsure what to do. Upon impact, he'd expected the cowshed to explode into a ball of flame, but all the star-ball seemed to have done was make a dirty great hole in the roof. He had heard Bessie's moo, so knew she was okay, but didn't know whether he should risk going inside. No, whatever it was, it couldn't be good news. The sensible thing to do would be to head back to the farm and lock the door. Whatever it was, it could wait until morning. Yes, that would definitely be the rational, logical and safest thing to do . . .

Five seconds later, Elliot slowly pushed at the big door of the cowshed.

As the door creaked open, Virgo realised she was completely unarmed. She retreated to the mush and grabbed the nearest thing to hand to await her attacker.

Elliot didn't really know what to expect as he entered the murky darkness of the dilapidated cowshed, but he certainly wasn't prepared for what he found. As his eyes learned to read the darkness, he could make out a figure in the gloom. Stood in the large pile of cow dung in the corner was a girl, no older than himself, dressed in a white fancy dress toga with a long silver wig. Her big round eyes were as dark as the night outside and she was doing her best to twist her delicate features into a ferocious stare, but only ended up looking like a slightly grumpy china doll. And she was pointing a large, yellow rubber glove threateningly in Elliot's direction.

'Don't move mortal, I'm not afraid to use this,' she said, waggling the rubber glove menacingly at the young, fair human who had appeared before her.

'I've seen where the vet puts that glove,' said Elliot to this strange, angry girl. 'Trust me, I'm not coming anywhere near you.'

Virgo inched closer to Elliot, never taking her eyes from his.

'Where am I?' she asked.

'In the cowshed,' Elliot replied.

Virgo looked straight at him. She had never heard of the Cow Shed region of Earth and didn't know if the inhabitants were friendly.

'Tell me Madam Bovinor,' she whispered over her shoulder to Bessie, 'can this child be trusted?'

Turning and seeing Elliot, Bessie was relieved that food was on the way and let out a friendly moo.

'That's good enough for me,' said Virgo, putting the glove down and approaching Elliot. She held out her hand. 'I'm Virgo, Goddess of the Zodiac Council and Guardian of the Stationery Cupboard. And you are?'

Elliot took her hand tentatively. 'I'm Elliot. What the heck are you doing in my shed?'

'Looking for Thanatos, Mr What-the-Heck-Are-You-Doing-In-My-Shed. Is he here?'

'Is who here?'

'Than-a-tos,' Virgo spelled out, as if she were talking to a deaf baboon. 'Daemon of Death. Where is he?'

'Oh, Thanatos,' said Elliot sarcastically. 'Walk down the road to the nearest Yeti and take a left at the Bogeyman. Thanatos lives two doors down.'

'Don't be absurd,' said Virgo snootily. 'Everyone knows that the Bogeyman lives in Belgium. It's not your fault. I've heard how simple you mortals are. If you don't know where Thanatos is, I'll have to find him myself. Good-day.'

Virgo marched out of the barn into the cold night. Elliot instinctively knew that getting involved with this girl would be trouble. He knew he should just go back to the house and worry about how he was going to pay for the roof. And he knew he couldn't let a teenage girl, clearly suffering from some sort of concussion, go wandering around the lonely Wiltshire countryside on a cold, dark night.

He threw some feed into Bessie's trough and ran after Virgo, who was wandering aimlessly down the path.

'Hey,' he called after her, 'Goddess girl.'

'Virgo,' said the Goddess grandly.

'Yes, you,' Elliot said dismissively. 'Look, it's really late and it's really dark – come back to my house and you can call your parents or whoever to pick you up. You can't walk around here all night, you'll freeze to death.'

'I cannot do anything to death, human, I am immortal.'

'Yes and I'm the Queen of Sheba,' said Elliot impatiently. 'Come on, come with me.'

Virgo thought about it. The Earth boy seemed safe enough and there was some sense in what he said. She wasn't going to find Thanatos in the dark tonight and besides, she was curious to discover more about this odd new world and the simple creatures who inhabited it.

'Very well, your Majesty,' she said. 'Show me to your home.'

An hour later, the two strangers were in front of the cosy fire in the dark farmhouse. Elliot gave Virgo a pair of his old combats, trainers and a T-shirt to replace her ruined robes and offered her the bathroom to remove the worst of the dung from her long hair. He made them both a cup of tea on the gas stove and had spent the last half an hour trying to obtain any information that might explain where she came from. It wasn't going well.

'So let me get this straight,' he sighed for the umpteenth time. 'You're an immortal Goddess who lives in Ilium?'

'Elysium,' corrected Virgo.

'Right, there,' said Elliot, 'and you travelled to Earth from the sky in your big star-ball?'

'Constellation,' said Virgo, who was fascinated by how soggy she could make her biscuit before it plopped into her tea. 'Constellation travel is one of the most sophisticated transport systems in the immortal world.'

'So sophisticated it landed you in a pile of cow dung?'

'That was unfortunate,' snapped Virgo defensively. 'I haven't visited Earth before and got a little lost in all the pollution you humans have created. Your atmosphere is filthy.'

'And now you have to go and give that flask to this Thermos bloke?'

'Thanatos.'

'Yeah, him, and then you'll just turn back into stars and whizz back up to Elision?'

'Elysium,' Virgo repeated impatiently.

'Yes, there. And you're like, a million years old?'

'Actually,' said Virgo huffily, as the last of her biscuit fell into her tea. 'I'm thirteen thousand, nine-hundred and seventy-four.'

This was getting silly. Elliot knew girls were funny about their ages – his Maths teacher, Mrs Goodwinge, had been 38 for the past five birthdays – but this was ridiculous.

'Are you sure I can't call your parents?' he sighed yet again.

'How many times, child – I don't have parents. I am a Goddess of the Zodiac Council, sent here to deliver ambrosia to an imprisoned death daemon. But if that's too much for your feeble human brain to comprehend,' she said matter-of-factly, rising to leave, 'then I'll be on my way.'

Elliot didn't know what to do. He really couldn't let this mad girl leave on her own, but if she wouldn't let him call anyone . . . it was better if she stayed here tonight. At least that way she was safe and tomorrow he could take her into the village and find her some help.

'No, don't go,' he said, 'please stay. But it's late, we both need some sleep. We've got loads of rooms here, I'll find you a bed.'

'Thank you, kind Elliot, but immortals don't require sleep.'

'Of course you don't,' said Elliot, too tired to argue with this crazy girl any more. 'Well, if you change your mind, there's a quilt on the sofa and you can sleep under that. Promise me you won't run off in the night?'

'I swear it on the River Styx,' she said solemnly. 'Immortals cannot break their oaths.'

'Marvellous,' said an exhausted Elliot. 'I'll see you in the morning.'

'Sleep well, human child,' said Virgo.

'Stay awake, loony star girl,' mumbled Elliot as he climbed the stairs and hauled his exhausted body off to his bed.

Chapter Three

The Swimming Lesson

Despite his tiredness, Elliot had a lousy night's sleep. The thought of Virgo – or whatever the delusional Goddess constellation nutter called herself – stealing the family silver kept him tossing and turning for half the night. The fact that his family didn't have any silver helped him to sleep for the other half, but barely had the new day broken before Elliot was pulling on his clothes and heading downstairs.

He expected to find Virgo snoring beneath the patchwork quilt that hid the holes on the back of the sofa. But as he reached the bottom of the stairs, he saw she was wide-awake in front of the telly. From what he could tell, the sofa hadn't been disturbed, but nor did Virgo show any signs of having been awake all night as she scowled at the TV.

'Morning,' said Elliot cautiously.

'Good morning Elliot,' said Virgo, still watching the television. 'I hope you enjoyed a better night than I did.'

Elliot was about to launch into a tirade about how actually, a lunatic head-case crashing into his cowshed had rather disturbed his evening. But something more important struck him. Virgo was watching television. They had electricity.

'What, how?' he mumbled sleepily, trying to find words that had yet to wake up.

'Well I must say that your hospitality puts your fellow mortals to shame,' launched Virgo, clearly relishing the chance to have a moan. 'These little people who live in this box are incredibly rude.'

Elliot looked at the soap opera Virgo was watching on the telly as he tried to figure out how the power had been miraculously restored to his home.

'I have been trying to make conversation with them all night,' she huffed. 'But every single one has completely ignored me. I didn't mind so much earlier when some of them had to go and fight werewolves – we've all been there – but these people are downright stupid. Take this woman,' she said, pointing to a well-known soap actress. 'I tried to advise her against running away with this man, but would she listen? Now she's trapped in a car with a man who killed his own mother only twenty minutes ago. And he ran over the neighbour's dog. And pretended to be his own sister. Oh and I re-routed your electricity through your neighbour's circuit. This place was like a cave.'

Elliot stared at Virgo through his sleepy red eyes. The mad star girl was also an electrician. Interesting. And he only had one neighbour – Patricia Porshley-Plum. Virgo had 'borrowed' electricity from Mrs Horse's Bum without paying for it. That wasn't right. Elliot knew what he had to do.

'So show me how to do that?' he asked Virgo as he went to make Mum her tea and toast.

Half an hour later, armed with a basic knowledge of how to re-route his electricity courtesy of Mrs Horse's Bum, Elliot gave Virgo her flask and bundled her out of the door before Mum could see her. As the initial excitement of another financial problem temporarily solved faded, Elliot's lack of sleep started to catch up with him. The two curious strangers walked in silence down the path and onto the track that led to the nearby village. Elliot wasn't a morning person at the best of times, and now, courtesy of his sleepless night, he was even grumpier than usual.

After they had been walking for a few minutes, Virgo spoke up.

'I have a feeling, young Elliot, that you might not entirely belicve what I've been telling you,' she ventured.

'No. Really?' Elliot grumbled as he chewed on his toast, wishing he had peanut butter. Or any butter.

'It's true,' she said, oblivious to his tone. 'I appreciate it must be confusing for your small mortal brain, but I really am an immortal Goddess, sent to administer this ambrosia to Thanatos.'

'Actually, I don't care,' snapped Elliot, stopping to face her. 'I don't care that you think you're an immortal tea-lady. I don't care that you're a walking fireworks display. I don't care if the Easter Bunny forgot your birthday and the Tooth

Fairy cancels your lunch plans. I have real problems in the real world and this whole weird fantasy of yours is really getting on my wick.'

Virgo considered his outburst.

'Well that's up to you,' she said calmly. 'Although I'm sorry the Tooth Fairy bothered you with our social arrangements. She can be thoughtless like that.'

'Oh for—' Elliot hissed as he stormed away.

Virgo ran to catch up with him.

'But if nothing else, I can prove to you that I am immortal,' she said, looking around. 'I just have to find a way not to die.'

'Don't try too hard,' grumbled Elliot, refusing to slow down.

Virgo lit upon a river that flowed a few metres away from the track.

'Aha,' she said. 'Here we are – follow me.'

She ran from the path and over the grass to the riverbank. Again, Elliot considered leaving her to her lunacy. But again, his better self made him follow this strange girl to the water's edge.

'Right,' said Virgo, 'if I were a mere mortal, I could stay underwater for thirty seconds maybe?'

'Something like that,' said Elliot, arms folded, refusing to play along.

'Okay then,' nodded Virgo as she walked down the bank and waded, fully clothed, into the river.

With a guilty heart, Elliot realised this had gone far enough. 'Look, you don't have to prove anything,' he said, snapping out of his bad mood. 'Don't do anything stupid, let's just find someone who can help you.'

'Urgh, it's cold in here and this water is just revolting,' moaned Virgo, striding on regardless. 'Does it not occur to mankind to keep anything just a little bit clean? After all, it won't all be here forever and then you'll be right in the glug, glug, glug—'

The remainder of Virgo's complaint was lost as her silver head disappeared under the rippled surface of the river, which swallowed her up with a gentle suck.

'She even talks underwater,' Elliot said to the empty space beside him as he glanced at his watch. He didn't need to worry – Virgo hadn't even paused for breath – she'd be out of there in no time.

Twenty seconds. Elliot looked around for the tell-tale bubbles that would show where Virgo was, probably already heading to the surface to warm up. Nothing. Not even a ripple. She was stubborn, that was for sure.

Forty-five seconds. Fair play, the girl could hold her breath. She'd come bursting out of that river with an almighty gasp any second now. Any second at all. Absolutely any second now. Elliot started looking around for something to warm her with when she'd finished her silly stunt. Virgo might be a pain in the bum, but he didn't want her to catch pneumonia.

One minute and fifteen seconds. Elliot felt his heart quicken. He'd been so busy getting cross with Virgo, it suddenly occurred to him that maybe she actually believed all this rubbish. What if she really did think she was immortal and was floating unconscious down the river whilst he stood there like a lemon? He could be responsible for the life of a seriously unwell young girl. What would he tell her parents? What would he tell the police?

Two minutes. Elliot was now in a full-blown panic. He'd stood by and let this poor sick girl drown herself just because he'd had a crummy night's sleep. He was going to prison and rightly so. He was a horrible human being. There was nothing else for it. He had to go in after her.

Elliot kicked off his shoes, pulled off his grandfather's watch and ripped off his T-shirt. He was about to lose his jeans, but looking at the early morning mist rising from the cold water, he quickly thought better of it. With a deep breath for air – and another for courage – Elliot plunged into the freezing cold river. The water bit him with a thousand icy teeth, but he didn't even notice as he thrashed around, frantically shouting Virgo's name. Once, twice, three times he dived beneath the murky surface, but he couldn't see or feel Virgo anywhere. He stood breathless in the middle of the river, desperately looking for any sign of the girl he'd left to drown. He threw his hands into the water in despair. She had gone. And it was all his fault.

'Let's hope you're immortal,' called Virgo as she suddenly

popped up from the water behind him and calmly walked up onto the bank, picking up Elliot's discarded T-shirt to dry her soaking hair. 'Or you're going to freeze to death in there.'

Elliot whipped round at the sound of her voice. This was impossible. She'd been underwater for nearly five minutes.

'What? How? You should be—' he spluttered.

'Well here we are again' sighed Virgo. 'Hello. I'm Virgo. I'm immortal. Shall we move on?'

She held out her hand to help a shivering Elliot out of the river. He took it gingerly, as if Bigfoot had just offered to shake hands. Virgo handed him his soggy T-shirt, which he put on in a silent stupor, his mouth still agog from what he had just witnessed. He shivered in a wet, confused, trembling puddle.

'Hold my hands,' the young Goddess instructed the freezing boy, who obeyed her in a daze. As they stood together by the river, Virgo closed her eyes and muttered mystical words that sounded like a song with no tune. At her chant, a million tiny stars crept from every millimetre of her body, trickling out into the air in wisping curls of light. These golden strands reached around them both, intertwining and forming an embrace of light, surrounding them both with a warm starry glow. Elliot felt the gentle heat seep into his soaking clothes and beyond, penetrating his skin and warming him from the core of his body. In seconds, Elliot was warm and dry.

'Better?' asked Virgo.

'Better,' answered Elliot, scouring every inch of his immortal companion's face for clues.

'Now, can we please find what I'm looking for?'

'What's that?'

'When the Gods imprisoned Thanatos, they marked his prison with a circle of stone. I know it's around here somewhere—'

'You mean Stonehenge?' said Elliot.

'Maybe,' said Virgo. 'Is it a prison?'

Elliot thought of the umpteen tedious school trips he'd been forced to endure at the prehistoric tourist attraction in hours of cold, wet boredom.

'Yup, that's the one,' he said. 'It's about ten minutes walk that way. I'll take you.'

'Excellent,' said Virgo. 'I'll be back in Elysium for pudding.'

She strode off across the fields, forcing Elliot to run to keep up with her confident pace. They walked in silence as Elliot reassessed all the information Virgo had given him since they met.

'So who is this Thanatos?' he asked.

'Thanatos was – well, technically still is I suppose – the ruler of the daemons,' explained Virgo.

'Is he like you?'

Virgo pulled up in indignation.

'You mean is he a God? He most certainly is not,' she huffed. 'Gods are flawless. Daemons are a nasty breed, who delighted in doing all the unpleasant jobs that the Gods didn't want when we ruled over humans. They looked after illness, old age, misery, all of mankind's ills. Thanatos was the Daemon of Death. It was his job to decide when a mortal's time was up, then he'd escort them down to the Underworld, where they'd be judged by Hades about where they'd spend eternity.'

'Kind of like the Grim Reaper?' said Elliot.

'That old softie?' laughed Virgo. 'Grim's a puppy dog next to Thanatos. He sells life insurance these days. No, Thanatos is a nasty piece of work by all accounts. Hates mortals for living, hates Gods more for never dying.'

'So what's Thanatos doing at Stonehenge?' asked Elliot.

'He's under it,' explained Virgo as she strode along. 'Zeus imprisoned him there three thousand years ago.'

'Three thousand years! Why?'

'Because he did something wrong.'

'Like what?'

'I don't know.'

'You don't?'

'Why would I?'

Elliot stopped in his tracks, bemused.

'So this bloke has been imprisoned for three thousand years and it's never occurred to you to ask what he did?' said Elliot.

'I have been told what I'm supposed to do. That is all I need to know.'

Elliot slowly started walking again.

'But who decided his sentence? What if didn't do anything? And even if he did, that's one heck of a punishment.'

'Don't worry about matters that your little human mind can't understand.'

'I understand justice,' said Elliot a little louder than he'd intended.

'Our systems are perfect. They have worked for thousands of years.'

'Doing something wrong for a long time doesn't make you perfect,' said Elliot. 'It makes you really wrong.'

'I don't expect you to understand,' said Virgo breezily. 'But these are the rules and I will follow them.'

'And do you always do what you're told?' asked Elliot.

Virgo paused for a moment as she remembered her hasty departure from Elysium the day before.

'Yes,' she answered plainly, trying to understand the strange feeling in her chest as she spoke.

'So why are you taking him that?' said Elliot, pointing to the flask of ambrosia Virgo was holding. 'Why not just leave him there to rot?'

'Gods are noble and just,' said Virgo. 'We all live by The Sacred Code, a set of rules about what we can and cannot do. Thanatos is still an immortal. The first rule of the code is the basic right to ambrosia, which we all have to drink if we're to stay young. Otherwise we'd just get older and start falling to bits without dying. That is every immortal's worst fear. Not to mention a litter hazard. The Zodiac Council is responsible for administering the immortal community and making sure he gets his dose every 250 years.'

'So you're just going to give this bloke a drink and then leave?'

'No,' replied Virgo. 'I'm going to drop the flask into the prison and return to Elysium. The rules forbid any contact with the prisoner.'

'That's cruel.'

'That's the rule. And we're here.'

Elliot had been so caught up in Virgo's story, he hadn't noticed that they had already reached the outer boundaries of Stonehenge. He had never seen the excitement of the ancient lumps of rock before, but now he knew what they were for, they suddenly seemed more appealing.

Now the busy summer season was over and the day had barely begun, the mystical stones were eerily quiet. The only figure to grace this ancient site was Cyril, a lone guide who was on hand to answer any potential questions from any potential visitors. Although on this cloudy, damp day, the only answer he wanted to give was 'milk and two sugars'.

Virgo turned to Elliot and shook his hand.

'Well thank you Elliot Earth-child for your begrudging hospitality and cantankerous company. It has been curious knowing you and I wish you well in your uneventful mortal life.'

And with that, Virgo hopped over the barrier and strode

towards a huge stone, set apart from the stone circle, which Elliot recalled from the school trips was called the Heelstone. Elliot watched agog as Virgo happily wandered across the hallowed ground and stopped by the Heelstone, as yet undetected by Cyril, who was looking in the opposite direction trying to decide if a cloud was the shape of an ice-cream or something ruder. Virgo crawled around the base of the stone, searching for something in the grass.

'Elliot,' she bellowed, causing Elliot to wince and Cyril to spin around. 'Would you mind giving me a hand?'

It took Cyril a moment to comprehend the full horror of the scene before him, as a silver-haired teenage girl stood up and kicked the sacred Heelstone of Stonehenge.

'Oi!' he yelled, reaching for the whistle around his neck. 'Stop right there, you hooligan!'

He blew three sharp blasts on the whistle, which instantly summoned two burly, if portly, security guards from the car park. They ran straight towards Elliot, who looked around for an escape route. But with Cyril approaching from the other direction, he had no choice but to run towards Virgo at the Heelstone.

Oblivious to the fuss around her, Virgo yanked up tufts of grass at the stone's base, tearing the soil around the sacred stone and throwing it carelessly over her shoulder. After countless handfuls had been tossed around her, she finally found what she was looking for – a small golden handle buried beneath the overgrowth.

'There you are,' she chirped and muttered some mystical words as she pulled up gently on the handle, which lifted the enormous rock above it as easily as if it were made of papier maché. As Elliot hurtled towards her, with Cyril puffing in one direction and the two security guards wheezing in the other, Virgo lifted the stone up over her head and threw the flask into the gap.

Elliot was fast approaching the Heelstone, but the security men were approaching even faster. They were gaining with every step and Elliot knew he couldn't outrun them for much longer. As Virgo started to lower the Heelstone to the ground, Elliot quickly realised his only escape. Diving at the shrinking gap between the Heelstone and the Earth, Elliot threw himself at Virgo, bundling him and the Goddess into the gap beneath the ground. It was a blind, frantic leap into the unknown – and as the almighty Heelstone fell to the ground, Elliot's flying feet just squeezed through the closing gap as the massive rock came crashing down on top of him.

Chapter Four

Negotiating Daemons

Grandad had always said that when one door closes, another one opens. Unfortunately for Elliot, his grandfather's wisdom didn't apply on this occasion, and as Elliot threw himself and Virgo headlong into the hole beneath Stonehenge, he had no time to concern himself about what lay beneath the stone – nor how he was going to get out of it again as the Heelstone locked securely back into place above him.

The first thing that Elliot established was that this wasn't a hole at all – it was in fact a staircase, made very clear as he tumbled down every hard stone step. Two things prevented him from breaking every bone in his body. Firstly, there were only five steps between him and solid ground, which Elliot found a little faster than he would have liked. Secondly, his fall was broken by a soft landing, which spared his skull from the cold and solid ground.

'What have you done?' hissed the soft landing, throwing Elliot off her and onto the floor.

Elliot lay on the cold ground, spitting out a mouthful of

dirt and teeth. He lifted his dazed head to see where he had landed. He was on a narrow platform at the top of some dirt steps and was staring straight into a pair of his old trainers.

'Trying not to get clobbered by the security guards you summoned, mouth of the South,' Elliot whispered back to Virgo, hauling his bruised body upright.

'We're not supposed to be here – we have to leave,' hissed Virgo.

'No,' said Elliot matter-of-factly.

'Yes!' Virgo hissed as loudly as she dared.

'Not a chance,' Elliot hissed back. 'Those men want to wring my neck. Some of us don't have the luxury of immortality.'

'We can't be here. It's against the rules.'

'Well we are here. So the rules will have to deal with it.'

Virgo let out a frustrated grunt. This was not going to plan at all. She could imagine the patronising faces of her fellow Council members if they could see the mess she was making of a simple job. She needed to get them out of here, but the boy was right – they couldn't go back out the way they came for fear of capture. She would have to go into the cave and find an alternative exit. It was the logical thing to do. She picked up the golden flask at her feet.

'Alright. But you have to stay here.'

Elliot never did like being told what to do. 'Where?'

'Where you are.'

'You mean I can't move at all?'

'No.'

'Why not?'

'You just can't,' said Virgo, failing to find a good reason. 'It's the rules.'

'Your rules. Not mine,' said Elliot as he took a big step to the left. 'I fancy standing here.'

'Don't be ridiculous, mortal. Stay still.'

'Nope, don't fancy it,' said Elliot, doing jumping jacks on the spot. 'I think I'll stand here.'

'Stay still!'

'Or here?'

'Elliot, stay still!'

'Or . . . ?'

'*Who's there?*'

It could have been the shock of the new voice, or simply jumping around that did it. But whatever the reason, at that moment Elliot lost his footing on the narrow platform and went crashing into the darkness several feet below.

Elliot had broken his collarbone twice in his life and knew enough about the searing pain in his chest as he hit the ground to know that he'd just done it again. He yelped in pain.

'I told you to stay still,' said Virgo as she hurtled to where Elliot was lying in a heap, dropping the flask as she went. 'If only you'd – you're hurt.'

She looked at the young mortal boy, who was clutching

his shoulder in silent agony. This was not going well at all. Not only had she brought a mortal to this secret place, she had now broken him.

'Right – er – now, if we just think about this logically for a minute—'

'Help,' spluttered Elliot, looking like he was going to be sick. 'Please—'

Virgo never panicked. She'd never needed to. But as she looked around the gloomy, empty cave with nothing to help her, this seemed like an excellent moment to start. What was she going to do?

'*Bring the child here.*'

The thin voice sliced through the dank silence of the cave like a spear. Virgo sought out the voice in the darkness, but only the cave's great, black emptiness stared back at her, like an open mouth between a pair of gaping jaws.

She picked up a torch from the wall and took a few faltering steps into the gloom. The weak light from the ancient torch cast a small halo around her, illuminating a few inches ahead of her tentative footsteps.

'Thanatos?' she called out quietly, a slight tremble in her voice. 'I should warn you, I'm—'

She looked at her T-shirt and untied trainers. She had to admit, she wasn't the most terrifying threat.

'I'm from the Zodiac Council. I've brought you ambrosia,' she said through dry lips.

'*Come closer. Let me see you.*'

Virgo squinted through the gloom for any indication of how far she needed to go. She held the torch higher to help her see into the distance. Surely the cave couldn't be that big?

A cold hand suddenly grabbed Virgo's arm in the darkness. She screamed and dropped the torch, plunging the cave into darkness again.

'Virgo?' Elliot called, trying to pull himself up with his good arm. 'Are you okay? Virgo?'

The torch suddenly burst into flame again, burning more brightly this time. It slowly lifted off the ground. But Virgo wasn't holding it. As the light flickered up from the ground, the body of the eternal prisoner was illuminated one inch at a time. His filthy bare feet were covered in millennia of dirt, reaching up his skeletal legs to his emaciated body. What was once a black robe clung to the bones on his arms and the light seared up his neck, until Elliot was staring into the gaunt, pale, hollow face of death, from the limp black hair at the top of his head, to the thin beard that brought his long face into a sharp point. His black eyes bored into Elliot's face.

'Come here, child,' rasped the daemon. 'I can help you.'

'Let her go,' said Elliot, motioning to Virgo, whose arm was still in the prisoner's thin grip.

Thanatos looked down at Virgo, who was still on her knees on the cave floor, glued to the spot as she looked up Thanatos's thin, wiry body. There was a long pause as the three figures froze like statues in a tomb.

'Of course,' said Thanatos. 'I was merely helping the young lady to her feet. Are you quite alright, my dear?'

He pulled Virgo quickly to her feet, before releasing his grip on her arm. Her right hand instinctively felt her left arm, but apart from a bitter chill to her skin, there was no harm done by the daemon's grasp.

'Thank you,' she said quietly, taking the torch and moving back towards Elliot.

With the brighter light now rebounding off the cave walls, Elliot was able to get a better look at the daemon who had spent three thousand years in this forsaken place. Daemons conjured images of impish, wicked, magical creatures in his mind's eye. But the figure that stood before him couldn't have been further from his imagination. Surely this pitiful creature couldn't be the death daemon Virgo had described?

The scrawny prisoner before Elliot's eyes was a cowed, weak man who didn't look like he possessed the strength to fight a kitten. What little flesh he had clung to his bones, every last one of which was visible through his pale skin. His dark, sallow face was barely visible through the knotted mass of limp hair that hung from his head. The wretched man didn't look immortal at all. If anything he looked minutes from death as he leaned weakly against the post that held sullied golden chains around his arms and feet. The only life Elliot could detect came from Thanatos's dark eyes, which still had a flicker of something, maybe pride, anger, pain . . . Elliot didn't know what it was. But he was glad for the man that he still had it.

'I wonder if you might be kind enough to fetch me some water,' he said meekly, gesturing to a cup near the stream at the cave's back wall. 'It's been so long since I—'

'My orders are to only allow you ambrosia,' said Virgo to the cave floor. 'Anything else is forbidden.'

'I understand,' said Thanatos. 'We must all do what we think is right. Thank you for your troubles young Goddess. I shall trouble you no more.'

Thanatos slumped against his post and slumped to the floor, closing his eyes at the effort it had taken him to stand.

Virgo returned to Elliot.

'Let's get out of here,' she said.

Elliot's feet stayed rooted to the spot. Whatever Thanatos had done, to leave him here in this awful place seemed inhuman. His good hand helped him to his feet as he started for the river that flowed along the cave's back wall beneath an ancient olive tree.

'Elliot, no!' the Goddess whispered. 'The rules are—'

Elliot dipped the cup into the cool stream, filling it to the brim with icy water. He looked back at Virgo.

'Your rules. Not mine.'

He winced as he stood, his collarbone jarring at the awkward movement. He walked back towards Thanatos, whose piercing stare was fixed on Elliot.

'Here you go,' he said as he offered the cup to the prisoner. 'Drink.'

'Thank you,' said Thanatos as he took a slow sip. 'Elliot, isn't it?'

Elliot nodded his head.

'Elliot, it's time to leave,' said Virgo more urgently, looking around for any way out of the prison.

'The boy's hurt,' said Thanatos. 'I can help him.'

'He doesn't need your help,' said Virgo. 'He has me.'

'And a fine job you're doing,' said Thanatos. 'I'm sure the Council will commend you.'

Virgo dropped her head.

'I can heal you,' Thanatos said to Elliot. 'All I ask is that you free me from this unjust punishment.'

'Elliot, don't even think about it,' said Virgo, grabbing his shoulder to pull him back, yanking his broken bone again.'

'Aaaargh!' yelled Elliot as the pain ripped through his arm. He needed a hospital. But doctors asked questions. Elliot knew they'd call his mum and it would take any doctor with five minutes of medical training to know there was something wrong with her. But he couldn't carry on like this, it was agony.

'Even if I wanted to, how would I free you from those?' he asked, looking at the heavy chains.

Thanatos lifted the chains off the ground.

'My bonds are strengthened by immortal charms. They

hold me. But they wouldn't hold you. Gods and mortals have different restraints. These chains would dissolve at your touch.'

'Why do I have to free you?'

'You don't. I'm asking you to. In return for fixing your shoulder.'

Elliot considered the situation. This man had been imprisoned for three thousand years. He was a frail half-man who barely had the strength to stand. What was the worst he could do? And Elliot really needed his shoulder fixed.

'Heal me first,' said Elliot. 'Then we'll talk.'

'You're an excellent negotiator,' Thanatos smiled. 'Fair enough. Come closer.'

'Elliot—' warned Virgo again, as Thanatos's skeletal hand reached towards Elliot's throbbing collarbone. His fingers inched closer, closer to the wound as all three figures transfixed on the thin fingers.

'Elliot – don't!' Virgo yelled – but it was too late. Thanatos's right hand suddenly slammed against Elliot's injured bone, causing him to scream in pain as the left grabbed Elliot by the wrist. Elliot tried to free himself, but the grip was superhuman and the pain was too much. Where Thanatos made contact with Elliot's skin, Elliot felt coldness like never before, a frozen current spiking through his body, making him feel as if he'd never be warm again. Elliot looked up into Thanatos's face, which was contorted into a wild stare, a smile playing on his lips as he watched Elliot writhe in pain beneath him.

With one final almighty blast, Thanatos pushed Elliot away, back onto the cave floor. Virgo ran to where her companion lay, watching Thanatos's exhausted body slump back against his chains.

'Elliot? Elliot – are you alive?' said Virgo trying to process the strange sensation that everything was not going as perfectly as it should be.

'No,' groaned Elliot as he pulled his head off the ground, shivering as the last icy sensations left his body. He looked over at Thanatos.

'What was all that about?' he said to the smirking God.

'I said I could heal you. I never said you'd like it,' said the God, toying with two olives between his fingers. 'Here – catch!'

Thanatos flicked one of the olives to where Elliot had landed. Instinctively, Elliot raised his perfectly fixed right arm to catch it. He pulled his arm back down slowly – the pain had disappeared.

'But it works,' said Thanatos, popping the second olive into his wiry mouth.

'Thank you,' said Elliot, pulling himself slowly to his feet. He looked at Thanatos's heavy chains. Surely he'd never be able to break those?

'It's a curious job, being given power over life,' drawled Thanatos, his searing gaze never leaving Elliot. 'I can take it away, sure. But I can also make it so much better.'

'Elliot, it's time to leave,' said Virgo, pulling at Elliot's sleeve.

'Make it better how?' Elliot asked the daemon, his feet rooted to the ground. 'Well that would have to depend,' said Thanatos, absently glancing around the cave. 'I could heal a young girl who had never walked, for instance. Or ease the headaches that ruin a man's life, or—'

Thanatos's eyes darted straight back to Elliot's soul.

'Or I could cure a mother whose mind is starting to fail before anyone knew there was a problem.'

'How do you—?'

'Elliot!' snapped Virgo. 'We're leaving. Now.'

Elliot's mind was whirring at a million miles an hour.

'Why were you put here?' he asked.

'The same reason anyone hides anything,' said Thanatos. 'Because they don't want it to be found.'

'Don't listen to him, Elliot,' Virgo hissed. 'He'll trick you. That's what daemons do.'

'And yet I'm the one in chains,' said Thanatos. 'I think you'll find someone tricked *me*.'

'You're here because you broke the rules,' said Virgo.

'And who says the rules are right?' said Thanatos, looking straight at Elliot. 'The rules say I should have received a fair hearing. Instead I've been left here without a trial for three thousand years. Whose rules are those?'

'Why should I free you?' said Elliot.

'Why should I stay here? And can you live with knowing that I am?' Thanatos shot back.

'How do I know you won't kill me the second you're free?'

'I swear on the Styx that I won't a lay a finger on you.'

Elliot drew a halting breath. The idea of his Mum back to her old self, back to the happy, healthy woman that he loved and needed overwhelmed him. Months of holding back the worries and fear as he watched his Mum slip away from herself started to well up from deep inside the pit of his stomach and Elliot had to force them back down his throat before they burst out of his mouth. Thanatos could cure his Mum. All he had to do was pick up the chains.

Before his brain even knew what his feet were doing, his left foot took a slow step towards the daemon. Virgo pulled harder on his sleeve.

'No – don't,' she said, grabbing his arm. Elliot shook her off as his right foot overtook his left, bringing him closer to Thanatos's thick golden chains.

'Elliot, you can't,' Virgo demanded, standing in front of the advancing boy. 'The rules clearly state—'

Elliot stopped and looked into Virgo's terrified face, breaking his eye contact with Thanatos.

'Her rules,' said Thanatos's voice in the cave, or maybe in Elliot's own head. 'Your life, Elliot. Do it.'

There was an eternal pause as Elliot looked between the silver-haired Goddess in front of him and the dark daemon behind her.

'I'm sorry,' said Elliot to someone. 'I have no choice.'

Virgo and Thanatos held their breath while this mortal child decided which one of them he was going to listen to.

The answer came rather suddenly.

With an almighty shove, Elliot pushed Virgo to one side and made a frantic dive towards Thanatos. Before the Goddess could figure out what had happened to her, Elliot landed just a few inches from the chains. Elliot scrabbled to his knees to give him the stretch that he needed. But Virgo was quick. She got to her feet first and zoomed at light speed across the cave to grab Elliot's legs. She grabbed him by the ankles and pulled him to the floor just before his fingertips could reach the chains.

'No . . . you . . . don't . . . know . . . what . . . you're . . . doing . . .' panted Virgo as she tried to claw handfuls of Elliot's legs back towards her.

But Elliot was possessed with the strength of someone a moment away from the thing they wanted most in the world. With the chains held in Thanatos's outstretched, bony fingers, Elliot gave one almighty kick to free himself from Virgo's grip. He hauled himself to his knees and threw himself forward one last time.

And this time, he made it.

No sooner had his fingers made contact with the massive gold chains, then as Thanatos promised, they simply melted away to dust in his hands. The coil that had seemed so massive simply dissolved like sand going through an egg-timer and Elliot watched as the chains disintegrated and melded with the dust on the cave floor.

The world stopped for a moment. Thanatos was the first

to shatter the silence as he slowly rose to his feet and dusted himself down.

'Thank you Elliot,' he said as he towered over the boy on the floor. 'That's much better.'

Thanatos stepped carelessly over the boy and went to where Virgo was still lying on the floor. Freed from his shackles, he seemed somehow taller, broader, barely resembling the shred of a man for whom Elliot had felt so much pity.

'I've done what you asked,' said Elliot, pulling himself off the cave floor. 'You said you'd cure Mum.'

'Not necessarily,' said Thanatos, stepping over the prostrate body of the young Goddess.

'You did,' said Elliot frantically. 'You said—'

'I said that I could,' said Thanatos, grabbing a handful of Virgo's silver hair and yanking her clear off the floor. The young Goddess screamed in pain as she dangled powerlessly from his arm, her feet too far from the floor to relieve her burning scalp. 'I never said that I would.'

'You lying, cheating—' shouted Elliot, holding back angry tears, charging at the daemon, who sent him flying against the cave wall with a mere flick of his hand.

'And as for you, my dear,' said Thanatos with glee, his eyes burning with delight. 'It's time you went back to the Council where you belong. Now which piece of you shall I send first?'

Virgo screamed again as Thanatos shook her by her hair. Elliot pulled his winded body upright once more.

'You can't kill her,' said Elliot shakily, unable to look at Virgo's tortured face.

'True enough,' said Thanatos, wrapping his fist more tightly around the hair. 'But I can really enjoy not killing her.'

Thanatos walked slowly towards Elliot, dragging Virgo on the floor behind him as if he were taking out the rubbish. The Goddess held her screaming head in her hands through gritted teeth as Thanatos towered once again over Elliot's bruised body.

'I'm very grateful to you, Elliot,' he began. 'And as a token of my gratitude, I'm not going to let you see what I'm about to do to your girlfriend.'

'You're letting me go?' said Elliot, looking at the heap of Virgo on the floor.

'Absolutely. I gave you my word I wouldn't lay a finger on you and I won't. Immortals cannot break their oaths. You're free to go. Besides, I might have use for you again.'

Thanatos stood to one side and gestured towards a tunnel beneath the staircase with a flicker of daylight at its end. Elliot looked to the safety that lay beyond. But this time his feet wouldn't move.

'What about her?' said Elliot, gesturing at Virgo with his head.

'You didn't care about her a few moments ago,' said Thanatos. 'I suggest you don't start now.'

Elliot locked eyes with Virgo, whose fearful gaze betrayed her fixed jaw.

'Just leave,' she said shakily. 'This doesn't concern you.'

'Ah – finally,' trilled Thanatos. 'Some advice worth listening to. Goodbye Elliot. I'll be seeing you again.'

Elliot took a few slow steps towards the tunnel. Virgo couldn't die, he knew that. But there were worse things than dying. He knew that too. He looked back to where Thanatos was still holding Virgo by her silver tresses. The death daemon waved his fingers in a gesture of dismissal.

'Run along now. There's a good boy.'

Elliot released his breath. There was nothing he could do for Virgo now. She couldn't die. But he could. And who would take care of Mum if he did?

He started to trudge slowly towards the steps as Thanatos turned back to his prey.

'Now then, my dear. Where were we?'

Elliot tried to block out Virgo's screams as he reached the foot of the stairs. He crouched down to crawl through the tunnel, where the sunlight was desperately trying to pierce the dank darkness of the cave.

The coast was clear. Elliot could go back to his life and no-one would ever know. Except for him. He would know everything.

Elliot looked back into the cave one final time. Thanatos was dangling Virgo like a puppet on a string, oblivious to the shrieks of the young girl ready to pass out from the pain.

As Elliot looked away into the bright morning sunshine, a golden glint drew his eye. The sunlight caught something lying on the floor. It was the golden flask Virgo had been carrying. The flask containing Thanatos's ambrosia. The same flask she had dropped when coming to rescue him. Elliot picked it up off the floor. Once again, he had no choice.

'Thanatos,' he yelled into the cave. 'Your ambrosia's here.'

'It'll keep,' the daemon shouted back. 'I expect I'm going to work up quite a thirst here. I'll drink it when I'm done.'

Elliot came back into view, opening the flask as he went.

'Not necessarily,' said Elliot tipping the now open flask so the liquid teetered on the brink of the rim. 'Let her go.'

Thanatos looked murderously at the boy, who was about to tip his life-giving elixir into the dirt.

'Don't be foolish,' Thanatos hissed. 'You've made a powerful ally today, boy. Don't turn me into an enemy.'

'You can't hurt me – remember?' said Elliot.

'I said I wouldn't lay a finger on you,' laughed Thanatos. 'I can still hurt you. Believe me. Put the flask down, child. This will the be the last time I ask you.'

'And this will be the last time I ask you. Let. Her. Go.'

'I mean it, child!'

'So do I,' said Elliot allowing a drop of the sacred liquid to spill onto the ground.

The two adversaries stood motionless with their bargaining chips, Thanatos suspending Virgo in mid-air, Elliot suspending the flask at a precarious angle.

'I'll put her down when you throw me the flask,' offered Thanatos.

'No. You first,' said Elliot.

'I said that I will put her down.'

'Swear it,' said Elliot, his latest lesson in daemon negotiations fresh in his mind. 'And that you won't throw her, give her back in pieces or damage her in any way,' he added, quickly running through the most likely loop-holes, letting another drop of ambrosia run out of the flask to underline his point.

'Fine,' said Thanatos as the second drop plopped onto the ground. 'I swear it on the Styx. Let's each let go in One . . . Two . . . Three!'

'Elliot – duck!' screamed Virgo as she and the flask simultaneously hit the ground.

And this time, Elliot listened. For no sooner had the flask left his hand then a bolt of black smoke shot out of Thanatos's hand, blasting a hole in the rock where Elliot's head had been moments previously.

'You stupid boy,' drawled Thanatos advancing towards where Elliot lay on the floor. 'How dare you challenge me, you fetid, mortal vermin. You presume to think that you are worthy to bargain with me, the most powerful daemon there has ever been? I offered you a choice. I spared your life. A mistake I will not make again.'

Elliot shrank as Thanatos approached him with a raised hand.

'For the second and final time, Elliot,' Thanatos whispered, 'goodbye.'

Had Elliot wondered what it would be like to have his body obliterated by a bolt of pure immortal evil, he could never have imagined the soul-splitting pain and agony that awaited him from Thanatos's palm.

But two things prevented him from finding out.

As the smoke shot out of Thanatos's hand, instead of blasting Elliot to pieces, it simply bent around his body, taking another chunk out of the rock behind him. Thanatos froze for a moment – how was Elliot still alive?

But before he could take another shot, a massive bundle of stars blasted through Thanatos, whipped Elliot up into their warm glow and whooshed him down the tunnel in a shower of golden light.

Chapter Five

Patricia Porshley-Plum

Patricia Porshley-Plum always got what she wanted. When Patricia was eight, she wanted a puppy. Her father, who had inherited his vast wealth from his great-aunt, told her she needed to learn the value of a hard day's work. So Patricia took all of Daddy's expensive designer suits to a jumble sale and sold them for £25. Her father – a man who admired an enterprising spirit – cheerfully bought her Bonnie the puppy.

When Patricia was thirteen, she wanted a pony. Her father, who phoned from the golf course to point out that we can't always get what we want, told her to contribute half herself. So Patricia sold Bonnie the dog and poured black paint all over Daddy's red Ferrari, claiming the insurance money to cover his half. Her father – a man who wasn't sure about red anyway – nervously bought her Bess the pony.

When Patricia was twenty, she wanted a car. Her father, who retired at 35, wanted to tell her to get a job and pay for it herself. But as his daughter pulled out a box of matches and a petrol can in the front parlour, her father – a man who now feared for his life – simply asked her what model she wanted.

Now Patricia was forty-something (but knew she could pass for 37), she wanted Home Farm. Yes, that vile ramshackle farmhouse would have to be squished and the fields of weeds bulldozed, but underneath lay a valuable piece of land that was ripe for development. Patricia could build dozens of cheap houses on the plot and make a fortune – the poor people stupid enough to afford them could find out all the problems with them for themselves. If only she could make Josie Hooper see sense. But that repugnant boy Elliot wouldn't let her near his mother and Patricia was beginning to run out of patience. Patricia Porshley-Plum was not getting what she wanted. And this was unacceptable.

Like anyone who has too much, Patricia had no sympathy for anyone who didn't have enough. She loathed poor people. Patricia treated poverty like most people treat a nasty case of flu – a horribly catching disease that required plenty of hand-washing whenever you went near it. Besides, poor people only had themselves to blame. If you couldn't look after your money, you didn't deserve it. Which left plenty of it for her. And those ghastly Hoopers were as poor as a cold lobster bisque.

What made the situation even more intolerable was the fact that Patricia knew something fishy was going on. She didn't believe Elliot's contagious illness routine for one tax-efficient minute and she was determined to get her hands on Home Farm. And that £20 the little blighter had stolen from her purse. Yes, Mrs Horse's Bum might have been a selfish, interfering, heartless old bag who couldn't pass for 37 with a time-machine – but she wasn't stupid. Something was up. She just needed to find out what.

Most normal people would have given up long ago – she had been told any number of times that Home Farm wasn't for sale. But Patricia Porshley-Plum wasn't most people. And she wasn't especially normal. Giving up hadn't won her the 1983 Pony Princess Rider of the Year – although poisoning all the other contestants had helped – and she wasn't about to give up now. Patricia Porshley-Plum had waited long enough. It was time to get her hands on that farm.

And so when Patricia saw Elliot leave the farm early that Saturday morning with a silver-haired girl – young people were so ridiculous with their hairstyles nowadays, a nice soft perm had done her perfectly well for years – she decided it was time to make her move.

'When opportunity knocks, answer the door,' her father had said to her before he died. Or at least she assumed he was dead – she hadn't seen him since the day she claimed he'd gone potty, put him in a home and taken his fortune. There was no time like the present, especially since her electricity seemed to be playing up at home that morning. Patricia Porshley-Plum decided that today was the perfect opportunity to get what she wanted.

Armed with a home-made Victoria sponge – well, it said that someone had made it at their home on the label – as soon as Elliot was out of sight, Patricia made her way back up the stupidly precarious path to Home Farm. She knocked gently on the door.

'Coo-ee! Josie-kins! It's Patricia!' she chirped like a canary on candy floss. 'Fancy a cuppa?'

The footsteps on the stairs assured her that risking that awful path hadn't been in vain and she plastered on her largest, least sincere smile in anticipation.

The door opened a fraction and the delicate blonde features of Josie Hooper peeked out the door.

'Hello Pumpkin!' gushed Patricia. 'Shall we have some cakey?'

The mind is a complex machine and, although Josie's day-to-day memory had been getting worse, her long-term memory was as clear as a spring morning. So, at the sight of her friendly neighbour, Josie ignored Elliot's warnings not to let anyone in the house and thought nothing of opening the door to Patricia Porshley-Plum, like Grandma letting the Big Bad Wolf in for a cup of tea.

'Hello Mrs Horse's Bum,' she said cheerily. 'Do come in.'

Even without the insult, Patricia thought Josie looked dreadful. She hadn't seen her for some months, but even so, the woman was ageing horribly. That's what happened when you didn't spend money on expensive beauty creams that were packed with dynoflavinemperorclotheazines to keep skin firm. And Josie wasn't even dressed yet! Shuffling around in her dressing gown – had the woman no shame? Of course not. She was poor. Poor people were so very, very lazy.

Patricia crossed the threshold into the cosy confines of Home Farm. As she looked around the cherished house that was stuffed with joyful souvenirs from all the branches of the Hooper family tree that had lived there, Patricia happily imagined what it was going to look like the day her bulldozers flattened it to the ground. She might even take the first swing herself.

'Can I get you a cup of tea?' Josie asked kindly, ushering her guest through to the kitchen.

'How lovely, dear,' said Patricia, offering Josie the sponge cake.

'Thank you,' said Josie as her neighbour sat gingerly at the kitchen table, wishing she could run an anti-bacterial wipe over the seat first. Or that her cleaner could do it for her. 'Would you like a cup of tea?'

'Er . . . yes – thank you again,' laughed Patricia. 'Just as it comes please. Milk in first, only three dunks of the bag, two and a half sugars stirred anti-clockwise and a teaspoon. Silver if you have one, but I'm not fussy.'

'Right,' said Josie, looking confused as she put the kettle on to boil. 'Thank you for the cake, Elly will be so pleased.'

'Isn't he growing up to be quite the . . . young man,' said Patricia, through clenched jaws as she sprayed some hand sanitizer on her palms under the table.

'Oh he's wonderful,' said Josie happily. 'He takes such good care of me. He's a real gift.'

'Let's hope you kept the receipt,' muttered Patricia under her breath as she looked out over the neglected fields. She could see it now. Rows upon rows of identical houses where these pointless green fields now stood. 'Dairy Mews' – that's what she'd call the new development. The idiots who bought her flat pack houses liked a bit of character. Patricia felt richer just looking out the window.

'Do you take sugar?' asked Josie, assembling the tea on a tray.

'Yes please, two and a half,' said Patricia trying to keep the irritation out of her voice. Not only was the woman poor and lazy, she was clearly stupid as well.

Josie set the tea tray down on the table and Patricia took in the chipped and mismatched crockery.

'I was so sorry about your father, Poppet. He was a lovely man,' Patricia lied, knowing perfectly well he had been the inventor of the Horse's Bum nickname that followed her around the village like one of those frightful charity collectors.

'Thank you,' said Josie quietly pouring the tea. 'It's been a difficult time.'

Patricia reluctantly accepted the stained cup making a mental note of a wilting plant that would be grateful for the drink when Josie's back was turned.

'Shall we have some cake?' she said breezily, working out

how she'd avoid another piece of Hooper crockery.

'You brought cake?' said Josie cheerfully. 'How lovely – Elly will be so pleased.'

Josie stood up to fetch the cake she had put down moments earlier under Patricia's curious gaze. She'd never spent much time with Josie before – why on Earth would she? But she didn't remember her being this dopey.

'May I use your facilities?' Patricia asked.

'Of course,' said Josie, rummaging around in a cutlery drawer for the big knives that Elliot had hidden. 'The toilet's just down the hall on the right.'

Patricia shuddered at the unmentionable word. Just because they existed, it didn't mean that 'toilets' needed to be mentioned out loud. Just like 'famine victims'. Or 'tax returns'.

She left the kitchen and immediately headed for the front room. Patricia had no intention of going to the unmentionable in this house, heaven only knows what she'd catch from the unmentionable seat. No, she wanted to have a nosey around to see what was going on at Home Farm.

Patricia peered around the front room, which was littered with photographs of happier times. In a fading golden frame were Wilfred and Audrey Hooper on their wedding day in 1975. A chipped black wooden frame showed Josie proudly cradling a newborn Elliot in her arms. And along the wall were Elliot's school photographs, showing the young man growing up – although the most recent one was two years old. Patricia turned her nose up at this pointless tat. All the walls in Patricia's own home were painted magnolia and hung with expensive paintings by artists who were so exclusive that no-one had ever heard of them.

Papers littered every spare surface and, checking that Josie was still rummaging around in the drawer, Patricia started to turn some of them over. They came from everywhere imaginable – gas companies, phone companies, overdue council tax demands, final reminders – and on top of them all was The Really Scary Letter.

Patricia Porshley-Plum's shrivelled heart danced a tango as she picked up the letter threatening Elliot and Josie's cherished family home. She read The Really Scary Letter like most people read a winning lottery ticket. A lazy mother and that idiot child couldn't possibly find the twenty thousand pounds being demanded in this letter. But nor could Patricia allow the farm to fall into someone else's hands once those tiresome Hoopers had been thrown out onto the street. Home Farm was going to be hers. And now she could get it for a bargain.

Folding the letter up and putting it back where she found it, Patricia skipped round to the unmentionable, took a deep breath and flushed it with her hand inside her sleeve. That blouse would have to be burned now. But it had been worth it.

Patricia swaggered back into the kitchen with a smile that could carve an ice sculpture. But Josie was no longer there. She walked out of the open back door to find Elliot's mother in the vegetable garden pulling up weeds.

'Er – Muffinpops? Your tea's getting cold,' Patricia trilled.

Josie looked up from her work and smiled warmly at her neighbour as she rose to her feet and brushed the soil off her dressing gown.

'Oh hello Mrs Porshley-Plum – how nice of you to drop round. Would you like some tea?'

Patricia leaned against the door-frame. The penny finally dropped. Josie Hooper wasn't being lazy or stupid or slow. She was seriously unwell. This usually bright young woman had the mind of an old lady. So that's why Elliot had been keeping her tucked away. Patricia realised that she was dealing with someone who wasn't capable of making a sound judgement on her own. Josie now needed a teenage boy to take care of her, to make important decisions, to keep her safe from harm. The woman was utterly defenceless. There was no way Patricia could buy Home Farm for a bargain price now.

It would be much cheaper to steal it.

'A cup of tea would be lovely, Sweetie-pie,' said Patricia with a smile that almost reached her eyes. 'And then after that, I thought the two of us might take a little outing . . .'

Chapter Six
Bad Council

One of Elliot's secret dreams had always been to fly in an aeroplane. As his family had never been able to afford a holiday abroad, he had yet to sample the delights of aviation and had always wondered what it would be like to view the world from thousands of feet up in the air.

But after five minutes of flying by constellation, Elliot swore that his feet would never leave the ground again.

He knew that Virgo's quick thinking had saved his life when she whisked him away from Thanatos's deadly blast. But Elliot now worried that he was in grave danger of losing it again as his body spun wildly in the air, climbing ever higher in the blinding glare of Virgo's constellation. As his body turned over and over, up and down, around and around and in a few directions that had yet to be invented, Elliot felt like a sock in a tumble dryer. One that was just about to throw up its breakfast.

Just as Elliot lost all sense of which end was up, his flight came to an abrupt halt, leaving him dangling about six feet over a lush green meadow.

'Oh thank goodness,' he began, just as he was dumped on the ground and Virgo's constellation flowed elegantly down to the ground to reform as her physical self. 'Ouch! You didn't have to drop me.'

'You're lucky I didn't drop you halfway across the Aegean Sea,' said Virgo, running her fingers through her long silver hair. 'You're heavier than you look. And you're welcome.'

'You too,' Elliot replied, encouraging his dizzy legs to stand. 'Where are we?'

'This is Elysium,' Virgo announced grandly. 'Welcome to my home.'

His vision still a little blurred from the flight, it took Elliot a moment to adjust to the sunlit scene before him. But when he did, he was in the most perfectly beautiful place he'd ever seen. The cloudless sky looked down on the luscious green meadow in which they stood, filled with fruit trees straining under the weight of their laden branches. In the distance one way, Elliot could make out a sparkling ocean by a tree-lined golden beach and in the other, a flawless glass pyramid that sparkled on the horizon like a vast diamond.

'Wow,' he whispered as he took in the paradise before him.

'We'd better get to the council chamber,' said Virgo, gesturing towards the pyramid. 'They need to know what you did.'

'What I did!' Elliot shouted indignantly. 'I saved your shiny head!'

'Which wouldn't have been in danger if you hadn't set Thanatos free. I told you not to trust a daemon.'

Elliot knew that he had a perfectly good answer to that point. He just didn't have it at that moment.

'What will they do?' he asked quietly, still smarting from his last encounter with the immortal community.

'Something brilliant,' Virgo said breezily. 'The Zodiac Council has been tending to the needs of the immortal community for thousands of years. I'm sure this kind of thing happens all the time. They'll have a plan. It'll all be perfectly fine.'

'YOU DID WHAT???!!!!' Aries shrieked over the commotion in the chamber as the council erupted in outrage.

'Well, it was all a bit of an accident really,' Virgo began, every eye in the room boring into her skull. 'You see, Elliot wasn't supposed to be in the cave.'

'*You* weren't supposed to be in the cave!' shouted Pisces. 'You were supposed to be ordering paper clips!'

'I know, but—'

'You are a young, inexperienced junior Goddess,' yelled Aries. 'You disobeyed express orders not to visit Earth. In one short day, you've managed to release the most dangerous daemon the world has ever known, reveal our existence to a mortal and miss the final stationery order deadline this month. Explain yourself!'

Elliot remained hidden behind the pillar that Virgo had

suggested as she gave a detailed account of the past few hours. The sight before him was the cherry on the icing of a very strange day. There were half-sheep, half-bulls, whole crabs, fish people and a lion all yelling over each other as they fired questions at Virgo.

Elliot looked around the magnificent chamber, which was adorned with beautiful works of art and vast bookshelves along the walls. One volume on the shelf in front of him caught his eye. He quietly picked up the enormous leather-bound book and opened the first page:

The Sacred Code (12,349th Edition)*

1) The Gods will ensure that all immortals receive ambrosia
b) The Gods cannot break mortal laws
7) The Gods cannot herd giraffes on a Tuesday
xic) The Gods cannot keep mortal money
F2) The Gods cannot wear socks with sandals
39.4) The Gods cannot break an oath
xy) The Gods cannot push cotton buds too far into their ears

**all rules subject to change with any or no notice*

And so on and so forth. The rules went on for endless pages, every one of which was stuffed with notes, bits of extra paper clipped onto the pages and scribbled amendments over every spare space. Elliot silently replaced the volume just as Virgo was coming to the end of her tale.

'. . . and so I felt that the most sensible course of action was to return here immediately so that I could file a full report. I used my initiative,' said Virgo.

'Shame you didn't use your brain,' shouted Scorpio, pouring a large glass of something that didn't look like water.

'Have you any idea how serious this is, Virgo?' Aries demanded.

'Yes,' replied Virgo, looking distinctly like she didn't.

'Haven't you ever studied Thanatos's history? It's surrounded you for millennia.'

Aries pointed to the walls, where Elliot – and Virgo – studied the beautiful murals that adorned it for the first time. They depicted the story of a great battle. In the first scene, a mighty grey-haired warrior – he knew that was Zeus – was hurling a thunderbolt towards an army of trolls, monsters and other dark creatures led by a now all-too familiar face – the gaunt features of Thanatos. The battlefield was littered with the bodies of stricken mortals, who were being terrorised by Thanatos's dark minions with all manner of ghastly tortures.

Flanked by two women in full battle dress – one dark-haired, one golden-haired, and a shorter, hunchbacked soldier wielding an almighty axe, the second mural showed Zeus and his army bravely battling Thanatos, bathed in golden light as their righteous crusade fought valiantly on.

The third was a victory scene, with all the Gods raising their weapons in happy salute. The hunchback was binding Thanatos with golden chains, locking him deep beneath the Earth. In Zeus's palm were four beautiful gems: a sparkling diamond, a blood-red ruby, a brilliant emerald and a deep-blue sapphire.

In all her years on the Zodiac Council, Virgo had never been allowed to finish a sentence. For the first time, she realised this could be an advantage.

'That's right, it's all coming back now,' she said. 'Thanatos . . .'

'. . . and his daemon army nearly destroyed humankind,' said Aries.

'Of course. The daemon army,' said Virgo. 'The one that . . .'

'. . . followed Thanatos into battle when he decided to overthrow Zeus,' said Sagittarius. 'Terrible business. Daemons sending pestilence and plague across the Earth, turning brother against brother with hatred and greed and all of man's ills. It was awful.'

'That's right,' said Virgo. 'I read all about it. But now the daemon army is . . .'

'. . . locked away in the very depths of Tartarus, thank goodness,' said Leo. 'The army can only be freed by the Chaos Stones.'

'Absolutely. The Chaos Stones,' said Virgo authoritatively. 'Because they can . . .'

'. . . control the elements,' bleated Aries. 'Earth, Fire, Wind and Water. It's how Thanatos kept the mortal population under control. And the only way he can free his army. Tartarus can only be opened by earthquake, fire, hurricane and flood.'

'Sounds like the average British summer,' muttered Elliot.

'If Thanatos ever got his hands on the Chaos Stones, he could free his daemon army, and none of us would be safe again,' said Aries. 'But thankfully, noble Zeus won the stones on the honourable field of battle.'

Elliot's mind snapped back to earlier that day. Thanatos said he'd been tricked. By whom?

'Last time Thanatos was at large, he and his daemon army nearly destroyed humankind,' said Capricorn. 'And three thousand years underground is unlikely to have changed his mind. If it wasn't for the noble victory won by the Olympians, we'd all be the ones locked away.'

'We can't change what has happened,' said Aries. 'The question is how we as a Council deal with it. We have a dangerous fugitive on the loose who is a known danger to man and immortals. We have to follow protocol.'

There was a long pause as the Council silently agreed its decision.

'Deny all knowledge,' shouted Aquarius.

'Precisely,' agreed Aries. 'Our official line is that we know nothing of Thanatos or his escape.'

'Excellent,' said Sagittarius. 'And I table a motion that we deny all knowledge of denying all knowledge.'

'Seconded,' said Scorpio. 'This Council knows nothing.'

'Agreed,' said Leo. 'When the history books are written, we will be remembered as the Council that knew nothing about anything.'

'Er – hang on a minute,' said Elliot, emerging from the behind the pillar to the astonishment of twelve council members and the annoyance of one.

'Elliot!' spat Virgo. 'I told you to stay there!'

'Elliot?' asked Aries. 'This is the mortal child of whom you spoke?'

'Yes, I was going to—'

'You've brought a mortal to Elysium?' roared Leo. 'Are you out of your mind?!'

'No, you see Thanatos was about to—'

'No mortal has ever set foot in Elysium!' shouted Cancer.

'Well it looks like I picked a good time to start,' said Elliot, slightly offended that the half-fish creature to his right was eyeing him up and down as if he were the oddity. 'Forgive me if I'm wrong, but didn't you just say that Thanatos was a threat to mankind?'

'I'm afraid we know nothing about that,' said Aries dismissively.

'You just said that he was a dangerous fugitive.'

'No he didn't,' said Capricorn. 'He didn't say anything.'

'So you're denying that Fleecy Features over there just

said that there's a death daemon on the loose who might just wipe out mankind with his daemon army?'

'No, he said that he'd need the Chaos Stones to unlock Tartarus, free his daemon army and wipe out mankind,' said one Gemini twin, before receiving a sharp nudge in the ribs from the other. 'Not that I have any knowledge of that.'

'So you've been put in charge of looking after the immortal community and the first time something serious happens, you're not going to do anything?'

'We are a council,' explained Pisces. 'It's not our job to actually do anything. We just have to file the correct paperwork.'

'It's not up to us to wage war on murderous death daemons,' added Taurus. 'Not that there are any of those. And if there were, we'd know nothing about them.'

'So this is your perfect system?' Elliot said to Virgo, who had sunk under the table until only the top of her silver head was visible. 'This is the world that is so much better than mine?'

All eyes turned to Virgo. Or the top of her head.

'The child has a point,' she finally squeaked from beneath the table. 'If Thanatos is as dangerous as you say he is, shouldn't we at least try to recapture him?'

'If Thanatos is as dangerous as we say he is, perhaps you shouldn't have let him go in the first place,' said Libra to a wall of death stares. 'Not that he is. Dangerous. Or even exists. I know nothing about it.'

‘Well on behalf of humankind, you’ve been a huge help,’ said Elliot, turning to leave. ‘Now if you could just beam me back to my endangered mortal life, I’d be very grateful.’

‘Virgo can show you the way. She’s just leaving herself,’ said Aries.

‘I am?’ asked Virgo, poking back up over the table.

‘You are,’ Aries pronounced. ‘Virgo, Goddess of the Zodiac Council and Guardian of the Stationery Cupboard. The Council hereby suspends you until further notice.’

‘WHAT???!!!’ shrieked Virgo. ‘You’re suspending me from the Council?’

‘No, child,’ said Aries grimly. ‘We are suspending you from immortality.’

Chapter Seven

Café Hero

Given the enormity of the sentence handed down to Virgo, Elliot expected something incredibly dramatic to happen when she was stripped of her immortality. He waited for the sparks to fly, for her body to be beamed up in a ray of light before being cast down onto the floor, a broken mortal shadow of her former immortal self.

But in fact, all that Virgo had to do was sign a few forms and hand over the keys to the stationery cupboard.

Elliot had no idea what to say to the now ex-Goddess as they walked away from the council chamber across the tree-lined plaza.

'I'm sorry you lost your job,' he finally offered.

'The Council has spoken,' said Virgo sadly. 'And the Council is always right.'

'A right bunch of—'

'It's my own fault. If I had obeyed the rules, none of this would have happened. Everything was perfect before.'

'So why did you leave?' Elliot asked.

'Because, I, er—' Virgo had absolutely no idea.

'Look, I'm sorry for your troubles and I'm really grateful for you saving my life and everything, but I really need to get home to Mum. Let's get into your whizzy star-ball thing and get back to the farm.'

'There is no whizzy star-ball thing now,' Virgo sighed. 'I'm mortal. We're going to have to take public transport. Bleurgh.'

They came to a halt by a beautiful river that lapped gently at the banks of the meadow. Virgo pursed her lips to whistle, but the only thing that came out of her mouth was a shower of spit, most of which landed on Elliot.

'Eugh – gross,' grumbled Elliot, wiping his T-shirt. 'Here, let me.'

Elliot put his thumb and forefinger into his mouth and let out a shrill and clear whistle. He and Grandad had spent hours perfecting that whistle. Grandad had known how to do so much cool stuff and Elliot had learned any number of useful tricks, including pickpocketing, semaphore, starting a fire and burping the alphabet.

'Try again,' said Virgo impatiently. 'This is so archaic.'

Elliot raised his fingers to give another blast, but before he could, he was violently drenched from head to foot by a huge wave that burst suddenly out of the river. The force of the water knocked him flying, and as he spluttered and choked on the grass, Elliot mopped the wet hair from his eyes to see what had caused this unexpected tsunami.

'At last,' said Virgo, who had remained inexplicably dry. 'It's here.'

Rocked by its own waves in the middle of the river, sat a long wooden boat, the kind Elliot recognised from Viking books. At the head was a carving of a ferocious lion and at the back, a serpent's winding tail. A pair of wooden oars balanced the boat on the river and a black sail hung from the tall mast, concealing the identity of the sailor onboard.

The boat was filled with passengers, who were even more bizarre than the ones Elliot had seen on a London bus once. There were two young goblins blowing bubble gum into a warlock's long grey hair, while a satyr was getting disapproving looks from an elderly fairy for playing heavy metal music on his pan pipes.

'Do you mind?' the fairy huffed, pointing to a sign of crossed out pan pipes on the mast.

'Whatevs,' muttered the satyr as he plugged some headphones into the pipes and returned to his thrash guitar solo.

'Hello Charon,' yelled Virgo. 'Room for two more?'

The black sail was drawn aside, and Elliot tried not to stare as he took in the sailor. The man, if that's what he was, was deathly white – Thanatos had been pale, but this guy was almost transparent. His stringy yellow hair hung limply down to his chin and a pair of pale grey eyes stared out of their dark sockets. Charon raised his finger and pointed straight at Elliot's heart.

'Come hither, mortal,' he said in a shaky, high-pitched voice, 'if you dare to ride the Ship of Death.'

Elliot decided that he didn't dare at all.

'Don't be ridiculous, Charon,' said Virgo impatiently, positioning the gangplank to reach them on dry land.

'Whatever do you mean Lady Virgo?' trembled Charon, shifting awkwardly in the boat.

'You sound like you've sat on a mouse. Use your real voice you fool.'

'Alright darlin', you got me,' laughed Charon several octaves lower, shrugging his shoulders with a chortle. 'Sorry mate, the tourists love all that stuff – come aboard.'

Elliot waited for Charon to whip off his disguise, but it appeared that the boatman was unfortunate enough to really look that way. He tentatively walked up the gangplank and onto the boat as Charon assumed his position at the oars.

'Welcome aboard mate,' said Charon with something that was supposed to be a smile. 'Nice to have you with us. I'm Charon, proprietor of Quick Styx Cabs. *You won't wait an eternity for us*. Made that up meself.'

'Well done,' said Elliot uncertainly, taking his place on a narrow bench next to a gorgon eating a particularly pungent egg sandwich.

'We need to get to back to Elliot's farm, it's . . .' Virgo looked to Elliot for instructions. 'You tell him. Charon can find anyone or anything.'

'Done the Eternal Knowledge,' said Charon proudly. 'I can take you anywhere you want to go. Except for the Underworld. Gods and mortals aren't allowed there – I don't go south of the river.'

'Home Farm? Little Motbury? Wiltshire? England? The World?' said Elliot, unsure how much detail to give an immortal cab driver.

'What river's it on?' asked Charon drawing the gangplank back in.

'Near the Avon. I think.' said Elliot.

'Right-o, we'll take the Severn – the Wye's murder this time of day. Hold on and off we go.'

And with an almighty tug on the oars, Charon eased the boat away from the bank and started along the glistening water. It was a nice change of pace after a hectic day, although Elliot was increasingly concerned that Mum had been on her own for too long.

'Excuse me Charon – how long will it take, please?' he asked the oarsman.

'We'll be there in two shakes of a hydra's tail,' assured Charon.

'And, er, how exactly are we going to row through the sky?' asked Elliot casually.

'We're on the River Styx,' said Virgo. 'It's the boundary between the Earth, Elysium above it and the Underworld below it. All the rivers on Earth run into it at some point underground, making it a very convenient way for immortals to get around unnoticed.'

'Back in the good old days, I used to take the souls of the dead from one life to the next,' explained Charon wistfully. 'Made a tidy earning too, ferrying spirits to the Underworld, getting a few coins for me troubles. But these days everyone makes their own arrangements when they snuff it. Nah, there's no money in the afterlife game anymore, I've had to branch out. Of course, it's all a conspiracy.'

'Oh don't start, Charon,' Virgo huffed. 'Not everything is a conspiracy.'

'That's what they want you to believe,' whispered Charon, tapping the side of his pasty nose, allowing a stray oar to whack a leprechaun off his seat. 'But I'm in the know.'

'You're in Cloud Cuckoo Land, Charon,' said Virgo with a shake of her silver head.

'No I'm not,' said the driver defensively. 'Besides, that's 637 miles due west, straight through the Asphodel Fields and second left after Dorking. Nah, we've all been fed a big pile of centaur droppings over the years. Take the creation story, if you really think that Uranus . . .'

Elliot started to zone Charon out as he looked over to a mournful Virgo staring wistfully out of the boat.

'What are you going to do?' he asked her.

'You heard them. I have to redeem myself.'

'How?'

'There is only one way,' said Virgo heavily.

'. . . and if you seriously believe that Hercules performed all twelve labours himself then you're dafter than Medusa's hairdresser . . .' Charon droned on.

'You're going to catch Thanatos,' said Elliot as Virgo nodded her silver head. 'Tell me something. If Zeus beat

Thanatos in the war, why did Thanatos say he'd been tricked?'

'Truthful daemons are rarer than wooden horse dung,' muttered Virgo. 'He was probably lying.'

'. . . and Theseus slaying the Minotaur? Do me a favour,' Charon scoffed. 'That boy couldn't win a food fight . . .'

'Thanatos doesn't have any reason to lie,' said Elliot. 'But perhaps whoever put him there does.'

'Zeus would never lie!' Virgo cried. 'He's the King of the Gods – well, retired. He will have fought that battle nobly and honorably.'

'Until he cheated,' announced Charon.

'What now?' said Virgo.

'Zeus beating Thanatos,' said Charon plainly. 'He cheated. Must have done.'

'What are you talking about?' sighed Virgo.

'Now listen, when it comes to the war, I'm as neutral as a magnolia living room in Switzerland. I get on fine with all sides. I've always been mates with the Olympians and I used to work with Thanatos,' said Charon. 'But if you believe that Zeus won those Chaos Stones in a fair fight, you're as blind as a Cyclops with an eye-patch.'

'Charon, you are full of as much poop as King Augeus's stables,' Virgo scoffed.

'I don't know how he did it,' said Charon. 'One minute Thanatos has all but won the war, the next Zeus has the Chaos Stones and it's game over. Thanatos would do anything to get them back. He loves those stones like a dung beetle loves diarrhoea.'

'What are they like?' asked Elliot.

'Well, they're small black beetles that like dung,' said Charon.

'The Chaos Stones,' said Elliot rolling his eyes.

'Oh them,' said Charon. 'Cor, they're a sight. Four of the most beautiful jewels you've ever seen. The Fire Stone is a deep red ruby, the Water Stone a boundless sapphire, the Air Stone a beautiful emerald and the Earth Stone, a brilliant diamond. Whoever owns the stones owns the elements – that's why Zeus couldn't beat Thanatos without them. If you've got the stones, you can create fires, floods, hurricanes, tsunamis – not to mention become as rich as King Midas. Before he invested all his wealth in seafront property in Atlantis.'

Elliot's ears pricked.

'Rich? How?' he asked, trying to sound casual.

'It's that Earth Stone,' said Charon. 'You think about it. If you control the Earth, you can find oil, gold, gems – you'd be minted in a minute.'

'And where are they now?' asked Elliot more keenly.

'Zeus still has them I guess,' said Charon. 'Although why he has to keep marrying all those rich women if he's got the Earth Stone, I dunno. Still, all work makes Zeus a dull boy.'

Elliot's mind was whirring a million to the dozen. A

stone that could make him instantly rich? A stone that could pay off his debts and buy his house back? A stone that could help him to kiss his money troubles away forever? Now that was a stone he needed to find.

'So Zeus is still alive?' Elliot asked.

'Must we have the immortal conversation again?' said Virgo. 'Of course he is, duh.'

'So he'll have the stones?' said Elliot. 'And if you're going to catch Thanatos, you're going to need some help.'

'Pah – you offering?' said Virgo condescendingly.

'Maybe,' said Elliot, the vision of the games console he was going to buy with the Earth Stone dancing in his head. 'But you need someone with experience. Someone who knows Thanatos well. Someone who has caught him before.'

Virgo looked as though she'd been hit by a thunderbolt.

'Oh my Gods!' gasped Virgo. 'Of course!'

'Took you long enough,' scoffed Elliot.

'Zeus, Athene, Aphrodite, Hephaestus – they caught him before. They can catch him again. You're not nearly as stupid as you seem.'

'Gee thanks,' said Elliot. 'So where are they?'

'Keeping a low profile. They retired millennia ago and blended into mortal life. You've probably walked past them and don't even know it.'

Elliot was pretty sure he'd notice a group of ancient Greek deities in the Little Motbury post office, but kept it to himself.

'Charon – can we make a stop on the way?'

'So where to?' Charon asked his passengers.

'I need to find Hermes,' said Virgo.

'That's easy,' said Charon with a nod of his pale head. 'This time of day – he'll be in that Café Hero having one of their fancy coffees. Now that whole business is dodgy if you ask me – they have more coffee shops than Dionysus has had hangovers.'

'To Café Hero,' said Virgo, finally brightening up. 'I think this is all going to work out perfectly.'

A few stops later and the Ship of Death pulled up outside a subterranean coffee shop.

'Here we are,' announced Charon as they came to a sudden halt outside a brightly-lit coffee shop on the side of the underground river. 'Café Hero.'

'Thanks Charon,' said Virgo.

'No problem,' said Charon. He looked down at the abacus on the front of the boat.

'That'll be three thousand drachma,' he said cheerily.

Virgo looked over at Elliot, who looked blankly back.

'What?' he said.

'Well I haven't got that sort of money,' she said. 'I was only coming here for the afternoon. You'll have to pay him.'

'I'm sorry,' said Elliot to Charon, rummaging around in his pocket for the £3.76 he'd stashed there earlier in the day. 'This is all I have.'

Charon's eyes became the size of saucers.

'Mortal money!' he whispered. 'Can I, can I really?'

'Of course,' said Elliot, trying not to wince at the thought of losing his entire week's spending money. But as Charon's hand withdrew from Elliot's, Elliot saw that the boatman had only taken a single 2p piece.

'I love these ones,' he said. 'They're the biggest. And if you ask me, the drachma is an unsustainable currency, it'll crash any minute. Which is what they want, of course.'

'Are you sure?' said Elliot, not wanting to cheat the man who might just have solved all his financial woes.

'Oh I'm not trying to rip you off mate, that includes the tip,' said Charon, still staring at his fare.

'Well, great – keep the change,' said Elliot, bemused for the millionth time that day.

'And here,' said Charon, fishing around in his pocket, producing a small piece of parchment. 'Here's my card. If you ever need me, just drop this in the nearest water and I'll come and find you.'

'Thanks Charon,' said Virgo.

'Right-o, ta-ra kids,' he said, pulling out a newspaper and a sandwich with something horrible wriggling inside it. 'Zodiac Council to Lower Taxes,' he read on the front page. 'Believe that, you'll believe anything . . .'

At first glance, Café Hero could have been any normal high street coffee shop above the ground. The brightly lit windows advertised a warm interior and inviting aromas floated out of the door as Elliot and Virgo made their way through it. Inside, a large coffee bar stood in the centre of the shop, steaming away with bubbling machines and whirring blenders, surrounded by glass cases full of the most tempting cakes and pastries – and the occasional slimy thing with elaborate icing on top.

High tables and long stools dotted the floor and cosy booths lined the walls of the room, which was filled with the gentle hum of coffee and conversation. But a quick look at the inhabitants revealed that this was no ordinary café. The tables were filled with extraordinary creatures of all shapes and sizes, from dragons, to fairies, to . . . Elliot didn't even know what half of them were. He looked around the nearby tables. To his left, a couple of Furies were doing crosswords over an espresso, while on his right, a unicorn fed her foal from a giant blueberry muffin on the end of her horn.

Even the two members of staff were fantastical creatures, both with long necks supporting at least a dozen heads each and countless arms, which sprang from every part of their torso. It was an inspired arrangement for their jobs, as the server could simultaneously take umpteen orders and prepare them all at once, and the waiter could clear at least ten tables at a time, whilst merrily chatting to several different customers around the café.

'Hecatoncheires,' Virgo explained, 'hundred-handed ones. They run the most successful chain of coffee houses in creation – they're springing up everywhere. 'Hi Kottos,' she called, in return to the forty or so hands waving in her direction. 'Now where is he? Ah – Hermes.'

Virgo's gaze fell on a tall, tanned man standing in the long queue for the counter between a sphinx and a troll. He was dressed from head to toe in designer labels, from his super-trendy T-shirt to his fashionable jeans. The outfit was topped off with a trilby hat and designer trainers, both of which had small, feathered wings on the side.

'Hermes! Hermes!' yelled Virgo over the hustle and bustle, but Hermes continued looking around the café, singing to himself and gently bopping on the spot.

'Great,' huffed Virgo, as she and Elliot worked their way down the queue, narrowly missing a bite from a grumpy werewolf and apologising to a hydra for stepping on one of her tails. Eventually, having irritated most of the queuing customers, they reached the winged messenger and after a deep breath to calm herself, Virgo tapped him on the shoulder. Hermes spun his handsome head around, taking a moment to recognise the young Goddess standing before him. But within seconds, he had thrown his hands to his face in a delighted gasp.

'Da-a-a-a-a-a-rling!' he screeched at a pitch Elliot had never heard a man use before, waking a nearby pram of baby goblins. 'So sorry lovely, *totally* plugged into my iGod – The Sirens have released a new album and I just can't switch it off. Hang on a jiffy.'

Hermes fiddled around in the small leather satchel slung across his body and produced a gold music player with a tortoiseshell back. He pulled two golden earphones out of his ears and turned to hug Virgo.

'How are you, sweet thing?' he squealed. 'It's been mi-llenn-i-a darling, love what you're still doing with your hair, it's sooo Golden Age. And who's this handsome chap – finally giving three thousand years of spinsterhood the elbow, you little minx?'

'Good to see you Hermes, this is Elliot, I'll introduce you later, but listen, I need your help.'

'Not another word, sweet thing,' interrupted Hermes, 'whatever you want is yours for the asking. Gossip, scandal, hair that suits your face shape – you name it.'

'I need to find Zeus. It's urgent.'

Hermes could see from Virgo's worried face that this was no time for questions.

'Of course,' said Hermes. 'But darling, you're not going to get one word of sense out of me until I've had my nectarchino – give me one quick seccy-tick.'

Elliot wasn't confident they were going to get word of sense out of Hermes anyway, but waited patiently whilst Hermes ordered a skinny-double-frappa-something-or-other and sat with him at one of the tables as he took a sip.

'Oh thank the Gods,' said Hermes dramatically, refreshed by his drink. 'Okay, the quickest way to find old man Zeus is to look on the gossip pages, he's usually in there somewhere.'

He reached back into the leather bag, which had a rolled newspaper sticking out of it. Hermes handed it to Virgo, who unfurled its pages while Elliot went behind her to read over her shoulder.

The newspaper was printed on browning parchment, with a large central banner across the top. '*The Daily Argus,*' it pronounced in classic Greek type, '*Keeping an eye on the Immortal Community*'. Small boxes around the edges advertised the paper's contents, from the weather forecast by the Delphi Oracle to horoscopes by Cassandra.

Hermes pulled out another copy of *The Daily Argus*, which had magically appeared in the apparently small bag, and thumbed through the pages.

'Here we go – *Catty Catullus's Cat Calls,*' Hermes pulled the page down to speak to Elliot. 'I know it's trash, but I just can't get enough of it. Oh look, Cerberus has had another baby.'

He read from the paper:

DOTING DADDY

by Catullus, Births and Re-Births Correspondent

The Hound of Hell is proud to announce
A baby girl, five pounds and one ounce

She's already got a big sister and brother
Let's hope that the children don't eat one another

'Ah, how sweet,' said Hermes.

'Hermes!' chided Virgo.

'Oh yes, sorry sweetie, attention span of a goldfish. Blah, blah, blah – okay, here we are. I might have known, he's in the Engagements section again, listen to this:

JUST MARRIED . . . AGAIN

By Homer, Society Editor

You've gotta admit it, old Zeus has some faith
He's married more women than Henry the Eighth
His heart has been won by the mortal Petunia
Who's roughly twelve thousand and four years his junior
They're planning a wedding, it's true love of course
Zeus promises this time he's got a divorce
Given his record, the bride must be plucky
You know what they say, three-hundredth time lucky
The honeymoon's planned for the island of Malta
Provided they make it as far as the altar

'The sly old dog,' said Hermes with an admiring shake of his head. 'But wait a gorgon-slaying mo – the wedding is in an hour!'

'Can you get us there?' Elliot asked.

'Can supermodels wear slingbacks?' Hermes announced confidently, positioning a pair of expensive sunglasses on his nose, admiring his reflection in the shop window. 'Kottos! I'll take my nectarchino to go. We've got a wedding to get to.'

Chapter Eight

For Better or Worse

Elliot honestly believed earlier that day that travelling by constellation was the most terrifying experience he was ever likely to have. But that was before he had travelled on Hermes's moped.

At first, the prospect of riding on the messenger God's funky motorbike had seemed incredibly awesome – there's no way Mum would ever let him ride a bike like that.

But as Hermes weaved crazily beneath the Earth, swerving around, blasting through or occasionally flying over (his moped had wings to match his shoes) any obstacle in his path, Elliot found himself clinging on to Virgo for his mortal life as they rode behind the God.

'Should be there in no time,' yelled Hermes back to his two passengers, who were clutching on behind him. 'Hang on – this bit can be a bit bumpy . . .'

Virgo and Elliot exchanged nervous glances as the bike suddenly took off towards the open sky above, speeding up with a jolt to make the climb to the Earth beyond. The scooter whizzed out of the ground and landed square in the middle lane of the M56.

'Don't mortals think that's strange?' Elliot shouted to Hermes, who revved the bike up another gear.

'Not at all,' Hermes yelled back. 'They're so busy hating anyone on a bike that they won't stop to think where I came from.'

The bike charged on up the motorway, finally turning off at the A784573, signposted to The Royal Withering St Stan's Golf Club.

'Nearly there,' yelled Hermes to a relieved Elliot, who hadn't had blood in his fingertips for seven junctions.

The bike drove for a few quick miles down a country road until it reached a grand blue sign for The Royal Withering St Stan's Golf Club. Hermes swung into the car park alongside cars that seemed the size of Elliot's cowshed. At last, the moped came to a welcome stop. Elliot dismounted quickly, his legs still vibrating from the scooter's relentless engine.

'Slumming it again, Zeus,' grinned Hermes as he took in the grand façade of the Golf Club, a stately home set in acres of lush green golf course. 'I wonder who the lucky girl is this time?'

'Exactly how many times has Zeus been married?' Elliot asked.

'You'd have to ask him,' said Hermes. 'He wouldn't have a clue either, but he'd probably come up with a better lie than me. Come on – we've got five minutes.'

Elliot looked over to an elaborate gold carriage, in which he could see nothing but an enormous white dress. Three salmon-pink bridesmaids were struggling to free the bride from her carriage, but the circumference of the wedding dress had her wedged firmly in the door. As the carriage rocked and jolted, the beautiful white horse pulling it struggled to keep still, releasing an irritated whinny. His eyes had been blasted on the back of Hermes's moped, but Elliot could have sworn the horse actually rolled its eyes.

They joined the groups of well-dressed wedding guests bearing elaborately wrapped wedding gifts. The ladies wore furs, the gentlemen wore tuxedos. Hermes looked woefully at his T-shirt and jeans.

'Oh this will never do,' he said, pulling the iGod out of his bag. He started to scroll through the machine. As he scrolled the dial in the centre, his outfits changed from sportswear to beachwear to a pair of lederhosen.

'Hermes, we don't have time,' snapped Virgo. 'We need to get to Zeus. Quickly.'

'There's always time to look sharp, sweet thing,' said Hermes, finally settling on a designer tuxedo. He offered the iGod to Virgo. 'Your turn?' he said hopefully.

'Hermes!' Virgo snapped.

'Suit yourself,' he sighed. 'You can lead a unicorn to water.'

They tucked in behind a woman wearing a fox fur around her shoulders.

'Well of course we all know that the only reason he chose

Petunia rather than me is because of her cheese scones,' said Mrs Fox to her companion, who was also draped in dead animal. 'I hope he enjoys them. And the massive hips they're giving her.'

The dead fox head looked mournfully at Elliot. Not only had it been snatched from the prime of life, but it was now stuck around the neck of this ridiculous woman.

'Bride or Groom?' asked the usher.

'Neither, you fool,' Mrs Fox announced. 'I'm a guest.'

Elliot entered the grandiose room. Every surface was covered in wood. There was so much wood everywhere, the overall effect was like being inside a rabbit hutch, but it was the most expensive rabbit hutch Elliot had ever seen. It looked as though a wedding had thrown up everywhere. Flowers adorned every surface, pink balloons filled every corner and there was even a huge chocolate fountain at one end of the room with a plastic bride and groom dangling their feet into it.

The guests were taking their seats, most people looking suspiciously at their neighbours as if they'd never seen them before and were glad that they hadn't.

'Now where is he?' Hermes said, hovering slightly off the ground to see over the throngs of people to the front of the room. 'Ah – there we are!'

Elliot followed Hermes's finger to the figure, which quite obviously belonged to the King of the Gods. Even with his back to them, Elliot could see that this tall, broad man had the bearing of a regal God – noble, strong and brave. Hermes, Virgo and Elliot fought their way through the chattering guests towards this towering presence, Elliot wondering what on Earth he would say to such a great immortal being.

Although as the man turned around, he didn't have to wonder long.

'Champagne sir?' said the waiter, offering a glass to Hermes.

'Oooh – don't mind if I do,' said Hermes, taking the drink gladly.

'You'd better top me up too, old boy,' boomed a voice behind him. 'Condemned man and all that.'

'Zeus!' Virgo gasped gladly as the waiter moved aside to reveal the real King of the Gods standing behind him.

Mythology was one of the few subjects that Elliot enjoyed at school and so he was familiar with the images of Zeus, with white hair flowing down his broad back and his strapping chest bursting out of a toga as he hurled thunderbolts at his enemies.

So he was rather surprised to find Zeus in a badly-fitting light blue tuxedo with a frilly shirt, holding a cheese and ham vol-au-vent. The long white hair was there, albeit badly slicked back with hair gel. And it wasn't a strapping chest bursting out of his clothing. It was a gigantic belly.

'Virgo! Hermes!' said Zeus warmly, taking Virgo into a

big bear hug. 'So good of you to come. Such a special day. This one's a keeper. Whatever her name is. And who do we have here?'

He extended a crummy hand towards Elliot.

'Elliot, Your Majesty,' said Elliot, looking into the smiling deep blue eyes set in a lined face. 'Elliot Hooper.'

'Smashing to meet you Elliot,' boomed Zeus. 'Lovely to have you here. I do love a good wedding.'

'He just doesn't enjoy the married bit afterwards,' smirked Hermes.

'Behave, you young whippersnapper,' laughed Zeus, hitting Hermes so hard on the back that he fell over. 'Good show.'

'Zeus – I desperately need your help,' said Virgo. 'I've done something terrible.'

'There, there, can't be that bad,' said Zeus. 'No worse than these vol-au-vents anyway. I've had better food from Tantalus's Takeaway.'

The organ struck up a chorus of *Here Comes the Bride*.

'Oh cripes,' gulped Zeus, dropping the vol-au-vent and wiping his crummy hands on his suit. 'Here we go again.'

'But Zeus, I—' started Virgo.

She was drowned out by the chorus of 'ahh' announcing that Petunia, the bride, had made it out of the carriage and onto the aisle.

Petunia had waited a long time for this moment. At fifty-five years old, she'd found Mr Wrong, Mr Stupid, Mr Boring and Mr Married, but finally she believed that the man she knew as Gordon was her Mr Right. Yes, Gordon was the man she was going to settle down and share her considerable wealth with. And Gordon was happy to agree.

Trailing behind Petunia with faces like slapped bottoms were Petunia's three sisters, Ivy, Daisy and Willow, who were trying to look happy that their younger sister had found a husband before they had. And that she'd made them look like three tins of salmon as they shambled down the aisle behind her.

However, Petunia had made one significant miscalculation. When ordering the biggest wedding dress she could find, she hadn't measured the space it had to walk down. The dress was wider than the aisle. She pushed valiantly on for the first few rows, taking out the flower arrangements on the end of the rows, a baby's pushchair and her Aunty Ethel's walking frame. Petunia paused for a moment, swatting a bunch of lilies and a packet of wet wipes off her dress with her bouquet before forcing her way onwards. She took another step forward, but became wedged between two rows. Plastering a grin on her face, Petunia tried to free herself, but the more she struggled, the tighter her dress stuck.

She looked back to her sisters, who were shaking their heads after already freeing her from her bedroom door, the garden gate, into the carriage, out of the carriage and a particularly distressing incident in the Ladies. Petunia looked towards her future husband, who was turned away, apparently taking a swig of something from a bottle concealed in his tux.

'Zeus,' whispered Virgo. 'Zeus, I really need to—'

'Gordon!' Petunia sang down the aisle. 'Darling, I need you!'

Zeus continued to drain the dregs from his bottle, not remembering the false name he'd given his future bride.

'GORDON!' Petunia shrieked making Zeus drop the bottle in surprise and kick it hastily away.

'Yes, my fragrant flower! Ah,' said Zeus, seeing his bride's predicament and hastily striding up the aisle to save her. 'Don't you look tickety boo!'

Zeus quickly assessed the situation. The hoop at the bottom of the dress was firmly wedged between two rows. The only way to free Petunia was to free the hoop.

'Hold on darling, we'll have you free in a jiffy,' he said, grabbing the bottom of the hoop firmly. 'Hold tight now. One. Two. Three!'

Zeus gave the dress an almighty tug. It worked. The bottom of the hoop came unstuck. But such was the width and weight of the dress, the dress merely tipped backwards. Still stuck, Petunia was now stranded in mid-air with her legs dangling around in the breeze, flashing her frilly knickers at the registrar.

'Aaaargh! Gordon! Help!'

'Hold on old girl,' said Zeus, grabbing one of her legs.

'Hermes dear chap – grab the other one for me.'

At his king's bidding – and with some difficulty given the strength, size and motion of the bride – Hermes grabbed Petunia's other leg.

'Nice shoes,' he whispered to the stricken bride. 'And a lovely service.'

'Right, on my count – one, two, three . . . HEAVE!' Zeus counted before giving Petunia another great big pull as if she were a tug-of-war rope. Hermes followed his king's lead and the two men pulled the squealing Petunia.

'She's coming,' strained Zeus. 'Keep going, old boy.'

The two Gods continued to yank Petunia's flailing legs as the bride squeaked and squealed and her sisters tried not to wet their knickers laughing.

'Kicks like a mule,' Hermes muttered to Zeus.

'Sings like one too,' mumbled Zeus back. 'Hang on my precious, nearly there.'

With an almighty tug the Gods pulled Petunia one last time. And this time it worked. Petunia flew free. But sadly for her, the dress did not. Now dressed only in her frilly knickers and some underwear that made her look like an Egyptian mummy, Petunia popped out of her frock like a champagne cork, taking Zeus and Hermes with her as they tumbled down the aisle, before landing headfirst in the chocolate fountain.

Betty the organist didn't really pay much attention to weddings these days, but thought it was taking the bride a particularly long time to come down the aisle. She looked up to see what was going on and was surprised to see the bride still standing at the top of the aisle. And she could have sworn she was wearing a much bigger dress a moment ago. Clearly Betty had done too many weddings. She'd nearly come to the end of the song anyway, so she started *Here Comes the Bride* for the second time.

But Betty was right. The dress was different. In fact, so was the bride. Like Petunia, Enid had been waiting years to meet Mr Right. Like Petunia, she was delighted when a dashing man her age came into her life wanting to share her life and money. And just like Petunia, she had agreed to marry him on Saturday 15th October at Royal Withering St Stan's Golf Club.

'Frederick!' Enid shouted down the aisle to her groom, who was lying under the chocolate fountain beneath a big mass of support knickers and petticoats. 'What is the meaning of this?'

Zeus poked his head out from beneath a flap of petticoat.

'Enid. My angel. You're a vision,' he said.

'And you're a cheating ratbag!' howled Enid, picking up her dress and charging down the aisle, until she was stopped by Petunia's wedding dress and hysterical sisters. 'Wait till I get my hands on you, you old dog!'

With one bride still struggling to get out of the fountain and other fighting her way down the aisle, Zeus let out a shrill whistle, at which the beautiful white horse that Elliot had seen outside came thundering into the room.

'Pegasus! Over here!' Zeus yelled. 'SOS!'

Pegasus took a charge down the aisle, elegantly leaping over Enid, the bridesmaids and the wedding dress like a frontrunner in the Grand National.

'Quickly, up you come,' said Zeus, scrabbling his way onto the horse's back, helping Virgo and Elliot in front of him.

But by this time, the guests were in uproar, with Petunia and Enid's friends fighting over who had the greater claim to the wedding – not to mention the free champagne at the reception. Zeus looked helplessly at Hermes, who nodded with a cheeky smile.

Hermes calmly walked into the fighting crowd, touching the dead animals that were draped around the fat necks of their owners, muttering mystical words under his breath. At his touch, the furs suddenly snapped to life, yapping at their owners and chasing them around the room. It did the trick perfectly. The crowds cleared, giving Pegasus a clear run back down the aisle.

'Come on Peg – step on it,' said Zeus pulling the reins of his magnificent steed. Pegasus set his head down and charged out of the church, avoiding the furs scampering around the floor, finally taking revenge on their owners for years of suffering around their bloated necks. With Hermes fluttering discreetly behind, they headed out into the open air. Zeus took a cautious look behind him. 'Okay Peg – up, up and away!'

And with that, Pegasus took a run up the fairway, unfurled the almighty wings folded beneath his saddle as he gathered pace, spread them wide and after a few galloping steps, took off into the clear blue afternoon, as a chocolate-coated Petunia came running out of the golf club in her undies, pelting the retreating God with ham and cheese vol-au-vents.

It was the fourth time that day that Elliot had travelled by immortal transport and after some initial fears as his feet left the ground again, travelling by flying horse soon became his favourite. As the magnificent Pegasus climbed high into the sky, Elliot was treated to the most beautiful view of the world below, which spread out beneath them like an ornate patchwork quilt.

'Couldn't trouble you for a place to lay my hat, could I old boy?' Zeus yelled into Elliot's ear. 'Need to lie low for a minute.'

'Of course, Your Highness,' said Elliot, as he directed the King of the Gods back to the farm that so desperately needed the Earth Stone that Elliot was going to 'borrow' from Zeus the first chance he got.

An hour later, Pegasus touched down in the disused paddock of Home Farm. Zeus, Elliot and Virgo dismounted the steed. Elliot tried to look away as Zeus struggled to get his considerable girth off his horse. After an extraordinary effort, Zeus eventually managed to get both legs pointing in the same direction and dropped inelegantly to the ground. He pulled himself up, ripped off his tux and revealed a bright orange Bermuda shirt and Hawaiian shorts underneath.

'That's better,' he said. 'Been dying to get rid of that wretched thing.'

'The tux or the bride?' asked Hermes as he screeched to a halt on his moped.

Virgo dropped into a dutiful low curtsey, but Zeus dismissed her formality with a wave of his hand.

'Oh enough of that nonsense,' boomed Zeus, his bright blue eyes sparkling like sapphires. 'Come here and give your old king a hug.'

Virgo ran to her ruler with a relieved smile and was soon enveloped in a vast Bermuda bear hug.

'That's more like it,' laughed Zeus, his twinkling gaze lighting on Elliot. 'Wonderful to meet you too Elliot, can't thank you enough for getting me out of a tight spot there. Some call me Jupiter, others call me Brontios. To at least five of my ex-wives, I'm a plumber called Dave. But you can call me Zeus.'

Elliot accepted a giant handshake, trying not to wince as the God crushed his fingers with his friendly strength.

'And over here,' said Zeus, gesturing towards the winged white stallion behind him, 'this fine fellow is my trusty steed, Pegasus.'

At the sound of his name, Pegasus trotted over to the small gathering. Elliot had loved the horses they'd had on the farm and this one was a truly majestic specimen. Elliot gently lifted his hand to stroke the horse's elegant head.

'Hey boy,' he whispered gently.

'If you require a dog to fetch you a stick, then please carry on,' said Pegasus grandly, shocking Elliot into silence. 'But if you are referring to me, my name is Pegasus. And I'm gasping for a mineral water.'

'You can talk,' said Elliot pointlessly.

'I'm a flying horse,' said Pegasus pertly. 'Talking's the easy part. And I prefer sparkling with a twist of lime.'

Elliot looked blankly around him, having never catered for a talking, flying immortal horse.

'Oh don't mind him,' said Zeus dismissively. 'Get off your high horse, Peg. There's a water trough over there, that'll do just fine.'

Pegasus looked over at the rusty trough filled with murky brown water and released a disdainful whinny.

'I suppose a few ice-cubes would be too much to ask,' he huffed as he sauntered over to it, sticking his nose as high into the air as he possibly could.

'Well this is all just super,' said Zeus cheerily.

'Zeus – we've got a problem,' said Virgo, unable to look her king in the eye. 'I've done something dreadful.'

'I'm sure we can fix it,' said Zeus. 'I've got a brilliant lawyer if we need one. He could get an Athenian out of a labyrinth. And make the Minotaur pay costs. Elliot, could we trouble you for somewhere to sit and chat please?'

Instinctively feeling that a chubby God, a flying fashion model and a talking horse might be too much for Mum, Elliot ushered everyone towards Bessie's cowshed, where they pulled up some hay bales and sat around in a circle. Pegasus strode in behind them, earning a flirtatious moo from Bessie, whom he haughtily ignored and settled himself for a rest on a pile of straw.

'Well isn't this delightful,' boomed Zeus, looking around the ramshackle shed as if he were sat in the Ritz. 'So, who is going to fill me in?'

Virgo and Elliot recounted their meeting with Thanatos in as much detail as they could remember, while Hermes and Zeus listened intently.

'And that's when I thought I should find you,' said Virgo at the end of their story, hanging her head towards the floor. 'I'm sorry Zeus, this is all my fault.'

'We'll have no more of that,' said Zeus kindly. 'If anyone is to blame, it is me, Virgo. Thanatos was my responsibility and I should never have left it to anyone but myself.'

'Charon said that you tricked Thanatos out of the Chaos Stones,' said Elliot. 'Is that true?'

'Oh for goodness' sake, Elliot – I'm sorry, Zeus, Charon's been filling his head with—'

'Yes,' said Zeus. 'I'm frightfully ashamed to admit that it is.'

'What?' gasped Virgo.

'Ah. Well. You see, thing was that the war against Thanatos was a frightful business,' Zeus began. 'Mortals massacred in their thousands, Gods sustaining terrible injuries that couldn't heal. I used every trick and tactic I knew, but whilst Thanatos had the Chaos Stones, I couldn't get near him. He controlled the elements, you see. So every time we got near him, we'd get blasted back again by a hurricane, or washed away with a tidal wave. He just couldn't be defeated while he still had those stones.'

'So you fought him and won the stones. No harm, no foul, darling,' said Hermes. 'If all Thanatos wants is the Chaos Stones, Zeus will have them locked up tighter than jeggings in January. Won't you, boss?'

Zeus's attention was suddenly drawn all around the shed as he started to whistle quietly.

'Zeeeuuuuus?' asked Hermes suspiciously. 'You have got the stones, right?'

'Not... exactly,' said Zeus sheepishly.

'So where are they?' Elliot asked, his heart sinking as his money troubles moved a step closer again.

'There's the rub,' said Zeus, rubbing his hands on his trousers. 'I can admit it now, Thanatos was more powerful then me. I just couldn't get near him. I wasn't able to win them in a fair fight, so I rather . . . well . . . sort of . . .'

'You cheated!' gasped Hermes dramatically, holding his drooping jaw in his hands.

'In a manner of speaking. Well – yes,' admitted Zeus. 'Thanatos wasn't only making enemies with us. As the war went on, many of his daemon comrades became jealous of the power the stones gave him. I struck a deal with four of his closest followers – the daemons Mammon, Lilith, Leviathan and Amon. They wanted the power of the stones for themselves. They could get close to Thanatos and agreed to steal the Chaos Stones, robbing him of his power. In return, I had to promise that they could each keep a stone and would escape imprisonment when I won the war.'

'You made a deal with the daemons?' asked Virgo in disbelief.

'What else could I do?' said Zeus. 'The war was destroying Earth and Thanatos would never have rested until every last mortal was dead and every immortal was his slave. I had no choice. I made them swear on the Styx that the stones would never be used to harm mankind and warned each of them that I never wanted to see or hear from them again. I've never seen them or the Chaos Stones from that day to this.'

Zeus hung his head in shame as his audience took his story in.

'Oh. My. Giddy. Aunt. Gertrude's. Pickled. Porcupines,' panted Hermes from the shed floor. 'I just can't believe it.'

Elliot felt winded. He had a week to find twenty thousand pounds and now this one ray of hope had faded too. Elliot needed that stone – and fast.

'I'm not proud, chaps,' said Zeus. 'But the important thing is getting to those stones before Thanatos does. It's hard to know whether he hates Gods or mortals more, but if he gets his hands on the Chaos Stones again, he can free his daemon army and then we'll all be in the soup. I'm going to need the girls.'

'Fifi and Trixie?' asked Hermes.

'No, no, no,' muttered Zeus. 'Although . . . No. I mean my girls, Athene and Aphrodite. And Hephaestus, he's always handy in a crisis. Elliot – may we trouble you for a place to stay tonight? This fine establishment will do nicely. It's getting late – we can fetch the girls tomorrow.'

'Yeah, why not,' said Elliot.

'Come Elliot,' said Zeus, pushing himself up to his feet. 'Give me a tour of this fine home of yours. I could do with stretching my legs after that long flight.'

Zeus looked out at the overgrown farmlands that had long since fallen into disuse. The crumbling soil was thick with weeds, which had been the only plants to grow on Elliot's farm for years.

'I'm ever so grateful to you, Elliot. I wonder if there is anything I might do to repay your kind hospitality, old chap?' Zeus said.

'Unless I can find twenty thousand pounds by the end of next week, there won't be any hospitality,' said Elliot. 'You don't happen to have it in your back pocket, do you?'

''Fraid not, dear boy,' said Zeus. 'And if I did, I'd owe

half of it to at least 57 ex-wives. Gods aren't allowed to keep mortal money. It's against . . .'

'. . . The Sacred Code,' sighed Elliot. 'I know. It was worth a try.'

'Money worries, eh?' said Zeus kindly.

'It might not look like much,' said Elliot looking out at the crumbling farm. 'But it's our home.'

'I understand,' smiled Zeus. 'Well it seems we both need a hand, so how about this? If you help me find the Earth Stone, you can use it to get some cash together quick smart.'

'We've only got a week,' said Elliot doubtfully.

'Plenty of time,' smiled Zeus. 'I can find a wife, get divorced and marry her sister in half the time. In the meantime, my sisters Hestia and Demeter run a very successful home makeover business and, with your permission, perhaps they could spruce things up around here?'

'Sure. Why not?' said Elliot, starting to tire after a very long and eventful day.

'Top hole,' smiled Zeus again as Hermes hovered towards them. 'You're tired, Elliot – we can manage from here. Why don't you head back home? Oh, and here,' he added summoning up a hamper from thin air, 'a few leftovers from the wedding. Shame for it all to go to waste. Again.'

'Thanks,' said Elliot, struggling under the weight of the food inside. 'I'll see you in the morning.'

'Toodle-pip,' said Zeus as Hermes fluttered down next

to him. The two Gods watched the young boy struggle back to the farmhouse with his supper.

'Thank the Heavens you found me,' said Zeus when Elliot was out of earshot. 'We need to stay close to Elliot – he's in terrible danger.'

'Do you think he's the one?' said Hermes. 'The one the prophecy foretold?'

'Almost certainly,' said Zeus. 'And I wouldn't wish that on my worst enemy.'

In a cramped bedsit above a betting shop, a different immortal was asking the same question.

'So I can't kill the child?' asked Thanatos as he sat before Pythia, Oracle of Delphi, conveyor of prophecies and manager of Bottom Drachma Bets in Twitching, Kent.

'Your liberator could be your killer,' said Pythia in a dazed trance. 'But your liberator may not be killed.'

Thanatos picked up the remote control and switched off *60 Minute Makeover*.

'Oi, I was watching that!' said a huffy Pythia.

'Pay attention,' snapped Thanatos. 'Are you telling me that this child has the power to kill me?'

'Look, I don't make this stuff up,' said Pythia, walking over to a battered computer and searching through her e-mails. 'I just give you the odds.'

Pythia hit the print button on her computer and an aged

printer slowly churned out a piece of paper. She handed it to Thanatos and he read his prophecy:

To: oracle@delphi.com
Date: 986BC
Subject: Thanatos (Plus how YOU can save on YOUR chariot insurance!)

The daemon restrained in the chains of gold
Can only be freed by a mortal not old
The child can't die from a terrible deed
By the hand of the daemon he generously freed
But daemon beware – your life with no end
Can now be cut short by your new mortal friend
As enemies you'll both keep your power alone
Unite – and you'll share the power of four stones

'Unite with a mortal? Don't be disgusting,' said Thanatos, tossing the paper aside. 'Does he defeat me?'

'I'm not psychic – I can't even tell you if they're going to wallpaper this sitting room in 60 minutes,' said Pythia. 'But while the mortal child is alive, the smart money's on him.'

Pythia flicked *60 Minute Makeover* back onto her small TV set. The conversation was over.

'I see,' said Thanatos, dissembling back into the mortal

disguise he arrived in. 'In which case, Elliot Hooper can't stay alive for very much longer.'

Excited by the prospect of a good meal after a long day, Elliot staggered back to the farmhouse as quickly as he could. He went to put his key in the lock. But the door was already open. The knot of fear tightened in his stomach again. Where was Mum?

But as he walked into the farmhouse, the sound of Josie's laughter reassured him that all was well. Until he saw who was sitting with her.

'Hello Honeybunches!' gushed Patricia Porshley-Plum, looking like that cat that got the cream the same day it won the mouse lottery.

Elliot's stomach clenched.

'What are you doing here?' he asked stiffly.

'Elly – don't be rude,' chided his mum.

'That's fine Josie, we've had the loveliest day, haven't we?'

'We went out for lunch, Elly!' said his mum in delight. 'I had steak!'

'That's great Mum,' said Elliot, his eyes not leaving Patricia's smug smirk. 'What did you talk about?'

'Oh you know girls – we chewed the hind legs off a donkey, Muffin!' Patricia guffawed. 'Anyway, you're back now, so I'll tootle off.'

Elliot looked at his Mum for any signs of trouble. But Josie simply looked like she'd had a lovely time.

'We should do this more often, Josie,' said Patricia as she walked past Elliot. 'It really has been the most wonderful day. Ta ta for now.'

And Patricia Porshley-Plum breezed out of the farm in a fug of over-priced perfume and self-satisfaction, leaving a bewildered Elliot feeling like the little pig who lived in the house of straw when there was a knock at the door.

Chapter Nine

Family Matters

Sunday dawned before Elliot's tired body was entirely ready for it. He'd spent a troubled night worrying about what Patricia Porshley-Plum had been doing with his Mum at her mercy for a whole day. He'd tried to find out from Josie where they'd gone and what they'd done, but the day was already a distant memory by the time evening came and Elliot didn't want to push his Mum's tired mind any further.

He felt uneasy leaving her again, but if he were to save their home, he needed to help the Gods find that Earth Stone. It was for the best in the long term – once he'd saved Home Farm, he could get back to taking care of Mum.

Making sure Josie had everything she needed for the day, Elliot headed over to the cowshed, which was already a hive of activity. As Zeus had promised, his sisters had come to the farm and as Elliot approached the shed, he was greeted by Demeter, a plump, ruddy-faced farmer walking around the newly-ploughed fields in her overalls, scattering seeds that were immediately springing up into every known variety of mouth-watering oversized fruit and vegetables. Elliot wasn't sure how he was going to explain the presence of giant banana trees in the middle of a damp Wiltshire farm to anyone who came looking, but he returned Demeter's friendly wave and rosy smile as she threw him an orange the size of a football.

Hestia, a petite, dark-haired Goddess dressed in a smart red suit, was marching around the shed with a clipboard and a pair of golden glasses perched on the end of her nose, leading a gaggle of knee-sized humans, who at Hestia's command, would whizz away in a cloud of smoke, returning almost instantly with a tape measure, piece of fabric or whatever other order they had received.

'Penates,' said Virgo through a mouthful of giant watermelon, taking Elliot by surprise. 'What they can't do with MDF and some sticky-back plastic isn't worth knowing,' she added as Hestia strode past shaking her head and muttering about colour schemes and creating space.

'I don't know what's wrong with me,' said Virgo, showering a nearby gaggle of penates in orange juice as she dug into Elliot's orange. 'I have this curious sensation in my stomach demanding that I fill it with food every minute of the day. I've only ever eaten for pleasure before. No wonder you mortals are so uncivilised if you have to spend this much time eating. And as for going to the toilet – who in Tartarus thought of that?'

Elliot left Virgo to her feeding frenzy and sought out Zeus, who was reclining on a makeshift hay sofa reading

The Daily Argus, apparently oblivious to the chaos around him. He spotted Elliot and gave him a warm grin.

'Good morning old boy!' he roared happily. 'Ready for the off?'

'Ready as I'll ever be,' said Elliot, wondering if today was going to be as eventful as the one before.

'Good show!' said Zeus, struggling off the sofa before it was scuttled away by some penates. 'First off, we need to get my daughters, Athene and Aphrodite. But I need your help – they're a pair of feisty fillies and they might behave a little better with a smashing new face around. We'll start with Aphrodite. You'll like her. Most boys do.'

Elliot had no time for nor interest in girls and doubted that Zeus's daughter would be any different, but smiled in polite agreement.

'Peg!' Zeus hollered at his horse, who was lying on the ground with a pencil in his mouth doing the crossword. 'Time to saddle up!'

'Imbecile,' shouted Pegasus as he rose from the ground.

'Steady on old chap,' said Zeus.

'Fourteen across – a stupid person, eight letters,' explained Pegasus. 'Although if the cap fits . . .'

'Virgo, are you joining us?' Zeus asked the former Goddess as she stood on a stool to unpeel a giant banana.

'Hermes and I are going to start looking for Mammon,' munched Virgo, gesturing at Hermes who was already typing away at his laptop. 'We find him, we'll find the Earth Stone.'

'Last one to find him is last season's sweaterdress,' chirped Hermes, jabbing away at his laptop.

'That's the ticket,' said Zeus amiably. 'See you later.'

If Virgo did answer it was forever lost inside her banana and she looked dangerously likely to join it as she dived into the skin headfirst.

Pegasus kneeled to help Zeus and Elliot clamber aboard. 'Come on Peg – giddyup,' yelled Zeus, spurring Pegasus on to a gallop and then one, two, three giant strides and they were climbing into the morning sky, leaving the industrious immortals – and one giant banana – far below.

It was another beautiful cruise through the sky, Elliot riding Pegasus in front of Zeus as they soared over the world below. But as they floated over the sunbathed countryside, there was something that had been playing on Elliot's mind.

'Do any of you have healing powers – the Gods, I mean?' he asked.

'I'm afraid not,' said Zeus gently. 'Our powers are mainly transformative. We can only change ourselves or other objects into something else.'

'I see,' said Elliot, trying to hide his disappointment. 'Why didn't Thanatos kill me yesterday? You know, back in the cave?'

'I don't think he can, dear boy,' said Zeus. 'Which is really rather jolly good news.'

'Why not?' asked Elliot.

'Before I built Thanatos's prison, I consulted the Oracle at Delphi, who told me that only a mortal could free Thanatos. That same mortal could kill him, but couldn't be killed by him. I didn't pay much attention to the rest – she can ramble on a bit, old Pythia – so Thanatos has good reason to be afraid of you. And you have good reason to be afraid of him.'

'I don't understand,' said Elliot. 'You just said he can't kill me?'

'I'm saying he can't do it himself,' said Zeus. 'Daemons are notoriously slippery things and you are a huge threat to him now. If he can, he'll find a way.'

'Right,' said Elliot. 'Does that mean I die or not?'

'I'm afraid prophecies are never that specific,' sighed Zeus. 'But I'm going to make bally sure you're safe on my watch.'

'But I can kill him, right – will that make me immortal?' asked Elliot excitedly.

'No. You'd probably just die a horrible death in the attempt,' said Zeus. 'Prophecies tend to work out better for immortals than humans. Thank the Heavens Virgo was there to rescue you yesterday.'

'Yeah,' groaned Elliot. 'She's mentioned it once or twice.'

'She's quite something that one,' laughed Zeus, 'I know legendary warriors who don't have half her courage. Mind you, I also know twenty-headed monsters who don't talk half as much either, but one thing I've learned about women is that you have to take the rough with the smooth. Ah – we're here, good-o!'

Pegasus gracefully descended behind some beach huts along Brighton beach.

'Be back in two ticks,' said Zeus as he huffed and puffed his considerable girth off the horse.

'Diet,' said Pegasus.

'Beg pardon?' said an affronted Zeus.

'Six down – a healthy eating regime, four letters,' said Pegasus pulling the paper out of his saddle bag with his teeth.

'Hmmm. See you later,' said Zeus, pulling his Bermuda shirt over his impressive belly as he ushered Elliot up the beach.

They walked up to the promenade and crossed into the winding streets of the seaside town.

'Now Elliot, here's the thing about my girls,' Zeus began as they stopped outside a bright pink door with "Eros" emblazoned across in lipstick red letters. 'They are both beautiful, powerful, intelligent girls who are a credit to their old Dad. But I can't tell a lie – put them together and they're like two Harpies fighting over a half-price handbag in the New Year sales. Need to handle this one with kid gloves, if you catch my drift.'

'Of course,' said Elliot, with precisely no idea what Zeus was talking about.

'Good chap, good chap,' muttered Zeus as he pressed the bright pink buzzer to enter the offices of Eros.

At the top of some narrow steps, Zeus and Elliot found

the reception area, which looked as though someone had lost a fight with a pink paint pot. Everything was pink – the walls, the ceiling, the lip-shaped chairs – even the receptionist's outfit was bright pink. Across every surface was the Eros slogan – *Married in a Month or Your Money Back* – Elliot recognised it from the adverts he'd heard on the radio.

'Welcome to Eros – where love don't cost a thing. Terms and conditions apply,' Sally the receptionist chanted.

'Well aren't you just a pretty little thing?' drawled Zeus. 'Can you tell Ms Venus that her old Dad's here to see her? And that I'd like to take her receptionist out for dinner sometime?'

Sally turned a shade of pink to perfectly match her suit.

'I'll give her a ring,' she giggled, picking up the top lip of the pink mouth phone.

'Carry on being so beautiful and I'll be giving *you* the ring, Sarah,' said Zeus to another cascade of giggles.

'It's Sally,' Sally giggled.

'It's irrelevant,' Zeus grinned as he picked up her hand and kissed it.

Elliot looked around the waiting room, which was filled with people clutching application forms, every last one of whom looked . . . single. Photographs of Eros success stories lined the walls, hundreds of married couples grinning at these hopefuls from every surface.

'*Daddy*!' chimed the most beautiful voice Elliot had ever heard.

'Hello my little pearl,' said Zeus, taking his daughter into one of his giant hugs. 'Come and meet my good friend Elliot.'

'Hi there Elliot,' said Aphrodite, shimmying across the room to meet the teenage boy glued to her office floor.

Elliot tried to speak, but all the words evaporated inside his mouth. It was hard to say exactly what made the Goddess of Love the most beautiful woman Elliot had ever seen, but as he gawped at her long golden hair, her twinkling blue eyes, her full rosy lips and the snug jeans and T-shirt that hugged every curve a woman could possibly want and more, he didn't honestly care.

Zeus nudged Elliot in the ribs.

'Your mouth called, old boy,' he whispered. 'It wants its tongue back.'

But Elliot was deaf to anything but the angel song in his head as Aphrodite walked towards him. He was hypnotised by the approaching Goddess and besides, he couldn't open his mouth for fear of dribbling.

'So you're our little mortal,' sang Aphrodite, or so it seemed to Elliot as she leaned down and gazed at him with her boundless blue eyes. 'Hermes has told me all about you. Lovely to meet you.'

'Hubhurghrumph,' garbled Elliot dreamily as he reached for her outstretched hand. With a wicked twinkle in her eyes, Aphrodite grabbed Elliot's hand and pulled him towards her to plant a big kiss on his cheek. At the touch of her lips, Elliot felt a blush begin twenty feet below the Earth, surging up through the ground beneath his feet before it burst through his shoes and erupted all over his face, giving him the appearance of a thoroughly happy teenage tomato.

'Aphy, could we have a word, please – bit of business to discuss with you,' said Zeus with a wink.

'Yes, of course – I'm just with a client at the moment,' she whispered, gesturing to the gentleman in the knitted pullover behind her. 'With you in a seccy, Colin!'

'Er, right-o, okay then,' replied Colin as he stood up, banged his knee on the desk and tripped over the chair, sending his thick black glasses flying across the office. Aphrodite looked lovingly at Colin as he blundered around the floor trying to find his spectacles.

'Bless. Such a catch. Just give me a mo,' she whispered.

'Aphrodite Venus?' a voice boomed across the reception. It belonged to quite the most enormous woman Elliot had ever seen without a shotput, a giantess dressed in a grey tweed suit carrying a briefcase that in her hands could have been a deadly weapon.

'That's me,' said Aphrodite sweetly.

'Millicent Tronglebom,' said the woman, striding across the room brandishing an ID badge. 'From Her Majesty's Revenue and Customs. I'm here to inspect your taxes.'

'Madam!' Zeus boomed admiringly, much to Sally's annoyance. 'You can inspect my taxes anytime! You are my kind of woman. Someone you can cuddle all week long and still have enough left over for sandwiches on Saturday.'

Millicent gave Zeus a look that could brew a verruca.

'We've discovered some irregularities on your account,' she barked, turning her attention back to Aphrodite.

'Ah. Whoopsie,' said Aphrodite mischievously.

'Whoopsie indeed, Ms Venus,' said Millicent, pulling herself up even taller. 'It seems that you haven't filed a single tax return. And if you can't come up with a reasonable explanation as to why, you can expect to spend some time in jail.'

'I see,' said Aphrodite, looking back at Colin, who was now walking around the office like a zombie with his arms stretched out, still without his glasses, but now asking for help from a hat stand. 'Won't you come through to my office? I'm sure we can come to an arrangement.'

With a wicked smile on her lips, Aphrodite ushered Millicent into the office, gesturing to Zeus and Elliot to follow her. She closed the door behind them and walked around the desk to take a seat at her heart-shaped chair. Colin had now given up on the unhelpful hat-stand and was once again crawling around the floor in search of his lost specs.

'Now, how can I help you?' Aphrodite asked Millicent sweetly, opening a small drawer in her desk and removing a pink leather box.

'According to our records, you haven't filed a tax return since . . . well, since forever,' said Millicent.

'That's correct,' Aphrodite said plainly, opening the box on the table.

'You don't deny it?' Millicent gasped.

'Why would I?' said Aphrodite. 'I have nothing to hide. Tax is boring. I don't do boring things. Besides, I give all my money away. Silly stuff really.'

Elliot wanted to argue that it was easy to think that about money when you didn't need it, but everything Aphrodite did was amazing and beautiful and wonderful.

'Don't you have an accountant?' asked Millicent.

'Nope,' said Aphrodite absent-mindedly, fiddling with whatever was inside the box.

'This is a very serious offence, Ms Venus,' Millicent roared. 'You could be facing—'

'Have you met Colin?' said Aphrodite, gesturing to the helpless soul floundering about on the floor.

'No,' sneered Millicent, peering down on Colin as if there were a pile of slug sick crawling around her feet.

'You two should get to know each other better,' said Aphrodite, suddenly standing up and yanking a pink Taser gun out of the box. 'I think you'll get along beautifully!'

'What the—?' gasped Millicent, but it was too late. Aphrodite fired the gun at an astonished Millicent, sending two wires flying out of the barrel. Both were tipped with pink hearts and sliced through the air towards their targets – one attaching to Millicent's magnificent bosom, the other onto Colin's scrawny bottom.

For a moment nothing happened, both parties getting over the shock of having a Taser fired at them in broad daylight. Elliot noticed the glasses were lying by his feet, so handed them to Colin, who was plucking the heart from his backside. Colin rose slowly from the floor, adjusting his glasses to fix his gaze on a dumbstruck Millicent.

'Millicent Tronglebom,' said Millicent softly, extending her hand towards a slack-jawed Colin.

'Colin Limpwad,' replied Colin, taking her hand as if it were a holy relic. 'You have the most beautiful name I've ever heard. Millicent Tronglebom. It's like a choir of heavenly hamsters singing your beauty.'

'Why thank you Colin,' giggled Millicent coyly. 'I hope you'll not think me forward, but I can't help but admire your lovely pullover.'

'Sweet Ms Tronglebom – my mother knitted this pullover for my 40th birthday. We live together.'

'Oh Colin – how I've longed to find a man who lives with his mother!'

'Sweet Milly – may I call you Milly?' asked Colin.

'Only if I can call you – schnookykins.'

'You can call me anything you want,' roared Colin, gathering the ample Millicent into his scrawny arms. 'I have yearned for a woman like you. A woman with grace. A woman with substance. A woman with a bosom I could spot my trains from. Marry me Milly!'

'Yes! Yes! A thousand times yes!' screamed Millicent, tearing Aphrodite's file in half. 'Let us go to Gretna Green this very afternoon!'

'If we hurry, we'll catch the 10.14!' cried Colin, picking up his Thermos flask and the cheese sandwich his Mum had packed. 'It's a class 390 Pendolino!'

'You can tilt my train anytime, my little Colly Flower,' shouted Millicent, shaking her hair free of its bun and scooping Colin up into her arms to carry him over the threshold as they ran out of the door towards the 10.14 and wedded bliss.

'And that's why I don't need an accountant,' grinned Aphrodite, replacing the Taser in the box and returning it happily to her desk drawer. 'Now. What can I do for you?'

Zeus was barely halfway through his explanation of events when Aphrodite pulled the keys to her sports car out of her handbag.

'I'm in,' she squealed. 'Sounds like fun!'

Athene, on the other hand, was going to take more persuading.

Zeus, Elliot and Aphrodite were in Athene's office at St Brainiac College, Oxford where Athene was an esteemed professor of philosophy. It was fair to say that it wasn't going well.

'You are such a boring-brained, library-lameo, boffin-bum!' Aphrodite shouted at her sister over the grand mahogany desk, which the siblings were leaning over in a heated discussion.

'How clever,' Athene shot back over the top of her tortoise

shell glasses. 'I see you've been studying the Big Book of Intelligent Insults again.'

Zeus looked over at Elliot with raised eyebrows. 'See what I mean?' Elliot could hear him say.

'I can't believe you'd rather sit here with your great big nose stuck in a book than out with us finding the Chaos Stones,' Aphrodite pouted. 'Just because you look like an old granny doesn't mean that you have to act like one.'

Painful as it was to disagree with Aphrodite, even in his own head, Elliot could see that Aphrodite was being very hard on her sister. With anyone else in the room, Athene would be the most beautiful woman there, her ebony hair piled into an elegant knot at the back of her head, her deep brown eyes radiating intelligence and grace. But next to Aphrodite, Elliot was convinced that all other girls looked like snotty warthogs.

'I am a Professor of Philosophy,' said Athene grandly. 'Some of us weren't fortunate enough to make a living duping people into making fools of themselves by falling in love with highly inappropriate partners. Some of us have to settle for improving humankind with brilliant thought.'

'I've given people beauty and joy,' replied Aphrodite. 'You've given them a headache and some boring books to keep in the downstairs loo. Besides, you weren't so grand when you were cheating on all those TV quiz shows . . .'

'I did not cheat!' said Athene defensively. 'I won those competitions fair and square.'

'Sure you did,' said Aphrodite with a naughty grin. 'Although with a few extra millennia to study than all the other contestants, any idiot could beat those poor mortals.'

'Not any idiot,' said Athene, looking straight at her sister.

'Come now girlies, this is no time for squabbling,' Zeus chided. 'We need to find those stones.'

'Yes Father, this pact with the daemons, surely you can't think that was wise?' said Athene, her dark eyes full of disapproval.

'Old news,' yawned Aphrodite. 'Moving on – Prissy Pants, are you in or out?'

'Out,' said Athene stubbornly.

Aphrodite opened her mouth to launch another string of insults at her sister, but was hushed by a hand on her shoulder from her father.

'We could really use your fabulous old bonce, sweetie,' said Zeus. 'But no is no. We'll leave you to it.'

With Aphrodite chewing her tongue, Zeus started to usher her out of the door. Elliot had never had siblings, but he'd seen enough of other people's to know how they worked. Besides, if Athene could help him find the Earth Stone, he needed her on the team.

'I'm sorry you won't be coming with us, Athene,' he said.

'I'm sorry too, Elliot, but I wish you well,' she said grumpily.

'That's really kind of you,' he said. 'Besides, it's probably the right decision. This doesn't sound like your sort of thing.'

'What makes you say that?' bristled Athene.

'Oh nothing. Just something Aphrodite said on the way here. Nice to meet you,' he added, starting out of the room under Zeus's admiring gaze.

'Wait. What did she say?' asked Athene, failing to sound if she didn't care.

'Nothing bad. Just that you preferred reading to fighting.'

'Well, that's not strictly true, I am a warrior Goddess.'

'And that you probably felt a bit old to fight this time.'

'I'm hardly any older than she is!'

'And that she had most of the ideas last time you fought Thanatos, so she didn't mind doing it again.'

'SHE SAID WHAT?' shouted Athene, slamming her hands on the desk, before hastily putting some books into a large bag. 'Aphrodite! Aphrodite, come back here – I'll show you who's the best fighter – I can practise on you!'

And in a blaze of fury, the Goddess of Wisdom swept out of the door and into Aphrodite's sports car.

'Good show, old man!' winked Zeus as they headed out of the university behind her.

With Aphrodite and Athene off bickering in Aphrodite's sports car to Home Farm, Elliot and Zeus boarded Pegasus again for the short flight to the small Surrey town of Greater Snubbington, where they landed behind the recycling bins in a posh supermarket car park. Or at least Elliot assumed it was posh – he'd never heard of Wright & Ripov, let alone shopped there.

'Last stop,' promised Zeus to Elliot. 'Nearly got the whole set.'

'A packet of Medjool dates wouldn't go amiss,' huffed Pegasus as he kicked an empty tin of organic coconut milk disdainfully with his hoof.

'Coming up, old boy,' said Zeus cheerfully, patting Pegasus on the bottom, a gesture his horse did not appreciate. 'Just one other thing on the shopping list.'

Elliot and Zeus walked through the automatic doors into the bright warmth of Wright & Ripov. *We See You Coming!* announced the signs all around the store, which was laid out like a market for customers who would probably never go to a real one.

'Now I know he's in here somewhere,' said Zeus, scanning the aisles. 'Ah – bingo – Hephaestus old boy!'

At the self-service checkout, dressed in the Wright & Ripov green and brown uniform, was the object of Zeus's search. He was a short, stocky man whose right shoulder was slightly higher than his left. He reminded Elliot of a troll action figure he'd enjoyed playing with when he was younger, although he decided quickly he wouldn't tell him that.

Hephaestus turned to the familiar voice, inclining his head slightly in greeting.

'Marnin',' he said to Zeus levelly.

'Hephy old bean, this is Elliot, a marvellous new friend. Elliot, this handsome chap is Hephaestus, inventor and builder extraordinaire.'

'How do,' said Hephaestus coolly, but not unkindly.

'Hi Hef . . . Hefist . . . Hefor . . .' bumbled Elliot, unsure how to pronounce his name.

'Heff. Ice. Tus,' Zeus whispered in his ear, 'but don't worry, no-one gets it right, darn awkward name.'

'Nothing wrong with me hearing, though,' said Hephaestus as Zeus smiled an apology.

'You there! Man! I need you!' yelled a shrill voice at the self-service checkout.

Hephaestus rolled his eyes and walked towards the grey-haired lady, who was dressed like a sailor, despite being a hundred miles from the coast. Hephaestus took a long, very bored breath.

'Welcome to Wright & Ripov,' he sighed. 'How may I be of service today?'

'I can't find Jerusalem Artichokes on this wretched machine,' she huffed.

''Ave you searched under 'A' for Artichoke?' said Hephaestus plainly.

'Well, no. I looked under 'J' for Jerusalem,' she pouted.

'There you go then, Madam,' said Hephaestus, returning to Zeus and Elliot, muttering 'Try 'I' for Idiot'.

'So,' he started. 'Whaddya want?'

'Well, thing is dear boy—'

'You there! Man! I need you again!' Mrs Sailor trilled once more.

Hephaestus spun around, getting to her rather faster, and considerably more annoyed this time.

'What do you . . . How may I help you?' he growled through gritted teeth.

'It's asking for proof of age for my amontillado sherry,' she said. 'Do I look 18 to you?'

'Several times over,' muttered Hephaestus as he jabbed at buttons on the screen, causing the machine to wobble. 'There you go.'

'Don't you want proof?' the lady asked.

Hephaestus eyed her up and down and walked away.

'I got eyes in me head,' he said.

'Well I hate to tear you away, Heffy old thing, but I could really do with your help,' said Zeus.

'Say no more,' said Hephaestus, yanking off his Wright & Ripov apron and throwing it on the floor. 'I'm in.'

They started to walk out of the supermarket, when Mrs Sailor piped up again.

'Man! Come here! I need you to verify my bags.'

Hephaestus stopped in his tracks and returned to the checkout.

'Let me see now,' he said, removing a small bronze axe from inside his jacket. He raised it above his head. 'One

. . . two . . . three . . . four,' he said, bringing the axe down on Mrs Sailor's shopping with every count. 'That verified enough for you?'

Zeus came to fetch his immortal colleague, stuffing a handful of jewellery into Mrs Sailor's stunned hand and taking what was now half a packet of Medjool dates out of her bag.

'Sorry dear lady,' said Zeus. 'New trainee.'

And leaving Wright & Ripov in stunned silence, Hephaestus limped out of the supermarket with Zeus and Elliot, as Mrs Sailor's checkout spluttered a broken '*Unexpected Item in Bagging Area*'.

By the time Elliot, Zeus and Hephaestus returned to Home Farm, Athene and Aphrodite were already there, huddled around Hermes's laptop next to Virgo, who was gorging on a sandwich the size of an encyclopedia. Elliot quickly popped in to check on Mum and introduce Hestia, who was now ready to work her magic on the house. All was well – or at least no more sign of Patricia – and Elliot headed back to the cowshed to find out how he was going to get the Earth Stone and save his home.

'Hooray, you're back!' squealed Hermes as Elliot walked into the shed. 'We've been busier than a photo editor in fashion week. We've found Mammon. He's here, in a list of the Earth's richest mortals.'

'Snordlesnot!' yelped Hephaestus as he hit his thumb with the golden hammer he was using to fix Bessie's water feeder.

'Mammon?' asked Elliot.

'Daemon of Greed,' explained Virgo, wiping some mayonnaise off her nose.

'He was Thanatos's henchman back in the day,' said Zeus. 'I wouldn't want to be in his shoes when Thanatos goes after him for the Earth Stone.'

'Well that's little use,' said Athene sharply. 'Mammon will have dissembled into a mortal form, he won't look like the daemon we know.'

'Hold your Hydras,' said Hermes, putting his palm up to Athene. 'Now where is my iGod? You're gonna love this.'

He scrabbled around in his small bag, delving his whole arm in up to the shoulder. He threw various items out of the satchel, including a stuffed panda, a green macaroon and the 1994 edition of the London A-Z, the last of which hit Hephaestus on the head, causing him to bring the golden hammer down on his thumb for a second time.

'Snordlesnot!' yelped the immortal blacksmith as he whipped the throbbing thumb to his mouth, immediately dropping the offending hammer on his foot.

'SNORDLESNOT!' he bellowed again, not knowing which injury to treat first, leaving him awkwardly sucking his thumb and hopping on his good foot for the five seconds it took him to fall over and bang his head.

Hephaestus polluted the air with a particularly colourful curse involving the inventor of the hammer and a donkey with wind problems, before struggling to his feet.

'Don't all rush at once, I'm fine,' he grumbled as he returned to his task.

'Here we are,' said Hermes triumphantly, puling the tortoise-shell device out of his bag. 'This is just fabby. I downloaded this from the Golden Apple Store just the other day. It's called Veritum, you put it over a photograph and it shows you the true essence of the person in the picture. Look!'

Hermes held the iGod screen over a picture of the first billionaire on the list, a bald bespectacled man, who had made his fortune in computers. At the touch of a button, the photograph changed from a normal looking middle-aged man, to a scrawny-looking chicken. Hermes nearly fell off his bale laughing. 'It's brilliant – you should see what happens when you Veritum some Hollywood actors – it's disgusting. Now let's see.'

Hermes went down the list, snapping the pictures as he went. The images variously changed from snakes to toads to rats, to one famous model who turned out be nothing more than a pair of plastic jugs.

'Ah – this one sounds suss,' said Aphrodite. 'Richard M Goldstein VIII, oil and precious gem tycoon. Try him, Herm.'

'Alrighty Aphrodite,' chimed Hermes, holding the iGod over Goldstein's bloated, piggy features. The picture instantly changed into a revolting brown troll, whose small, black eyes peered out over his big snotty snout, which covered his whole head in a thin layer of green slime.

'Urgh. That's Mammon alright,' said Zeus in disgust.

'Oooh, hasn't he done well for himself?' said Hermes, dropping his iGod on the hay bale next to him. 'Estimated wealth of five hundred billion pounds from his oil fields and priceless collection of jewels. He lives in a seventy-five bedroom mansion in the Highlands. What a show-off.'

'If we can find him this easily, so can Thanatos,' said Athene, as a copy of *The Daily Argus* flew into the cowshed out of nowhere, hitting Hephaestus and crashing the hammer down on his thumb in a symphony of 'Snordlesnots'. 'We need to get to Mammon first while we've got the element of surprise.'

'You can forget about that,' said Pegasus, eyeing the front page of *The Daily Argus*. 'Thanatos is headline news.'

Elliot surveyed the front cover of the newspaper. The lead story was illustrated with a black and brown picture of the kind Elliot had seen on the side of Greek vases. At first he couldn't make out what it depicted, but when he looked more closely, he saw that the picture was of Thanatos holding Virgo by the hair, whilst Elliot cowered in front of the daemon.

MORTAL PERIL!

By Ovid, Current Affairs correspondent

The Argus News has come across
The great escape of Thanatos
Virgo met the ancient crook

And let the daemon sling his hook
The Virgo girl was only due
To give the swine his usual brew
She took the drink for him to sup
And then she royally stuffed it up
'Cos when she crossed the sacred portal
The ninny brought along a mortal
The human child broke the spell
Now Thanatos will give us 'ell
The daemon villain's on the loose
Those silly kids have cooked our goose

'Crivvens!' cried Zeus. 'Hermes, get yourself to Mammon's mansion, quick smart. Find out where he keeps that stone. We have to get to it before Thanatos does.'

'Oh yippee, I love a good spy,' said Hermes, as his moped whizzed into the shed. 'I'll take the high road – Scotland, here I come!'

And he flew out of the barn in a flash, leaving a blizzard of hay in his wake.

'Well that's that,' said Zeus. 'Now we must give a thought to some security around here. Hephaestus – we need something around the farm, something that will keep Elliot safe inside and everyone else out, something big and tall, something strong, something . . . something like . . .'

'A fence,' said Hephaestus drily as he wrapped his bright red thumb in a dirty rag.

'That's the ticket!' said Zeus excitedly, as if Hephaestus had just invented the wheel. 'Get to it old man, good show.'

'I get all the good jobs, me,' grumbled the blacksmith as the water feeder started to work beautifully, before heading out of the shed with a tape measure.

Zeus glanced over at Elliot, who was barely able to keep his exhausted eyes open.

'You must go and rest,' said Zeus to Elliot. 'You're going to need your wits about you. Virgo, you stay in the house with Elliot at all times – until we know what Thanatos has in mind, we have to be on constant alert.'

Virgo nodded, stuffing a piece of cheese back into her mouth.

'Wait,' said Elliot. 'I have to go to school.'

'What an admirable attitude,' said Athene approvingly as she and Aphrodite magically transformed hay bales into sumptuous silk-covered beds, not realising that her sister was pulling faces behind her back.

'If I don't go to school, they'll come looking for me here,' said Elliot. 'And none of us needs that.'

'He's right,' said Zeus. 'And the less disruption to Elliot's life, the better. Virgo, you will go to school with him – you're a mortal now, it will be an excellent chance for you to blend in.'

Elliot looked at Virgo's long silver hair as she tucked into a whole wheel of Cheddar. Blending in was going to be tricky.

'Excellent,' said Virgo. 'I look forward to the opportunity to broaden my mind.'

'Clearly you've never been to my school,' muttered Elliot.

'You have to promise us you'll stay safe, old man,' said Zeus. 'We need you, Elliot, and we'll take care of you. Now go and sleep well, it's been a long day.'

Zeus watched Elliot and Virgo as they headed out of the shed and back up the path towards the farmhouse.

'You shouldn't make promises you don't know you can keep,' said Athene quietly from behind her father's back. 'There's no telling what Thanatos would do to that poor boy if he got his hands on him.'

'You know that and I know that,' said Zeus from the door, watching to make sure that Elliot and Virgo had made it safely into the house. 'But let's just hope young Elliot never, ever has to find it out for himself.'

Chapter Ten
An Old Fiend

Until very recently, life had been extremely good to Mammon, the Daemon of Greed. In fact, several lives had been good to him, enjoying as he was his 43rd different one. One of the challenges that faced a daemon living in the mortal world was keeping up the act – after all, no matter how stupid these humans were, everyone would start to get suspicious if you never aged and never died.

Mammon's solution was quite simple. Blessed, as all immortals were, with the ability to dissemble, making mortals see whatever he wanted them to see, Mammon simply dissembled into different human guises, ageing as time went by and then pretending to die before taking up a new identity straight afterwards. His favourite disguise was as a billionaire oil tycoon, and he was currently dissembling as the eighth Richard M Goldstein – although in actual fact he had also been the other seven. But no-one had been around long enough to join the dots and Mammon had been living the life of Riley these past few millennia.

As a daemon, Mammon had always enjoyed the supernatural advantages of living on Earth. But when Zeus gave him the Earth Stone in return for betraying Thanatos, Mammon possessed powers beyond his wildly greedy dreams. Wary of his oath to Zeus, he had never summoned the earthquakes or landslides that the brilliant diamond was capable of creating, but Mammon took full advantage of other aspects of the stone's potential that had never interested Thanatos.

To his greedy delight, Mammon quickly discovered that the Earth Stone could tell him where oil or precious gems were buried, glowing bright when they were near, then opening up the ground at his command. There wasn't a corner of the Earth Mammon hadn't plundered for its wealth, and Mammon – or whichever Goldstein he happened to be – had amassed a vast wealth. Not overly blessed with intelligence, he found this easiest of get-rich-quick schemes suited him perfectly and he had been happily living off his enormous fortune for thousands of years.

Or at least he had until yesterday. He never normally paid much attention to *The Daily Argus*, believing himself far above and beyond the mere immortals reported within it. But yesterday's front page had sent a fear through him, the like of which he'd not known in 43 lifetimes. Thanatos was free. And Mammon knew he'd be coming straight for him.

Like anyone who got something for nothing, the Daemon of Greed had always been paranoid about someone taking it from him. But after reading about Thanatos's escape, Mammon stepped up his already enormous security and gave every single guard strict instructions not to let anyone in. He didn't care if someone arrived claiming to be his long-lost son, or dying mother – Mr Goldstein didn't want anyone but him let into his Scottish mansion.

So the guards on the front gate thought nothing of allowing Richard M Goldstein VIII into his own home when he drove up to the massive gate that morning. His butler happily opened the door to allow his employer into the house while Trent, Mr Goldstein's personal bodyguard, gladly unlocked the door to his personal office when he said he had forgotten his key. Had they all checked with one another, they would have realised that Richard M Goldstein VIII had never left his office in the first place, but by the time Thanatos had dissembled them all and stood in the office of the daemon who had betrayed him 3,000 years ago, it was far too late.

'Hello Mammon,' said Thanatos slowly to the daemon quivering beneath the mahogany desk. Daemons were unable to dissemble each other, so Mammon knew precisely who had entered into his sanctuary and in a last desperate bid to save his immortal bacon, had dived beneath the table in terror.

'H-h-h-hello Master,' he stuttered, his warty brown head appearing over the table-top. 'How, how did you get here?

'That needn't concern you,' said Thanatos coldly. 'Let's

just say that an unfortunate air steward on Highland Airways found the emergency exit a little sooner than he might have liked. But you and I have more important matters to discuss. May I?'

Thanatos pulled a tackily elaborate golden chair back from the desk and sat down on its edge. He looked around the vast room with a sneer. Every spare inch of Mammon's office was stuffed to the brim with expensive artefacts, from old masters to priceless vases, to every gaudy antique, ornament and knick-knack imaginable. It was a tacky, tasteless Aladdin's cave and Thanatos looked around as if he were trapped in a portable toilet.

'Well they say that money can't buy you taste,' said Thanatos, contemptuously gazing around the office before casting his hateful stare on the quaking daemon. 'How kind of you to prove them right.'

'Thank you,' stammered Mammon eventually, surprised he was still alive this far into the conversation. Daemons were immortal creatures, but unlike the invulnerable Gods, daemons could be killed, so Mammon knew his chances of leaving the office alive were slim. But the dopey daemon decided he would try to improve his odds by engaging the ruler he betrayed to his immortal enemies in polite conversation.

'You look well,' said Mammon to relieve the tense silence.

'How kind,' said Thanatos flatly. 'Three thousand years locked in a subterranean cave doesn't do much for one's social life, but works wonders for the complexion.'

'Oh I can see,' enthused Mammon. 'You've got a certain glow about you, a shine even—'

'Where is it?' hissed Thanatos, rising sharply out of the gold chair, which clattered across the room at the force of his gesture, sending Mammon squealing back under the desk.

'I don't know,' he shivered, rocking backwards and forwards.

'There are only a few moments of your miserable wart-covered life left, you pestilent swine,' drawled Thanatos. 'Don't waste them by lying.'

'No, no, I'm telling the truth,' cried Mammon, daring to poke his snout above the desk again.

'I'm going to count to one,' said Thanatos.

'No, really, I- I- I-' spluttered the greed daemon.

'One,' said Thanatos reaching over the desk towards Mammon's slimy neck.

'No, please,' screeched Mammon, backing away from the deathly hand. 'I—'

'YOU WHAT?' shouted Thanatos, his patience expired.

'I LOST IT!' blubbed Mammon, crying like a newborn baby, his dirty tears running down his warty face into the snotty mess under his snout.

'You lost it. Of course you did,' said Thanatos, his eyes rolling in his gaunt head. 'You always did have the brain of a decapitated goldfish. Well at least this saves wasting any more time having to speak to you. Goodbye Mammon.'

He grabbed the daemon by his slimy head and lifted him clean off the ground.

'Wait, WAIT,' shrieked Mammon, 'I know where it is!'

Thanatos stopped, still holding Mammon aloft by his head.

'Care to enlighten me?' asked Thanatos.

'Well – it's a funny story actually,' snivelled Mammon.

'I seriously doubt that,' Thanatos groaned, dropping the daemon to the floor, where he landed with a squidgy splat. 'You have one minute.'

With no tissues around to deal with his grotty nose, a gasping Mammon blew it on his shirt-sleeve before pulling himself together to tell his tale.

'Back when I was Goldstein the Sixth – somewhere around the late 1800s – I heard about the biggest diamond ever found, called the Cullinan diamond,' he began. 'I thought I had every massive gem in the world, so when I heard about this one, I . . .'

'You had to get your filthy, greedy paws on it,' added Thanatos.

'Exactly,' said Mammon more brightly, giving his nose another wipe with his sleeve. 'I went to South Africa where the Cullinan diamond had been mined and offered the man who found it ridiculous sums of money to buy it from him. But I was too late. He told me that the King of England had already bought the diamond to put it in a new Imperial State Crown, the pride of the Crown Jewels. I was desperate. I had to have that diamond.'

'This story had better get somewhere soon, or I am going to kill you just to stay awake,' said Thanatos to his trembling servant.

'So I pretended to the miner I didn't mind, but asked, as a fellow diamond enthusiast, if I could at least take a look,' said a flustered Mammon. 'He agreed and took me to where the diamond was locked away. But the thing was, once I had the Cullinan in my hands, I couldn't help myself, so I . . . I . . .'

'You swapped it,' sighed Thanatos.

'I had to have it!' whined Mammon. 'So I distracted the miner by making him think there was a tiger outside and I quickly swapped the Cullinan for the only other diamond I had to hand.'

'My Earth Stone,' said Thanatos in a tone that could freeze water. 'You are truly one of an incredibly stupid kind.'

'Exactly,' said Mammon, on the verge of tears again. 'But I thought I could get it back. I knew that the miner was planning to send the diamond – which was now the Earth Stone – to England by steamer, so I dissembled into one of the sailors to steal it back. But when I got to the safe, it was empty. The whole thing had been a decoy – the miner actually sent the Cullinan diamond by post – he thought it would be safer.'

'I have things sitting in my nostrils that have more brains than you,' said Thanatos.

'But I do know exactly where it is!' said Mammon brightly. 'It's in the Tower of London!'

'So you are telling me that my Chaos Stone, which has the power to control the element of Earth, is now stuck on the front of the Imperial State Crown and locked away in one of the strongest mortal fortresses known to mankind,' said Thanatos slowly.

'Yes,' gibbered Mammon, brightly. 'I've tried to steal it back, but I can't get near it, security's too tight. But here, I've got the Cullinan diamond,' he added keenly, opening a safe beneath his desk and producing an enormous diamond. 'You can have that if you want.'

Thanatos snatched the priceless stone and threw it against the wall, where it flew straight through the nose of the Mona Lisa before falling to the floor.

'WORTHLESS JUNK!' he yelled, grabbing Mammon by the head once more, causing the wretched daemon to burst into uncontrollable sobs.

'P-p-p-please,' he whimpered. 'Please Master, don't kill me, I'll do anything you want, anything, just – please – don't—'

The rest of his begging was lost in a sea of snotty tears as Thanatos threw Mammon back over the other side of the desk.

'There is a service you could perform, which may just spare your fetid, pungent life, while I figure out how I will reclaim my Earth Stone,' said Thanatos.

'Yes Master, of course, anything you want,' dribbled Mammon gratefully, 'thank you Master, thank you.'

'Oh shut up you snivelling buffoon,' said Thanatos. 'I'm having a little trouble with a mortal child. It appears I can't kill him. So I need you to do it for me. Immediately.'

'Kill a mortal?' gasped Mammon. 'But I swore an oath never to harm mortals. What if Zeus finds out?'

Across the desk, Thanatos again grabbed the Daemon of Greed, who spontaneously wet his trousers with fear.

'I'd say that Zeus is the least of your problems right now,' he spat in Mammon's warty face. 'Are you going to help me or shall I dash your miserable brains out right now? If I can find a magnifying glass.'

'No, please my Lord, I'll do it, I'll do it,' moaned Mammon. 'Please, we'll go now, we can take my private jet. We'll be in England in a couple of hours, just leave my brains alone. Please.'

Thanatos threw Mammon down again in disgust and swept out of the room.

'Have a nice day Mr Goldstein,' said Trent the bodyguard as his boss swept past him in a furious hurry.

'Have a nice day Mr Goldstein,' said Trent again as another Mr Goldstein flew out of the office, looking exactly like the first, only with wetter trousers.

Trent removed the shades that always sat on his face and wiped his eyes. He'd been guarding the office all night. Clearly he needed a coffee.

Back inside the office, the discarded diamond sparkled expensively on the floor of the empty room. Or at least, it appeared to be empty. In his paranoia about *who* might enter his office, Mammon hadn't given any thought to *what* might already be inside it.

Had he paid closer attention, Mammon might have noticed that in amongst the expensive bric-a-brac that filled the room, a new and especially fabulous jewel-encrusted Grecian urn had appeared the night before. And had he looked even more closely still, he would have observed that the large handles on the side of the urn looked remarkably like a big pair of ears, flapping around to hear what might be said. The urn now started to wobble and shake, finally falling to the ground, where it immediately transformed back into the gasping form of Hermes.

'Oh my sainted sandals!' he panicked. 'The Earth Stone! Elliot! Everything! What will I do? Where's my iGod, I have to call home!'

Hermes delved his arm into his bag and rummaged around inside its bottomless depths. He pulled out a sock, a chandelier, a riding saddle and a ferret, but with each desperate grasp, he couldn't find his phone. His heart sank as he suddenly recalled his hasty departure from the cowshed. He could still see his iGod on the hay bale where he left it. He had no way of contacting the Gods. Even at full speed, he could never outrun Mammon's jet, but he needed to get a warning to everyone back home before Mammon could get hold of Elliot.

Hermes paced backwards and forwards, twittering to himself as he decided what would be best. Finally, inspiration struck.

'Hades!' he squealed to the empty room, running to the door to escape the tack-filled horror of Mammon's office. He paused at the door, before quickly trotting back to collect the Cullinan diamond.

'You're coming with me, gorgeous,' he said to it gently, before putting it into his bag and transforming into the bloated figure of Richard M Goldstein VIII.

'Have a nice day Mr Goldstein,' said Trent to the third identical man to walk out of the room. Trent rubbed his eyes again. He didn't need a coffee. He needed a doctor.

After a few hours whizzing through – and occasionally over – the rugged Scottish landscape and back into England at full speed, Hermes came to the neon lights of Blackpool twinkling into the sky. He flew along the promenade, past the tower, the roller coasters and any number of Kiss Me Quick hats, until he arrived, exhausted, at his destination. He parked discreetly in a side alleyway before rounding the front of a huge casino.

The massive building was fashioned like a vast rocky cave, with flaming torches dotted all over it, burning different coloured flames. Over the cave's entrance, in huge burning letters, the casino's name and slogan were scorched bright into the Blackpool skyline.

'TARTARUS,' it shone at the stream of gamblers walking in to try their luck. 'WHERE SINNERS ARE WINNERS!'

Hermes hurried through the casino's enormous gambling floor, past whirring fruit machines and excited dice throwers, around spinning roulette wheels and tense card games. In his hurry, his winged feet left the ground for greater speed, but everyone in the casino was so caught up in their own gambling dramas, or blurry from the free drinks, no-one even noticed a flying man zooming past the flashing lights.

At the back of the room was a huge black door, covered with small sculptures of men and women. '*Abandon All Money, Ye Who Enter Here,*' it said in bronze letters across the middle, '*Staff Only*'. The door was guarded by Buck, a burly security guard in a tuxedo.

'You have to let me in,' gasped Hermes, holding his exhausted ribcage in both his hands.

'I don't have to do nothing, Sir,' came Buck's reply. 'This area is restricted.'

'I have to see Mr Hades, I'm an old friend,' Hermes panted, trying to push past the man mountain in his way.

'Mr Hades ain't seeing no-one today,' said the guard, holding Hermes's head at arm's length. 'And that includes you.'

'You don't understand,' pleaded Hermes, 'I have to see him, it's an emergency.'

'Sure,' said the guard, 'you've spent your life savings or next month's rent. I see it all the time. Not my problem pal.'

'Oh for the love of little golden apples, I don't have time for this,' said Hermes, and with a nimble leap, he flew over the security guard's head and kicked the door open with his airborne feet, slamming it quickly behind him and locking it as he entered the office within.

Leaping up from a dark red velvet chair behind a huge wooden desk – which was no mean feat for a man of his bulky size – Hades quickly put his hand in a nearby drawer and produced a small black pistol, which he pointed straight at the dramatic intruder. But before he took his shot, Hades recognised the feathered heap of designer labels on the floor and dropped the gun before opening his arms into a welcoming hug.

'HOIMES!' Hades roared in greeting to his exhausted visitor. 'Geez, I haven't been that scared since I saw my last lawyer's bill. How you bin? It's been forever, get over here you great flying fuzzball.'

Barely able to hold his body up, Hermes crawled along the floor to his fellow Olympian as he struggled to catch his breath.

'Thanatos – Elliot – diamond – murder!' he gasped, clinging on to Hades's ankles as he desperately tried to tell his friend of his plight.

'Hey, Hoimes,' said a baffled Hades, running his hands over his receding slicked black hair. 'Are we talking or playing Charades here? Sit down, take a breath, have a drink.'

Hades went to a statue of Atlas holding the world on

his shoulders – then opened the globe to reveal an extensive bottle collection. He poured some golden liquid into a short glass as the exhausted messenger dragged his body to a nearby chair.

'Here – this nectar's been oak-casked and aged for 50 years,' said Hades. 'It's sweeter than a nymph's nougat.'

Hermes slumped his body into the chair. Then immediately jumped out of it again as a frantic banging started underneath the floor.

'You gotta be kidding me,' sighed Hades, guiding Hermes to another chair before pushing the first one out of the way and rolling away the rug to reveal a trapdoor hidden in the floor.

'Scuse me one minute,' said Hades to his guest as he lifted up the trapdoor. 'Hey Benny,' he shouted down the hole, 'you don't like your new digs, maybe next time you'll pay your hotel bill, you joik,' and he slammed the door back down on the dirty fingers that had peeked out of the gap and listened to the falling wail, until it hit the ground with a whimper.

'Sorry 'bout that, Hoimes,' said Hades, returning to his velvet chair. 'Now what's got your feathers in such a flap?'

As quickly as he could between heaving breaths, Hermes filled Hades in on Thanatos, Elliot, Mammon and the Earth Stone.

'And now he's on his way to squish that poor child and I can't get there fast enough to warn him,' gabbled Hermes hysterically, grabbing the lapels on Hades's suit. 'What are we going to do? What are we going to do! Ooh, nice suit.'

'Tell me about it,' said Hades. 'This suit cost more than the golden fleece. So getcha paws off.'

'Sorry,' whispered Hermes, returning to his chair sheepishly.

'So I'll tell you what I'm gonna do,' Hades began. But before he could finish, the door to his office was blasted open again, this time by an ageing showgirl, decked out in a sequined leotard with pink and yellow feathers, who was hurtling towards Hermes armed with a silver stiletto.

'You leave him alone you – oh, Hoimes, it's you! What you doing here, dollface?'

'Hi Persephone darling,' said Hermes, raising his cheek to accept her welcome kiss. 'Sorry for barging in, but I'm in a proper pickle.'

'It's okay sweetie, good to see you,' said Hades's wife, pulling up another chair. 'Security just called me from my show – that's one crowd ain't gonna find out what happened to Lola at the Copacabana, but what you gonna do?'

'Sweet cakes, why don't you go fix us boys another drink and let us get back to business, eh?' said Hades to his wife.

'Don't you tawk to me like that you big lug,' said an indignant Persephone. 'I'm on a six-month contract here and don't you ever forget it.'

'She's been saying that for two thousand years,' whispered Hades. 'She can't get enough of me really. But we need to get you on the road, Hoimes, come with me.'

Hades stood and turned to the huge bookcase behind him, which contained volumes and volumes of leather-bound books.

'Now where is it?' he asked as he ran his fingers along the middle shelf. 'Ah, got ya.'

He pulled a copy of Dante's *Inferno* from the shelf, which automatically turned sideways and opened up to reveal a small keyboard. Hades used his right middle finger to play the first few notes of the funeral march, which split the bookcase lengthways down the middle, creating a door that led to a dark tunnel.

Hades ushered Hermes and Persephone through the gap and grabbed a torch from the wall. They walked downhill through the long, dark tunnel until they reached an opening underground. Standing in the middle of the empty space was a huge black chariot drawn by four magnificent black stallions.

'Now here's what I'm gonna do,' Hades said to Hermes as he opened a small safe concealed in the rock. 'My chariot here is so fast it can outrun death. Which given the coicumstances, is really quite convenient. My boys can run you underground and take you wherever you need to go. And here,' he said, handing Hermes the ornate silver helmet he had removed from the safe. 'This is my invisibility helmet, I'm guessing you guys could use it.'

'We could use you, Hades,' said Hermes as he settled himself inside the chariot. 'Fancy coming along for the ride?'

'Nah,' said Hades. 'I gave all that God stuff up a long time ago. I gotta nice life here now and besides, I'm too old for that get up.'

'Nonsense,' said Hermes. 'You haven't aged a day since the Trojan War.'

'Get outta here,' laughed Hades. 'But I got eyes and ears everywhere – if I hear anything that could help you guys, I'll give you a call.'

'Thanks Hades,' said Hermes as the four horses turned the chariot to face one of the tunnels. 'We'll be in – aaaaarghghgh!'

The sudden charge of the horses cut him off mid-sentence as they suddenly dived down into the solid ground, which swallowed the chariot whole, charging Hermes at breakneck speed underground towards Home Farm and Elliot's endangered life.

Chapter Eleven

Sinking Feelings

While Mammon was spilling the contents of his mind and nose to Thanatos, Elliot was getting ready to return to school. Two days after the Gods had moved in, he was beginning to feel the benefits of living with a cowshed full of immortals, not least because of Hestia's considerable talents.

In a single day, the Goddess had transformed Elliot's tatty farm into a home that looked like it had jumped off the pages of a magazine. Some changes were simply the work of a good eye for interior design – the peeling walls were covered in fresh coats of bright paint, sumptuous fabrics covered the plush new sofas and armchairs and the bedrooms were given enormous fluffy beds that sank a foot when you slept in them.

Other alterations, however, suggested that this was no average DIY job. The bathroom now had a shower that flowed like a warm, scented waterfall, with a bathtub permanently filled with hot, bubbly water that was big enough to swim in. Even the toilets played Mozart when you sat on them. But Elliot's favourite changes were in the kitchen, which now boasted a self-emptying dishwasher, a washing machine that dried, ironed and folded clothes before spiriting them back into their drawers and – Elliot's personal favourite – a fridge and a kitchen cupboard that always contained exactly what you wanted to eat when you opened them.

Elliot had told Mum that some friends would be staying for a while to help around the farm and she accepted his explanation without question, even when Virgo came into the kitchen staggering under the weight of a tomato the size of a satellite dish, or when Hestia transformed their black and white TV into a top of the range flat-screen plasma, complete with DVD player and that expensive games console. If anything, Elliot thought Mum seemed a little more like her old self with the Gods popping in and out of the house, chatting to her about life on the farm and none of them batting an eyelid when she asked the same question several times or forgot the name they'd just told her.

While the cowshed was alive with building activity as the penates followed Hestia's instructions for its redesign – much to Bessie's bemusement – the Gods came up to the farmhouse for Demeter's breakfast, which would have fed a small army for a week. As Virgo was coming with Elliot to his school that day, Athene transformed Nan's old sewing kit into a spinning wheel and loom, from which she created two perfect Brysmore uniforms, consigning Elliot's tatty old one to the dustbin. The Gods had said nothing more about Thanatos and Elliot hadn't asked – he guessed they would talk to him if there was anything to tell and besides, the more he found out about the death daemon, the less rosy his own future looked.

But no matter how great the house appeared, he was still going to lose it unless Elliot could meet The Really Scary Letter's demands by the end of the week. The Gods were no closer to locating the Earth Stone and without it, Elliot had no idea how he was going to conjure up the twenty thousand pounds he needed. But after Aphrodite did his paper round in her car, the extra sleep and fullest stomach Elliot could remember for months left him feeling in decent shape for a Monday morning as he and Virgo walked across the fields to school.

'I still don't see why we couldn't have accepted a lift from Aphrodite,' grumbled Virgo as she pulled her shoes out of the mud for the third time.

It had taken more willpower than Elliot knew he possessed to decline the beautiful Goddess's offer of a ride to school in her sports car, but now more than ever, Elliot didn't want to arouse any suspicions about his home life. Besides, having been surrounded by people for two days, he wanted to enjoy the quiet peace of his walk. But Virgo had other ideas.

'I think today is going to be fascinating,' she struck up, no longer caring if Elliot joined in her umpteenth attempt at conversation. 'I haven't really had any formal education. Apart from a few lessons with Aries in Elysium, but I'm not sure that gorgon-slaying and hydra-taming are quite the same.'

'You're in for a real treat,' said Elliot. 'Gorgon-slaying's got nothing on algebra.'

'Well you might not appreciate the benefits of a good education, but I certainly will,' said Virgo haughtily. 'And I intend to make the most of this marvellous opportunity to broaden my tiny mortal mind.'

'Try a microscope,' muttered Elliot, earning him a punch from his companion.

Zeus had secured Virgo's place at Brysmore with a phone call to Call Me Graham, pretending to be the headmaster of a prestigious girl's boarding school. He spun a story that Virgo was Elliot's cousin who had just moved to the area and needed to continue her schooling. After presenting papers at the school office that Aphrodite had expertly forged, Elliot and Virgo rushed to their first class of the day, double history with Mr Boil.

'Just keep a low profile. We don't need anyone asking awkward questions,' Elliot had warned Virgo as they entered the history department under Boil's sneering glare.

Halfway through the two-hour lesson on Roman civilisation, Boil had just finished droning on about Julius Caesar when he woke his dozing class by slamming an enormous book about the Roman emperor on the table.

'And I hope that you were all making notes on today's

lesson, as questions about the Romans will feature in the end of term exam, in which I needn't remind you, you must score at least 85% to remain at Brysmore Grammar School,' drooled Boil, his pudgy face delighting at the bombshell he was about to drop. 'And just to help you along, I have set you a surprise exam on everything we have covered this term. Tomorrow. And those who receive less than 85% will receive an hour's extra tuition from me after school for the remainder of the term.'

Elliot joined his class in a chorus of groans. He didn't need reminding about the exam, but he did need a miracle. His history marks had been slipping for months and the chances of him scoring 85% in the end of term exam, let alone being able to pass one tomorrow, were worse than Virgo taking a vow of silence.

Virgo raised her hand. Elliot shot her a warning look, but she continued to keep her hand in the air until Mr Boil begrudgingly acknowledged her waggling arm.

'What do you want?' he snapped unpleasantly.

'Before we all commit your lesson to paper, I just wanted to make a few corrections,' said Virgo to a chorus of stunned giggles from her classmates.

'I beg your pardon,' spat Boil. 'Corrections to what?'

'To your lesson,' continued Virgo as the class gawped on in disbelief. 'I must say, for a teacher of history, your grasp on the period is very poor.'

'What on Earth?' seethed an incredulous Boil.

'I don't see how you can expect us all to pass a test on the subject when you've given us all the wrong information,' Virgo said blithely, the only other sound in the room the gentle bump of Elliot's head on his desk. 'You say, for example, that Caesar was killed in 54 BC. It was 44 BC. And if you think Caesar's last words to Brutus after he stabbed him were "Et tu, Brute?" you heard a far politer story than I did. Perhaps you'd like me to correct some of your other mistakes?'

'Perhaps you'd like me to give you detention for the rest of the term,' shouted Boil, even more furious when a quick peek at his book proved that Virgo's date was right. 'Miss – Miss – what's your name girl?'

'Anna Smith,' said Virgo moodily, unhappy with the mortal name Zeus had chosen for her.

'Well Miss Smith,' boomed Boil, 'clearly there are a few things you need to learn about the Brysmore rules. The rules state that students must treat teachers with respect at all times.'

'I always follow the rules and this is an excellent one,' nodded Virgo. 'Allow me to rephrase: Mr Boil, with the greatest of respect, you don't know what you're talking about.'

'I – what – how dare you!' spluttered Boil.

'Now if you can barely construct a sentence, how do you expect to shape the minds of these children?' said Virgo calmly. 'Don't worry, I can tell you everything you need to know about the Romans. Strange lot. Great builders, but they had some funny ideas about what made a good day out.'

'Stand up!' screamed Boil as Elliot sank his head into his hands. Virgo duly obliged, her fellow pupils unable to take their horrified eyes off her.

'I was going to let you off with a warning, but that little display has just earned you a detention,' quivered Boil, trying to keep his temper in check. 'And unless you change your hair colour by tomorrow, you'll earn yourself another.'

'Why, what's wrong with my hair?' asked Virgo, running her hands through her long silver locks.

'Silver hair is against Brysmore rules,' said Boil triumphantly.

'Then the Brysmore rules are ridiculous,' said Virgo plainly, making Mr Boil gasp at her outrageous blasphemy. 'I have no more control over the colour of my hair than you do over the lack of yours.'

The tension in the classroom was shattered as everyone inside it erupted into helpless fits of laughter. At the mocking giggles of his pupils, the history teacher began to shake with rage. A quivering in his hands trembled up his arms, until his head began to shudder. As the colour rose from his neck into his furious red face, the tremors from Mr Boil's bottom chins grew into an earthquake of fury, which caused all the independently wobbly bits of his body to vibrate as one furious whole.

'Go and see the headmaster!' he roared, barely able to form the words from his incensed mouth.

'Ah excellent,' said Virgo. 'I assume he's your superior? I

would be delighted to discuss some of my suggestions for improving this establishment. I must say that my experience thus far as been far from satisfactory.'

'Get out!' hissed Mr Boil in a fit, barely capable of speech. 'GET OUT! And you too Hooper, GET OUT!'

'But I haven't done anything!' cried Elliot.

'I don't care!' seethed Boil. 'Get out, both of you!'

'This is an outrage,' yelled Virgo. 'This is an injustice the like of which I haven't seen since Sagittarius the centaur was disqualified from the Cheltenham Gold Cup.'

'Just shut up,' said Elliot, bundling her out of the classroom as Boil continued to spit his incensed mumblings to a hysterical classroom.

'What a funny little man,' said Virgo as the door closed behind them. 'Are all your teachers that ignorant?'

'Most of them,' said Elliot, moving her away from Boil's death stare through the classroom window. 'Great way to keep a low profile, by the way.'

'Do the words "stay still" ring any bells?' she said snootily as Elliot guided her to Call Me Graham's office, where a sob story about her dog getting run over saved her from Boil's detention.

Apart from Virgo challenging a netball opponent to a discus duel, the rest of the day passed without further incident, and by three o'clock, Elliot and Virgo were walking back across the field towards home.

'So is Mr Boil always that much of a Minotaur dropping

or was today a special occasion?' Virgo asked Elliot.

'Nah,' said Elliot. 'He's always like that. Hates my guts.'

'Why?' asked Virgo. 'What have your guts done to him?'

'He doesn't like anyone who thinks for themselves,' said Elliot. 'And I might have sewed the odd sardine in his car seats. But he's determined to get me kicked out of the school – he'll do anything to get rid of me. But he needn't worry, these exams should do it for him. He knows I'll never get 85%.'

'All the more reason to prove him wrong, then,' Virgo said, the smile on her face quickly vanishing when her shoe caught in the mud again. 'Snordlesnot!'

'What does that mean?' asked Elliot, stopping again to wait for Virgo to pull herself from the mud. 'Hephaestus says it a lot.'

'Ah yes, well. It's not a word one should really use in polite company,' said Virgo, still trying to wrestle her foot from the ground. 'It's an ancient Titan curse. It's tricky to translate, but it roughly means, "May the Gods forever poke you in the rear end with a pointy potato and throw monkey dung at your sister".'

'Glad I asked,' said Elliot, trying not to laugh at Virgo's struggles with the damp English countryside. 'Oh come on, it'll be time to come back soon, let me help you.'

Elliot started towards the stricken girl, but he couldn't move his feet. He too was completely stuck in the muddy soil. Elliot walked this field every day – he'd never known it be like this before. He pulled and strained at his feet to try to free them, but the more he struggled, the further he sank into the ground.

'This is weird,' said Elliot as he looked over at Virgo, who was now sunk up to her knees in a mixture of mud and sand.

'This English weather is terrible,' she said, looking all around the field as the hedges, trees and fences started sinking along with them into the sandy mud.

But something else had caught Elliot's attention. From the safety of a nearby ridge, a large, brown troll was crouched on the ground, holding his palms to the soil and muttering a strange spell. His head snapped up as he realised he was being watched. He looked sadly at Elliot, mouthing what almost looked like an apology to him, before lumbering away before he could be spotted by anyone else.

'Mammon,' said Virgo, following Elliot's eyes. 'Elliot, we need to get you out of here.'

But neither of them were going anywhere – no matter how much they fought and struggled, they were now stuck in the sandy swamp up to their waists, unable to reach the surface or each other.

'Stop moving,' said Elliot suddenly, remembering something he had heard a long time ago. He waited an endless minute as they both stayed absolutely still, unable to move, but not sinking any further.

'It's quicksand. The more we move, the quicker we'll

sink,' said Elliot, keeping his body as still as he could. 'Okay, I think I know what to do. Try to lie back onto the mud.'

Virgo obeyed Elliot's instructions, tilting her silver head back into the muddy swap and arching her back until she lay on the slushy surface.

'Now spread out your arms and take some slow, deep breaths,' said Elliot on his back a few feet away. 'Your body should float up to the surface.'

They lay in silence to concentrate on their slow breathing. For the longest time, nothing seemed to happen. But then Elliot felt his legs slowly float up through the mud, until he was laid like a muddy star on the surface of the swamp. He looked over to see that Virgo had done the same.

'Now slowly, paddle over to firmer ground,' he instructed, making tiny movements with his hands to ensure he stayed afloat.

Inch by inch, Elliot and Virgo paddled their way slowly across the field, neither daring to speak for fear of sinking beneath the mud. Virgo was first to reach the safety of the ridge and immediately snapped off a tree branch to pull Elliot to the bank. Elliot grabbed the branch and scrambled to safety, both he and Virgo covered in mud and sand.

'How did you know what to do?' asked Virgo when they'd had a few minutes to gather their breath.

'My Grandad,' said Elliot. 'He read a lot and was always telling me stuff. I can also fold a napkin into a swan, but that probably wasn't so useful today.'

'We've got to get back to the farm,' said Virgo, 'Zeus needs to hear about this right away.'

'I think we'll take the road,' said Elliot, looking out at the field, which was a swampy mess of mud and sand.

Half-walking, half-running along the slower, but much drier road to the farm, Elliot and Virgo went straight to the house. They burst into the front room to find Mum and Athene sat happily in front of the fire, sewing a patchwork quilt together.

'Hello darling,' said Josie to her filthy son. 'Been playing football?'

'Something like that, Mum,' replied Elliot, running to give her a relieved hug.

'I'd better get these children washed up, Josie,' said Athene to Mum, a look of deep concern clouding her face. 'Will you be alright for a minute?'

'I'm fine, thank you,' said Mum, taking a bite out of a house brick-sized piece of lemon sponge. 'That lovely gardening programme's on in a minute. It looks so much better now I can see the colour of the flowers on the new telly.'

Elliot looked on gratefully as Athene tended to Josie, settling her comfortably in front of the TV before ushering the two children out of the room.

'Are you both alright?' she said anxiously, wiping some mud from their faces. 'Was it Thanatos?'

'No, Mammon,' said Virgo. 'He tried to kill us.'

'Come up to the shed, we need to tell Father all about it – are you sure you're both okay?'

Assuring Athene they were fine, the three of them headed up to Bessie's cowshed. Although it was no longer covered in swarms of penates, there was nothing from the outside, apart from the fixed roof, to show they had ever been there at all. Athene swung open the door.

'They're all in there,' she said, guiding Elliot and Virgo inside.

It took Elliot a moment to entirely comprehend what he saw as he walked into the shed. Where his rundown old cowshed had once stood, there was now a marble-floored palace, complete with fountains, statues and rows of olive trees growing inside the barn. On an upper level, a dozen different doors led to the Gods' sleeping quarters, which, Elliot could see, looked every bit as opulent as the downstairs, complete with feather beds in every shape and size and a library for Athene.

Although the outside appeared no larger, the inside of the shed now seemed vast, not least because of the two lush grassy fields growing on either side. To the left were Pegasus's quarters, a large hay-lined golden stable with a mineral water fountain flowing in the garden outside, where the majestic horse was reclined on a velvet bed reading *Black Beauty*. To the right was Bessie's new home, a luxurious hay-bed and giant water-feeder set in the softest grass Elliot had ever seen. His pet cow was clearly delighted with her new pad – although perhaps less pleased with the pink frilly knickers Aphrodite had put over her udders – and was happily leaping around the grass thanks to a golden caliper on her lame leg. Elliot could hear the chink of hammer on iron in Hephaestus's new forge underneath the shed and despite the cold, grey weather outside, inside the barn it felt warm and sunny as they approached Zeus and Aphrodite happily reclining on long velvet chairs, chuckling over something they had read in *The Daily Argus*.

'Ah, you're home,' said Zeus with a smile a mile wide, struggling to manoeuvre his portly frame off his comfy chair. 'Hope you don't mind the improvements, Hestia does like to go a bit overboard. If there's anything you don't like, just say the word.'

Zeus stopped as he saw the state of the youngsters and his daughter's worried face.

'Mammon attacked them on the way home,' said Athene. 'He's here, which means Thanatos can't be far away.'

Aphrodite rushed over and embraced them both, bringing Elliot out in another bright scarlet blush. 'Oh thank the Heavens you're alright,' she said, clutching them both to her. 'I said they shouldn't have to go to school,' she added, shooting a filthy look at her sister.

'The less we disrupt young Elliot's life, the better,' said Zeus, earning a grateful nod from Athene, who couldn't resist a 'told you so' glance at Aphrodite. 'But we are going to have to be a lot more cautious with you in future, Elliot. This is a sorry state of affairs indeed. Now has anyone heard from Herm—'

Zeus was cut short by an explosion of feathers through

the cowshed door as four stallions as black as night burst through the floor of the new shed and stopped so fast that Hermes flew out of the chariot and straight into the ornate fountain that flowed in the centre of the room.

'Mammon's coming, Mammon's coming!' the bedraggled messenger squealed as he slumped over the side of the fountain, spitting out a mouthful of water. He lifted his panting, soaking head and saw Elliot, alive and well in the middle of the shed.

'Oh thank the Gods!' shrieked Hermes as he propelled himself out of the fountain, leaving a long wet puddle in his wake. Elliot tried to retreat from the approaching soaking hug, but within seconds, he and Hermes were lying on the floor in a big, wet, muddy mess.

'He's alive!' Hermes sobbed. 'He's alive! He's – eughghgh – absolutely filthy. Does anyone have a towel?'

A short while later, when Elliot and Virgo had had a chance to clean up and Hermes was refreshed by a take-away nectarchino from Café Hero, the six Gods and Elliot were crowded around Hermes's laptop, which was powered by the artificial sun in the shed.

'Stealing this crown is going to be harder than air-dried mascara,' said Hermes. 'Security at the Tower of London is ferocious.'

'I should hope so too,' huffed Athene. 'Besides, breaking a mortal law is against The Sacred Code.'

'And I'm sure Thanatos will be holding a copy when he's pelting mankind with mountains, genius,' said Aphrodite sarcastically. 'Oh sorry Elliot, no offence,' she added with a dazzling smile.

'None taken,' mumbled Elliot, immediately bursting into his Aphrodite blush.

'Well the good news is,' said Zeus, 'if we can't steal it, neither can Thanatos. But we really do need to get our hands on that stone first.'

Everyone sat quietly as they waited for inspiration to strike. Elliot's mind was whirring. He needed that stone. And fast.

'What if we just swapped the crown?' said Elliot. 'That wouldn't break the code. After all, we've got the diamond that was meant to go inside it. Hephaestus, would you be able to make a replica?'

'I can make a ruddy better one,' snorted Hephaestus, mildly miffed at the questioning of his skills.

'Elliot's right,' said Athene. 'Then all we have to do is swap the original for our replica and take the Earth Stone – Hermes, when does the crown leave the Tower?'

Hermes typed away at his laptop and read down a page. 'Blah, blah, blah – right, here we go – "The Imperial State Crown is worn by Her Majesty the Queen at the State Opening of Parliament, which this year will take place on October 21st".'

'That's this Friday,' said Athene. 'Can we do it by then?'

'We'll have to,' said Zeus. 'We'd better get on with it.'

'And we'd better study for this history test tomorrow,' said Virgo. 'As much of an ignoramus as this Boil is, you don't need to give him any more ammunition, Elliot.'

'Why's that?' asked Zeus.

'Because this vile little man has it in for Elliot and is determined to see him thrown out of the school, even though he's twice as clever as anyone else, that's why,' gabbled Virgo. 'Not that I care,' she added quickly.

'Sounds to me,' said Athene, 'like you need to prove him wrong, Elliot.'

'Sounds to me,' huffed Zeus, 'like this Boil character needs a thunderbolt up the b—'

'Daddy!' screeched Aphrodite in delighted horror.

'Athene, can you give Elliot some pointers? He needs all the help he can get,' Virgo asked.

'Thanks a lot,' mumbled Elliot, who would much rather have hatched a plan to 'swap' the Crown Jewels with Zeus.

'So long as it doesn't involve cheating, I'd be happy to help,' said Athene solemnly.

'That's rich coming from you, Miss I-Want-to-Be-a-Millionaire-in-Seventeen-Different-Countries,' said Aphrodite.

Athene glowered at her sister, but refused to take the bait.

'Look, I'll walk the kids back to the house – I don't think we should leave them alone tonight,' gabbled Aphrodite, bundling Elliot and Virgo out of the door before anyone could object.

Virgo and Aphrodite chatted away up the path whilst a tongue-tied Elliot walked a few paces behind them. But when they reached the farmhouse, Aphrodite held Elliot back, waiting to see that Virgo was out of earshot before speaking.

'Now listen Elly,' she said, opening a locket around her neck and producing a heart-shaped pearl from inside it. 'Stuff the Fun Police back there, I'll give you some real help for tomorrow.'

She handed Elliot the pearl, which he turned slowly in his palm.

'This wishing pearl will grant you anything your heart desires,' she said, her eyes twinkling wickedly. 'Just hold it in your hand and make a wish at the start of the test – you'll ace it.'

'Wow – thanks,' said Elliot, stringing together the longest sentence he'd been able to say to the Goddess since she arrived.

'You're welcome sweetie,' winked Aphrodite. 'Besides, you might need it tonight. After five minutes of listening to Big Sis, you'll be wishing for some ear-plugs and a muzzle.'

And with a musical giggle, Aphrodite wiggled back to the cowshed, leaving a happy pink boy contemplating all the things he might wish for from a beautiful love Goddess.

Chapter Twelve

Be Careful What You Wish For

Athene was in fact a gifted teacher, and had Elliot spent more time listening to her, he would have realised that she could have taught him more in one evening than Boil had managed in over a year. But confident that Aphrodite's pearl was all the revision he needed, Elliot instead spent the lesson day-dreaming whilst tucking into a giant pizza. By the time he went to bed, he had an imaginative list of things he could use the wishing pearl for, but not one scrap of Athene's lesson had gone into his happy head.

There was no longer any question that he and Virgo could walk alone to school the next morning, but Aphrodite did agree to drop them discreetly around the corner and watch them into the school from a distance.

'I thought you'd be panicking,' Virgo said to Elliot as he jaunted happily along the short path to the school gates. 'You weren't even listening to Athene. I've been studying all night and I still don't think I can possibly pass this test.'

'Thing is Virgo,' said Elliot smugly, holding the pearl in

his pocket, 'you've either got it or you haven't. And I've really got it.'

'Well keep it to yourself,' said Virgo suspiciously, as Elliot swaggered into school.

'Morning Mr Boil, lovely day,' said Elliot to his nemesis as he passed the history teacher struggling to squeeze his porky body out of the compact car that seemed to permanently smell like old fish.

'Be quiet Hooper,' sneered Boil unpleasantly as he finally freed his backside from the door-frame of his Ford Fiesta. 'I'll be watching you today,' he added to Elliot's cocky form as it disappeared inside Brysmore's grand doorway.

Elliot and Virgo walked straight to the exam hall, where a straggle of fellow teenagers were trembling outside, clearly exhausted from a sleepless night of study and worry. Elliot sauntered past them all and joined the end of the line.

'Suckers,' he muttered under his breath as Emma from his class burst into tears and her boyfriend Dominic was sick in a wastepaper bin.

The smell of old vegetable soup announced that Boil had arrived and the sad gaggle of history students reluctantly trudged into the exam hall, not least because they had to walk under Boil's smelly armpit as he held the door open to count them all in. Boil sneered at Elliot as he filed into the room behind Virgo, meeting the boy's cheery grin with a hateful grunt.

Inside the hall, Boil slammed an exam paper down on

each individual's desk, delighting in making his petrified students jump with each one.

'You have one hour,' he announced with a ghoulish grin when he returned to the front of the hall. 'You may begin.'

Elliot watched scornfully as his classmates whipped over their papers and started furiously scribbling away, their horror-filled faces struggling with Boil's fiendish questions. Under Virgo's confused gaze, Elliot leisurely turned over his paper and read the questions with a derisive snort. He didn't have a clue how to answer a single one, but then he didn't have to. He made himself comfortable in his chair, waited until the patrolling Mr Boil had walked past his desk, then grasped the pearl tightly in his pocket and closed his eyes.

'I wish,' he whispered as quietly as he could, 'to pass this exam.'

Elliot sat completely still for a moment, his eyes still closed, his hand still clutching the pearl, waiting for his mind to fill with inspired historical knowledge.

But nothing happened.

He cautiously opened one eye to see if the exam paper had simply written itself. But there it was, as blank as it had been ten seconds before. He couldn't understand it. Surely Aphrodite wouldn't give him something that didn't work? He waited a few seconds more, before releasing the pearl and taking his hand slowly out of his pocket.

The second the pearl left his grasp, Elliot's hands snapped to his desk and grabbed hold of his exam paper.

Elliot darted his head around to check Boil hadn't heard the slam of his hands on the desk, but the history teacher was too busy towering over the trembling figure of tearful Emma, narrowly missing Dominic's second puddle of vomit. Elliot didn't understand, how could this possibly help him to pass the exam? He tried to let go of the paper, but his hands were clenched tightly around both sides of his exam and he no longer appeared to have any command over them.

'What are you doing?' hissed Virgo, seeing Elliot shake as he tried to control his wayward hands.

'I don't know,' whispered Elliot, 'I can't help it.'

'SILENCE!' roared Boil from the back of the hall, making every last candidate jump in their seats.

Elliot tried desperately to release the paper, but not only were his hands holding it fast, they now seemed determined to raise it off the desk.

'No, no, no,' whispered Elliot as his arms lifted off the table and veered sharply to the right, forcing Elliot's whole body to move sideways as his arms took on a life of their own. They continued to surge sideways, bringing Elliot to his feet as his arms pulled him over to Virgo's table to his right.

'What the blazes are you doing Hooper, sit down!' shouted Boil as he charged towards Elliot at full steam.

But Elliot was utterly helpless as his arms dragged him over to the next desk, finally plonking his exam paper heavily on a stunned Virgo's hand, his grasp immediately relaxing once the exam hit the desk.

'Ow!' she yelped. 'What's the matter with you?'

'Silence Smith!' said Boil arriving at her desk in a fury. 'Hooper! You have precisely two seconds to return to your seat before I give you an automatic fail.'

'Sorry Sir,' said Elliot, relieved to be free of the paper at last and turning to go back to his own desk. But his hands suddenly sprung to life again, this time grabbing Virgo's exam paper and jerking towards the table in front of her. This time they dragged Elliot forwards and forced him to deposit Virgo's exam on Emma's hands, who duly burst into tears again. The other students had all turned around to see what the fuss was about, and watched in bemusement as Elliot worked his way around the hall, picking up exam papers and passing them onto the next person with increasing speed.

'Everyone get back to work!' screeched a puce Boil as he chased Elliot around the hall. 'Hooper, I'll have your hide for this!'

But Elliot was completely out of control, frantically being dragged from one desk to the next, passing exam papers around the room as Aphrodite's pearl granted his wish to the letter.

'Help me,' he panted at Virgo as he rounded the room for the third time. 'Make it stop.'

Virgo ran over to restrain him, but was powerless against

the Goddess's wishing pearl and could only watch helplessly as an exhausted Elliot darted from her grip and passed the exam from person to person, whilst a panting Boil shouted every threat he could muster a few feet behind him.

'THIS EXAM IS OVER!' Boil eventually roared, seeing that Elliot would not stop and his exam was in chaos. At his words, Elliot's hands immediately dropped the exam paper he was holding and returned limply to his side, allowing the worn out boy to crumple to the floor in an exhausted heap.

'You've all failed!' Boil spat to a chorus of aggrieved groans as every last one of Elliot's classmates shot him filthy looks at the prospect of the rest of the term in Boil's extra history classes. 'Hooper and Smith, you're coming with me.'

Boil dragged Elliot up off the floor by the back of his blazer and frog-marched him and Virgo straight to the Headmaster's office.

Elliot was no stranger to Call Me Graham's luxurious office. This term alone he had sat in its leather armchairs on at least ten separate occasions. But he had always managed to talk himself out of serious punishment. Call Me Graham was renowned for being a soft touch and spinning him a tale of woe had always been enough to get Elliot out of trouble. But this time, Mr Boil accompanied Elliot and Virgo into the room and egged on by Boil's furious wobbling, no amount of sob stories could save them.

'I'm very sorry to hear that your great aunt has died. Again,' said Call Me Graham shakily to Elliot as he nervously flicked his fringe. 'But Mr Boil is right, this time you have gone too far. You will have to be disciplined.'

'Expelled!' cried Boil triumphantly.

'Oh really?' stammered Graham, turning to look at Mr Boil. 'I was thinking more along the lines of a stern letter home. Maybe. If that's okay.'

'The boy is a menace,' said Boil, not taking his piggy eyes from Elliot's angry face. 'And Smith has done nothing but cause trouble since she arrived. I will not let the Brysmore name be dragged into the dirt. You're expelled, both of you!'

'But that's ridiculous!' cried Virgo, nudging a belligerent Elliot into defending himself. 'It wasn't even a real exam.'

'Silence!' screamed Boil. 'Not another word from either of you. The Headmaster's decision is final.'

'But I haven't made a decision,' Call Me Graham quietly piped up.

'Yes you have. And an excellent one it is too,' said Boil, slamming his hand down on Graham's shoulder in solidarity.

'Right. Oh. Well then. Your parents will need to collect you and I'll want to talk to them,' said the Head to an enthusiastic wobble from Boil.

Elliot's blood froze. This was exactly the situation he'd been trying to avoid. There was no way he could ask Mum to come to the school. If Call Me Graham found out about his home life, he knew he would have to tell the authorities, then all the months he'd spent trying to keep Mum at home would have been in vain. He looked desperately over at Virgo, who gave him an understanding nod.

'I'll call my parents,' she said sweetly to Call Me Graham. 'They're Elliot's aunt and uncle, they'll be very disappointed in us both.'

Elliot shot her a baffled look, but she mouthed reassurances at him as she headed to the office. She dialed Hermes's number.

'Hello-dee,' the messenger chirped down the line after a few rings.

'Hermes, it's Virgo,' she whispered furiously. 'We're in trouble.'

'Mammon?' panted Hermes, leaping into the air and staying there.

'No. Boil,' said Virgo, 'I can't explain now, but we need some parents, quick.'

'Leave it with me kiddo,' said Hermes, instantly catching her drift. 'Two prize parentals coming up. Hang on in there.'

'Thanks Hermes,' she said and replaced the phone, quickly heading back to the Head's office before Elliot's mouth could get them in any more trouble.

Ten minutes later, Elliot and Virgo were relieved to hear the screech of Aphrodite's car tyres break the tense silence in Call Me Graham's office. There was a thundering knock on the Headmaster's door and Mr Boil sprang to answer it, delighting in his front row seat at Elliot's expulsion.

Boil's fat eyes nearly popped out of his fat head when he saw who was on the other side. Standing at the entrance to the office was the most beautiful woman he had ever seen, dressed in a smart, tight pink suit. Behind her was a huge, tanned man in his forties, taut muscles bulging from every inch of his enormous body, right up to a neck like a tree trunk, which supported a chiseled head with short cropped hair. Elliot didn't recognise the man from his face, but the Bermuda shirt and shorts gave his identity away.

'Hi,' boomed a transformed Zeus in an American accent, grabbing Boil's hand in a handshake so violent it nearly lifted Boil off the floor. 'I'm Brad. And this little cutie is my wife, er . . .'

'Bridget,' purred Aphrodite, extending her lovely arm out towards Boil's fat one, just giving him time to adjust the glasses that Zeus-Brad's shaking had dislodged. 'You must be Mr Boil. I'd know that handsome face anywhere from Elliot's description.'

Despite the peril of the situation, Elliot had to stifle a giggle as the two Gods sauntered into the office, Aphrodite throwing the youngsters a shifty wink as she walked towards them.

'Now what have you two scamps been up to?' she said, waggling a finger at Elliot and Virgo as she perched on the edge of Call Me Graham's desk. 'You know how important I think school is.'

Call me Graham had come out from behind the desk to introduce himself, but before he could say anything, Boil had breezed past him and sat in his chair, leaving the Headmaster looking rather lost in the middle of his own office.

'Well,' murmured Graham as he took a seat on a footstool to one side, 'they've disrupted a school examination.'

'And been insolent to a teacher. And it would take me all day to list your nephew's various crimes,' wobbled Boil.

'I'd happily spend all day with you, Mr Boil. All night too if necessary,' said Aphrodite breathily, leaning so far over the desk that Boil spat out the mouthful of Graham's tea he'd just slurped.

'Now kids,' said Zeus-Brad, hiding a smile and moving his huge new frame behind Mr Boil at the desk. 'Sounds like you owe Mr Wart here an apology.'

'It's Boil,' shouted Boil, tempering his volume when he realised the size of the man stood behind him. 'And an apology won't even come close. What little I've seen of your daughter doesn't impress me at all, but Elliot Hooper is a disgrace to the Brysmore name and should be expelled!'

'Oh come on now Graham,' boomed Zeus-Brad sternly, moving to the Headmaster and bringing a hand the weight of a bowling bowl crashing down on his weedy shoulder. 'I'm sure we can work this out between us. They're just a couple of excited kids.'

'I love the way your chins wobble when you get excited,' said Aphrodite to Boil, perching on the desk so that her lovely legs were right in front of Graham's trembling head. 'But expelled – and I just love the way the spit glistens on Mr Wart's lips when he says that – that's so, so final. Is there any way I could persuade you to give our little Elly one more chance?'

'Absolutely not,' gasped Boil, not taking his eyes from Aphrodite's long legs. 'He's disgraced himself too many times. And it's BOIL!'

'Aw you seem like a reasonable guy,' said Zeus-Brad, squeezing his huge hand on Call Me Graham's shoulder, releasing a pained whimper from the headmaster. 'Let's not be hasty.'

'Please,' implored Aphrodite, bringing her gorgeous face inches from Call Me Graham's, intoxicating him with her heady scent.

'Well – I – the Brysmore rules state—' spluttered Graham, earning him another painful squeeze from the hulk of a man behind him.

'Pretty please,' said Aphrodite, pouting her rosy lips at the gibbering Headmaster, who melted like butter at her batting eyes.

'I s-s-suppose Mr Boil here might have been a little harsh,' stammered Call Me Graham, wiping the sweat from his brow with a frilly handkerchief as Zeus released him from his iron grasp.

'Wh-WHAT?!' shouted Boil. 'No Headmaster, expulsion is the only possible answer—'

'I think you'll find that Graham here has given his answer,' said Zeus-Brad, walking over to Mr Boil and towering over him with his gigantic muscular form. 'Unless there's anything you want to add?'

'No – no,' whimpered a gibbering Boil. 'But they are both suspended. I don't want to see either of these children until Monday. And if they get half a percent beneath 85% in the final exams, they'll both be out of this school.'

'Oh thank you,' squealed Aphrodite, leaping off the desk and planting a big kiss on Call me Graham's clammy cheek, turning him a shade of pink that put Elliot's blushes to shame. 'You won't regret it. Now come along you naughty children, let's get you home.'

'Yes Mummy,' said Virgo, smiling gratefully at Aphrodite.

'Yes Bridget,' squeaked Elliot, tears of laughter rolling down his face.

'That's Aunty Bridget to you,' Aphrodite chided, her eyes sparkling with mischief.

'Sorry Aunty Bridget,' Elliot hissed, running out of the room before exploding with laughter in the corridor beyond.

'Good to meet you, Wart,' boomed Zeus-Brad, his blue eyes cold as steel as Mr Boil winced from the force of his handshake. 'I'll be keeping my eye on you, don't you worry.'

'IT'S BOIL!' shouted the incensed history teacher as Zeus slammed the door in his fat face, blocking the hysterical laughter coming from the corridor.

'Well I think I handled that very well,' said Call Me

Graham quietly from his footstool. 'Must be time for lunch.'

As Call Me Graham left for the canteen, tripping over some fresh air on the way, Mr Boil looked out of the door, where the quartet's giggles were still echoing down the hallway.

'Laugh it up, Hooper,' he muttered under his pungent breath. 'The last one will be mine.'

Zeus, Aphrodite, Elliot and Virgo couldn't stop laughing all the way home about the Gods' performance in Call Me Graham's office. But when they reached the farm, Athene didn't see the joke.

'Suspension is a very serious business,' she said sternly to the four heads hung before her. 'Think of all the school they'll miss. What were you thinking, giving Elliot that pearl?'

'Oh hush up,' pouted Aphrodite, knowing her sister was right. 'I was only trying to help Elly rub that pig-faced buffoon's nose in it. Besides, this suspension is just what we need – it's too dangerous letting them out of the house with Mammon and Thanatos on the loose. They're safer here and you know it.'

'Be that as it may,' Athene continued, 'you will both be having tuition from me for the duration of your suspension so you don't fall behind at school. And you are to stay on the farm at all times.'

'Except on Friday,' said Elliot.

'And on Friday,' said Athene.

'Except on Friday,' Elliot repeated. 'When we're all going up to London to steal the Imperial Crown.'

'We're swapping it,' said Athene quickly. 'And no matter what we're doing to it, there's absolutely no way you are coming on such a dangerous mission. You're staying here.'

'No way,' said Elliot, looking to Zeus and Aphrodite for support. But for once, all the Gods were in agreement.

'It's too dangerous, Elly,' said Aphrodite, coming over and giving him a squeeze. 'We have to keep you safe.'

'The girls are right,' said Zeus. 'The best thing you can do is take care of yourself, leave the silly stuff to us. Thanatos will be trying to get the crown in London and nothing can get past Hephaestus's new fence. You'll be safer here.'

'A mortal just isn't equipped for something as risky as this,' added Virgo in a superior tone. 'Your place is here.'

'So's yours,' said Aphrodite.

'What?' cried Virgo. 'Not a chance, I'm coming with you.'

'No you're not, old girl,' said Zeus softly, but firmly. 'You're mortal too now – your powers aren't strong enough for you to look after yourself and we need to concentrate on getting that crown. You need to stay here with Elliot, this isn't a mission for you.'

'Well that's not . . . I should . . . you all . . . Grrrr,' seethed Virgo as she stormed out of the barn in a huff.

'Are you sure you're alright, dear boy?' Zeus asked Elliot

with one of his soul-piercing looks. 'That must have been quite an ordeal.'

'I'm fine,' said Elliot. 'And thanks for helping out back at the school, you know, with the Brad thing. I just don't want them to—'

'You don't have to explain anything to me,' said Zeus knowingly. 'We're here to help. And to that end,' he added, foraging around in the pocket of his Bermuda shorts, 'I want you to have this.'

He opened his fingers to reveal a tiny silver thunderbolt in the palm of his hand.

'You may have had enough of our gizmos today,' said Zeus, handing over the charm. 'But if you ever need us, just throw this at the ground. We'll know where to find you.'

'Thanks,' said Elliot quietly, turning the silver trinket in his palm.

'You'd better go and find Virgo,' said Zeus. 'She may not have the power of an immortal, but she certainly has the temper of one.'

'Sure,' said Elliot, wandering back up the path to the farm, playing with the thunderbolt in his hand and wondering how he was going to explain to Mum what he was doing at home on a Tuesday lunchtime in the middle of the school term.

Chapter Thirteen

On The Wrong Track

Despite Elliot's best efforts to enjoy himself, Athene was determined that his suspension would not be the holiday he wanted. When the wise Goddess wasn't putting the finishing touches to the plan to steal – or swap – the Imperial Crown, Athene devoted every spare minute to tutoring Elliot and encouraged her fellow immortals to do the same.

Much as he tried to maintain his reluctance throughout her lessons, it was impossible for Elliot not to enjoy Athene's inspired teaching. It was much easier, for instance, to remember the elements of the periodic table when Athene turned bits of rock into pieces of gold and silver, or to remember who was who in *Romeo and Juliet* when the Gods performed the play for him – Hermes made an especially memorable Juliet. After two days of classes at the School of Immortality, Elliot had not only been coached in all his school subjects by Athene, but had also been taught how to throw thunderbolts by Zeus, fly in winged sandals by Hermes and swear in ancient Greek by Aphrodite.

Friday, the day of the State Opening of Parliament, came around in a flash. Having locked himself in his forge beneath the cowshed since Monday night, a grimy, sweaty Hephaestus finally emerged on Thursday night, proudly bearing a beautiful crown that was the spitting image of the Imperial Crown that the Gods intended to swap. The blacksmith proudly gave the Gods a demonstration of the 'improvements' he had made to the original, before reluctantly handing it over to Hermes, who was eventually persuaded to take it off his own head and place it in his bottomless bag.

As Friday morning dawned, the Gods had their plan rehearsed to the very last second. Athene would grow an olive tree at the far wall of the Tower, allowing the Gods to climb over the wall. While Aphrodite made the two soldiers guarding the Jewel House fall so passionately in love with one another they'd forget what they were doing, Zeus – disguised as a beefeater – would enter the Tower holding a large staff, which was in fact Hermes. The messenger God would then transform into one of the security guards, create a distraction as the Imperial Crown was removed from its case and swap the crowns over before they all made their escape on Pegasus, who would be disguised as one of the horses pulling the state coach.

'And me?' asked Hephaestus as Athene explained the plan earlier in the week, which she'd woven onto an elaborate tapestry.

'You just hang about with an axe, comrade,' said Zeus. 'You're our Plan B.'

'Too kind,' grumbled Hephaestus, returning to his forge.

They had been practising for days, recreating every stage of the process in meticulous detail thanks to the carriages, horses and guards the Gods were able to create from wheelbarrows, mice and each other. By Friday morning, the Gods were confident their plan was flawless.

But no amount of begging, sulking, shouting or moaning had persuaded them to take Elliot and Virgo along for the ride and as the Gods prepared to leave for London, they were watched by two very grumpy onlookers.

'We'll be back by lunchtime,' said Zeus as Pegasus circled for take-off outside the cowshed.

'I look ridiculous,' said Pegasus, who was decked out in full ceremonial regalia.

'Nonsense, you look splendid,' said Zeus as he mounted his steed in his beefeater outfit.

'Behave yourselves you little monkeys,' giggled Aphrodite, as she and Athene jostled for space on one side of Hades's chariot, with Hermes and Hephaestus squashed onto the other. 'Hold tight everyone, here we goooooooo!'

Elliot and Virgo watched with faces like thunder as Hades's chariot dived underground, a whirlwind of leaves the only evidence that it had been there at all.

'Chocks away,' cried Zeus as Pegasus soared into the sky, only remembering at the last minute to wear the helmet of invisibility, making himself and Pegasus vanish into thin air the second the helmet hit his white head.

'So,' grumbled Virgo, as she and Elliot stood outside the empty shed. 'Do you want to go over those equations Athene left us?'

'No,' sulked Elliot, kicking a stone in grumpy frustration. 'It's not fair, we should be going too.'

'I know,' said Virgo. 'We were managing perfectly well before they came along. In a kind of releasing-an-angry-death-daemon-and-nearly-getting-killed sort of way.'

They gave each other a sulky glance. But one look at each other's miserable faces was enough to make them both burst out laughing.

'Come on,' said Elliot. 'Perhaps if we get this homework done whilst they're away, sergeant Athene will give us the night off.'

Virgo nodded her agreement and they were about to return to the farmhouse when a rolled copy of *The Daily Argus* landed at their feet.

'I wish my paper round was that easy,' said Elliot, picking up the newspaper and unfurling its pages.

'The one that Hermes has been doing for you every day?' scoffed Virgo.

But Elliot didn't answer. He was reading the lead story on the front page of *The Daily Argus* and with every word his face fell further.

'Uh-oh,' he whispered before reading the story out loud to Virgo:

CROWNING GLORY
By Cicero, News Editor

The Argus can't see any reason nor rhyme
Why Zeus and his gang are resorting to crime
Word reaches our paper that those crazy fools
Are planning to pinch one of England's Crown Jewels
This morning they travel to fair London town
To sightsee, then nick the Imperial Crown
Hephaestus has made one from silver and gold
And Hermes will swap this new crown for the old
Her Majesty won't have a gracious response
To find that it ain't her crown sat on her bonce
This terrible heist truly beggars belief
The King of the Gods is a dirty old thief

'This isn't good,' said Elliot when he'd finished reading.

'No it is not,' agreed Virgo. 'The standard of journalism at *The Daily Argus* is utterly reprehensible – they have spies everywhere, but everyone has a basic right to privacy. This level of press intrusion—'

'Who cares about that?' snapped Elliot. 'If we're reading this, then so is every other immortal in the world, including Mammon and Thanatos. We have to warn Zeus.'

'Hermes's phone won't work in the Underworld, the reception there is terrible,' mulled Virgo. 'And they've taken all the transport with them. Unless you can drive Aphrodite's car?'

'I'm thirteen, you prune,' said Elliot.

'Of course you are,' said Virgo. 'You're such a grumpy old man I forget you're only a baby. Charon?'

'The river's a twenty minute walk from here,' said Elliot. 'It'll take too long.'

'Well come on?' said Virgo. 'You know how things work down here, how else can we get to London?'

'The train!' cried Elliot. 'If we run, we might just catch the morning train from the village station, we could be in London in a couple of hours.'

'Hurry up then,' shouted Virgo, already halfway down the path to the farm gate and on her way to the village. 'What are you waiting for?'

Elliot and Virgo sprinted down the track to the village, to the pretty train station in its centre. Elliot hadn't been on a train since before his Grandad became ill, but he had always loved their trips to London, going to visit a museum or a famous landmark. He felt a lump of sadness well up from his stomach as he thought of the good times he and Grandad had enjoyed from this station, but he didn't have time to dwell, barely having time to buy two tickets before the train came rolling into the station.

Elliot and Virgo hopped on board and sat at a table with four chairs in a quiet carriage in the middle of the train. In their haste, they hadn't noticed the large figure lumbering behind them the moment they left the enchanted safety of the farm, who watched them board the train and jumped on behind them undetected, and who even now was plotting the best way to ensure they never reached their destination.

On board the train, Elliot was counting the money he had left over from buying the tickets. As the Gods had provided everything he'd needed since they arrived, he still had much of his weekly spending money left and as he sat listening to Virgo ramble on about the disasters awaiting humanity if Thanatos got the Earth Stone first, his stomach started to rumble.

'I'm hungry,' he moaned.

'Me too,' said Virgo. 'I didn't have time for my fourth breakfast this morning.'

'I'm going to the buffet car. Stay here and try not to be weird,' said Elliot as he set off down the train in search of some food.

'Says the boy with the bottomless pit for a stomach,' muttered Virgo as she looked out of the window at the countryside whizzing past outside.

Brian the ticket inspector had not had a good morning. Ever since his alarm clock hadn't gone off, everything about today seemed determined to make life as hard for him as possible. There was the large lady in carriage C who had locked herself in the lavatory at Gillingham. And then there was the little boy in carriage J who had just vomited pink milkshake all over the businessman in front of him. The train was running fifteen minutes late, the passengers had been complaining all morning and all Brian wanted was to pass the rest of the journey in peace, leaving him free to enjoy the stamp-collecting fair that awaited him in London. He arrived at Virgo's seat.

'Tickets please,' he barked at the daydreaming girl.

'Sorry?' asked Virgo, startling at his sudden noise.

'Your ticket,' Brian snapped rudely. 'I want it.'

'Oh, I see,' said Virgo, her brow furrowed in confusion. 'But it's mine.'

Brian let out an impatient sigh. Today had been hard enough. The last thing he needed was some teenage know-it-all making his day any worse.

'Miss, if you cannot produce a valid ticket for your journey, I will be forced to charge you a penalty fare. Do you have a ticket or not?' he huffed.

'Yes, I have it here,' said Virgo, pulling her train ticket from her pocket. 'So you want this?'

'Yes,' sighed Brian.

'You want me to give you my ticket?'

'YES!' shouted Brian, his patience expired.

'Fine,' said Virgo, holding the ticket out. 'That'll be nine pounds and fifty pence.'

Brian gave her a look that could unblock a drain.

'I beg your pardon?'

'My ticket,' said Virgo. 'If you really want it, it'll cost you nine pounds and fifty pence, the same it cost Elliot. Be grateful I'm not trying to sell it on at a profit.'

'I am not going to pay for your ticket!' shouted Brian. 'Just give it to me.'

'I will not,' said the indignant young Goddess, withdrawing her ticket back into her pocket. 'We've all paid good money just to sit on your train – which is covered in some revolting pink mess by the way – and yet here you come, refusing to pay a penny and stealing everyone else's tickets. It's a disgrace.'

'That's it!' cried Brian, throwing his hat on the floor in a temper. 'Get off my train! Get off, you rude, obnoxious—'

'Come to think of it,' said Virgo, oblivious to Brian's ranting, 'I don't see why we should have to pay for this journey at all. The train was going to London whether or not we sat on it. Why should we have to pay for a service that you are using for free? No, not only will I not give you my ticket, I insist upon a full refund.'

As he staggered back down the carriage, Elliot could hear some choice language coming from further down the train and he hoped that it had nothing to do with the former Goddess he had left unattended while he went to buy some crisps. But as he opened the door to the carriage, he was greeted by the sight of Virgo standing on the table, trying to encourage fellow passengers to rise against the tyranny of South Coast Trains and demand a refund for their tickets while Brian jumped on his hat in temper.

But before Elliot could calm the situation down, the train jolted so violently, it threw everyone in the carriage from their seats and Virgo from the table where she had been preaching.

'What was that?' cried Virgo from the floor, rubbing her silver head.

'I don't know,' said Elliot, bracing himself between the seats as the train made another sudden jolt. 'But I'm guessing it isn't leaves on the line.'

'What the 'ell's going on?' shouted Brian down the emergency intercom to the driver.

'Er – there's a troll in my cab,' came the fuzzy terrified reply from the driver. 'He appears to be dismantling the brakes.'

'Mammon!' cried Elliot and Virgo, barging past Brian to make their way up the shaking train to the driver's cab. Thrown from one side of the train to the other, they forced their way through screaming passengers, the suitcases littering the floor and the scalding hot coffee that flew at them with every shudder. As the train rocked perilously from side to side, they made their unsteady way up the carriages, eventually bursting into the driver's cab at the front of the train.

The wind from the open window nearly blew them straight out again, but they forced their way inside against the blast of icy air. The driver was unconscious in his chair, knocked out by a huge rock on the floor. Elliot made his way to the open window and stuck his head into the raging wind, just in time to see Mammon tumbling down the track from where he had thrown himself off the train. As he scrambled to his feet, the Daemon of Greed jumped into the air, landing on the ground with such a thud, the surrounding Earth shook, causing the train to leap from the tracks. Mammon jumped again, making the train jump once more. But as it sped away from the daemon, Elliot could just make out something travelling towards the train at enormous speed.

At first it looked like a long black snake, slithering along the ground in a crooked line. But as Elliot watched from the charging train, he could see the snake getting wider and closer, until he realised that it wasn't a snake at all, but a long crack in the ground that was getting wider and bigger and charging towards the train's rear wheels.

'He's trying to crash the train!' Elliot shouted above the noise of the wind racing past them. 'He's going to kill us all!'

Virgo frantically jabbed at all the levers and buttons on the train's dashboard, but nothing would make the train slow down. The train shot through a station, throwing the waiting passengers all over the platform with the force of the gust it created, the crevice shooting along behind, throwing wooden sleepers into the air as it pierced through the Earth.

Elliot forced his head out of the window again as the crack drew even closer to the train's rear wheels. They were all doomed. Unless . . . Elliot suddenly remembered the charm Zeus had given him the previous evening. He pulled Zeus's thunderbolt from his pocket and held it out of the window, throwing it as hard as he could to the floor. The train immediately raced away from the spot where the thunderbolt had landed, but as soon as the silver charm hit the ground, an almighty clap of thunder and huge flash of lightning lit up the sky. Elliot looked back at the crevice – it was now just a few feet from the train's back wheels and it was only a matter of moments before it caught them, plunging the train and everyone in it into the gaping abyss opening up behind it.

Elliot and Virgo looked helplessly at each other as the train charged on through red signals, sending alarms ringing inside the train and out as the safety sirens screamed their warning about the runaway train. Elliot looked desperately around him, looking for something, anything that might save them. Virgo grabbed hold of his arm.

'What?' he cried, still looking for the miracle that would rescue everyone on board.

Virgo said nothing, but simply pointed up ahead. Elliot stopped to follow the direction of her finger, seeing nothing but a small black blob on the horizon.

'Wha —?' he started again, as the sound of another train's horn gave him the terrible answer. The black blob was getting nearer and taking shape every foot of the track it sped along.

It was another train. And they were heading straight for it.

'Where are they?' shouted Elliot, desperately searching the sky for any sign of the Gods.

'I don't know!' screamed Virgo. 'Elliot, we have to get off this train!'

'We can't leave all these people,' Elliot shouted back. 'Mammon will kill them all.'

'You can't help them,' Virgo screamed again. 'But you can save yourself.'

'NO, WE'LL HAVE TO SAVE YOU!' boomed an almighty voice beside them, as Zeus removed the invisibility helmet to reveal him and Pegasus galloping in mid-air alongside the train. At the same moment, Hades's chariot came bursting out of the ground, carrying the other four Gods, who looked on in horror as they hurtled along next to the train.

'Elliot! Jump!' cried Aphrodite from the chariot. 'We'll catch you!'

Elliot frantically signalled ahead to show the train thundering towards them and behind to show the enormous crevice trying to pull the train into its dark depths. The Gods huddled together for a few seconds. Decision made, they didn't waste another second setting to work.

'Hold on Elliot,' shouted Athene as Zeus spurred Pegasus

on, positioning his flying horse in front of Hades's chariot and the four black stallions that drew it.

'Hurry!' screamed Elliot from the cab, the black blob on the horizon growing larger with every speeding second.

With Zeus in position up front, Athene stood in Hades's chariot and jumped onto the back of the first horse. Whispering soothing words into the horse's ear, she stood on its back and jumped again, this time landing on the back of the second horse. Everyone watched with their hearts in their mouths as the Goddess bravely made her way along the charging horses.

She safely made the jump to the third horse, but just as she was about to jump onto the leading horse, the rear carriage of the train rocked violently as the back wheels slipped into the approaching ravine. The violence of the movement caused the whole train to rock, throwing Elliot and Virgo onto the floor and breaking Athene's concentration for the crucial split second she needed to make the jump.

As she leapt from one horse's back, only one foot found the back of the next. She teetered impossibly on one leg for a couple of infinite seconds, but she couldn't regain her balance and with a scream the Goddess of Wisdom toppled over the horse's flank and out of sight.

'Theney!' screamed Aphrodite, seeing her sister disappear from view, snapping her head behind the chariot to see if she had been trampled by the horses or the train. But Athene didn't appear. Hermes, Hephaestus and Aphrodite spilt over the side of the chariot to search for their immortal friend.

'Look!' shrieked Hermes, pointing to where Athene was being dragged from the front horse's bridle. 'She's there!' Aphrodite took one look at her stricken sister and instantly leapt from the chariot to the back horse, just as Athene had done before her. Elliot and Virgo, who had struggled to their feet again, watched anxiously as the love Goddess jumped nimbly from one horse to the next, finally landing on the front horse and clinging firmly to its mane as she reached her hand down to her sister.

Athene clung gratefully to Aphrodite's wrist and as the two women exchanged an understanding nod, they counted to three together. On the third count, Aphrodite gave an almighty pull as her sister kicked off the ground, sending Athene flying up into the air and landing her neatly behind Aphrodite on the back of the horse with a grateful squeeze. The two Goddesses wasted no further time in loosening the reins and throwing them up ahead to their father, who lashed the chariot to Pegasus. With a thumbs up to those behind him, he spurred Pegasus on, making the chariot surge ahead of the train.

With the chariot charging along the track in front of the train, Hephaestus leaned out of the back of the chariot, holding a hammer in one hand and a huge bolt in the other. He set to work attaching the front of the train to the back of the chariot, Hermes watching in terror as the blacksmith hung perilously out of the back of the chariot, inches from the careering train's spoiler. With the bolt nearly in place, Hephaestus leaned over to give it a final hammer, when the back of the train slipped once again into the crevice, causing another fierce jolt, sending Hephaestus tumbling out of the back of the chariot.

Hermes sprang into action and into the air. He grabbed the blacksmith's ankles as Hephaestus clung to the front of the train, both Gods hovering in the air as Hermes struggled to keep them aloft as the train rocked on its rails. As the train recovered its balance, so too did Hermes and, with some deft flying, he was able to negotiate himself and the blacksmith back into the chariot, allowing Hephaestus to deliver the final blow, attaching the train and the chariot together.

With Pegasus now leading the chariot, which was attached to the train, Hermes flew up to Zeus, who was keeping Pegasus on course along the track. As he understood that everything was in place, Zeus gave Pegasus a reassuring pat on the neck, replaced the invisibility helmet and spurred his horse on again. But this time, rather than charging forwards, Pegasus reared up into the sky, pulling Hades's chariot upwards behind him as he climbed up into the air. As the flying horse and the flying chariot soared up into the sky, the front wheels of the train came off the track and started to lift the front carriage off the ground.

'It's too late!' cried Elliot as the front carriage continued on its collision course with the approaching train and the rear carriage teetered on the brink of the crevice. But the Gods had sensed the danger and spurred all the horses on, who responded to their cries with a great surge up into the heavens. With the almighty force of five immortal horses pulling the train into the sky, carriage by carriage, the train gracefully came away from the track and started up into the air, flowing behind Pegasus and the chariot like the ribbons on a kite. The battered passengers, who had been screaming their prayers and curses as they awaited their doom, suddenly fell silent as the 8.42 to London Waterloo flew off invisibly into the sky, just missing the train that would have smashed them all to smithereens and stopping the crevice in its tracks, as the boy it was intending to kill drove a train off into the sky.

Forty minutes later, the train made a graceful landing just outside platform 10, fifteen minutes ahead of schedule. Aphrodite wandered through the train spraying a scent that calmed all the passengers and made them forget the past hour of their lives.

'Please remember to take all your personal belongings with you when you leave the train,' breathed Hermes down the microphone shortly after fluttering into the cab. 'Thank you for travelling with South Coast Trains. We hope you choose to fly with us again soon.'

Elliot and Virgo were still tending to the driver, who had

regained consciousness somewhere over Woking. As the paramedics arrived to take him away, concerned about a concussion that left him feeling like the train had been flying, the two friends slumped to the floor of the carriage.

'Next time we'll take the bus,' said Elliot, reeling from the third attempt on his life in a week. 'Thanks,' he said to the Gods. 'Stealing the Crown Jewels and saving a train full of mortals in a single morning. What's on this afternoon? So let me see the Earth Stone.'

The Gods exchanged nervous looks.

'What's wrong?' asked Virgo. 'Did Thanatos get the crown?'

'No,' said Zeus. 'But neither did we.'

'What do you mean?' asked Elliot, desperately clambering to his feet.

'Your signal came just as we were going to make the swap,' said Athene. 'We knew you'd never use it unless you were in terrible danger. So we came to find you.'

'So the Earth Stone's gone?' said Virgo.

'Not at all,' said Zeus, trying to sound upbeat. 'We still know exactly where it is. We might just have to wait another year before we can get our hands on it.'

'We can't. I need it now,' said Elliot desperately. 'They're repossessing my farm on Monday.'

'This isn't your fault, Elly,' said Aphrodite, coming over to give him a squeeze. 'You couldn't possibly have known that Mammon would have attacked the train like that. Your life is more important than your farm.'

'But if I'd stayed at the farm like you told me to . . . We have to get the stone.'

'It's done now,' said Zeus. 'Let's not dwell on it. The main thing is to find Mammon before he can attack you again. Thanatos must have him terrified if he's prepared to break his oath.'

'No,' said Elliot stubbornly. 'Today. Where's the crown now?'

'I overheard the guards say it was on its way to Buckingham Palace,' said Hermes. 'Apparently the Queen likes to practise with it before the ceremony. Hefty beast of a thing apparently. The crown I mean, not the Queen.'

'Right,' said Zeus, pacing around the floor. 'So we need to break into Buckingham Palace, distract the Queen, swap the crown and be back for an early bath. Huzzah!'

'Why don't we just go and ask her for it?' said Elliot quietly.

'Tremendous idea,' snorted Virgo. '"Excuse me Your Majesty, could we just have your priceless crown to stop a murderous death daemon, thanks." We'll be locked up in a dungeon before lunch.'

'Well, do you have a better idea?' snapped Elliot. 'We have to get that stone and this might be the only way. Besides, she always seems nice enough on the telly.'

'He's right,' said Zeus. 'It's worth a try. And Elliot, I think you're the man to persuade her.'

'Me?' said Elliot. 'No way. I can't do anything.'

'You can avert a rail disaster,' said Aphrodite.

'You can escape from quicksand,' said Athene.

'You can face down a death daemon,' said Virgo.

'You can wear anything with those eyes,' said Hermes.

'You sound like just the chap to me, Elliot,' said Zeus, as Hermes handed over the bag containing the crown. 'Take Virgo and Pegasus to Buckingham Palace. We'll go and find Mammon before he can cause any more bother. I know you can do it, Elliot. We all do.'

As the five Gods gave Elliot encouraging pats on the back, kisses for luck and a trendy new scarf (Hermes), Elliot took Hermes's bag containing the crown and went to where Zeus had parked Pegasus in a car parking space.

'I've had to fight off two white vans and a moped for this space,' snorted the horse as Elliot and the Gods approached. 'Parking in this city is a nightmare.'

'You're off to see the Queen, Peg,' said Zeus with a wink, stroking the horse's white mane.

'I wasn't aware I had granted her an audience,' said Pegasus snootily as he bent down to allow Elliot and Virgo on his back. 'But after my efforts today, I'm sure some sort of knighthood is in order.'

'Good luck, Elliot,' said Zeus to Elliot as the boy strapped the invisibility helmet to his head, instantly disappearing from view.

As an invisible whoosh carried Elliot and Virgo away, Zeus and his comrades looked up into the sky.

'D'ya really think a young lad like that can persuade a Queen?' said Hephaestus doubtfully as the Gods filed into the chariot when it appeared from beneath the ground.

'I think Elliot Hooper can do anything he sets his mind to,' said Zeus proudly as the four black horses reared into the air, before disappearing underground once more.

Chapter Fourteen

By Royal Command

The short journey to Buckingham Palace took no time at all and within minutes of leaving the Gods, Elliot and Virgo were flying around the outside of the palace on Pegasus, peering through the windows of the Queen's London home under the cover of the invisibility helmet. It was quite a view – they could see a maid pocketing some of the silver cutlery she was supposed to be polishing in the kitchen, and a footman trying on the Queen's dresses in the robing room. But they finally found Queen Elizabeth II in her private parlour, sipping a cup of tea and reading the newspaper, the Imperial Crown sparkling on the top of her regal head.

'What do we do now?' asked Virgo. 'We can't just smash through the window?'

'I suppose we knock,' said Elliot, unsure of the correct protocol for approaching the Queen of England on a flying horse. With Pegasus hovering steadily outside the window, Elliot leant over to the window and tapped out the politest knock he could manage on the glass.

The Queen looked straight at Elliot and Virgo, but returned to her paper.

'We've just been blanked by the Queen,' said Elliot indignantly. 'And to think my Nan had a mug with her picture on it.'

'That invisibility helmet suits you,' said Virgo with a sigh. 'It matches your invisible brain.'

Realising that he still had the helmet on his head, Elliot quickly took it off, making sure that Virgo received a good nudge in the ribs in the process. He took a deep breath and knocked again, hoping that the crowds of tourists below were too busy trying to make the guards in front of the palace laugh to notice the flying children who had suddenly appeared above their heads.

The Queen looked up again. If she was startled to see two children on a flying horse outside her window, she didn't show it. Elliot smiled politely and Virgo gave her an enthusiastic wave, which the Queen courteously returned. Not taking her eyes from the window, she slowly removed her glasses and put her newspaper down on the golden tea-table in front of her. She walked over to the window and opened it up to her visitors.

'Good morning,' she said calmly. 'May I help you?'

'Er – Morning Your Majesty,' said Elliot, attempting a clumsy bow on Pegasus's back. 'Can we come in, please? We have something really important to ask you.'

'I see,' said the Queen. 'To whom does one have the pleasure of speaking?'

'One is . . . whom are . . . am a . . . I'm Elliot,' he said, quickly abandoning any attempt at talking posh. 'Elliot Hooper. And this is Virgo. She used to be a Goddess.'

'Hi The Queen,' chirped Virgo with a big grin.

'How do you do,' said the Queen. 'Well you'd both better come in.'

As the Queen helped Elliot and Virgo dismount Pegasus and clamber through the window, Elliot became aware of an insistent snorting behind him.

'And this is Pegasus,' said Elliot as he landed on the soft carpet of the Queen's parlour. 'He's a flying horse,' he added, quickly realising that the Queen had probably worked that out for herself.

'Your Majesty,' said Pegasus grandly, dropping into an elegant bow fifty feet in the air.

'Welcome Mr Pegasus,' said the Queen, acknowledging his bow with a gracious nod of her head. 'I can honestly say that you are the most magnificent horse I have ever seen.'

'I can honestly say that you're right,' said Pegasus, sweeping into another bow as Elliot put the invisibility helmet over his white head to conceal him from view.

Elliot and Virgo fidgeted awkwardly in the middle of the room as the Queen closed the window and turned to greet her visitors.

'May I offer you some tea and crumpets?' she asked her guests.

'No thank you, we don't have much time,' started Virgo.

'Cor yeah,' belted Elliot, whose stomach had been rumbling since the Home Counties. 'With some peanut butter. If . . . you . . . have . . . some . . . please . . . Your Majesty,' he trailed off, as a sub-zero look from Virgo reminded him that this wasn't really the time.

'I'll see what I can do, Mr Hooper,' smiled the Queen, her eyes sparkling as she rang a small silver bell on the table. She sat back down in her chair, neatly positioned her flowing white gown and straightened the purple sash across her left shoulder.

'Now,' she said, folding her hands in her lap. 'What can I do for you, Mr Hooper?'

'Right,' Elliot began slowly. 'There's no easy way to say this, so I'm going to get straight to the point. That crown you're wearing contains a diamond that's really a Chaos Stone and has the power to control the Earth. We need to take it so that a really evil death daemon called Thanatos can't get his hands on it – nor the other three Chaos Stones – and release his daemon army and kill mankind with earthquakes and floods and fires and plagues and other really bad stuff.' He sighed at the lunacy of his own tale. 'You think I'm insane and you're going to lock me up in the Tower of London, aren't you?'

The Queen calmly took a sip of her tea and stared intently at the young boy before her.

'Your tale is incredible indeed, Mr Hooper,' she said evenly. 'But you'd be surprised what one might believe from two children who have arrived at my window on a flying horse. And for the record, I prefer to lock people up in Windsor Castle these days,' she added with a twinkle. 'The heating's rather better.'

She picked up the small silver bell and rang it again.

'I can't think what can be taking Jeffers so long, he's normally so prompt,' she said, looking at the white double doors to the room. Elliot wondered if Jeffers was the man they had seen in the robing room, who was probably struggling to undo the zip on the pink frock he'd been wearing five minutes ago.

'But to return to your request, Mr Hooper, do I understand correctly that you would like me to give you the Imperial Crown, so that you may guard this Chaos Stone from Thanatos?' said the Queen.

'Yes,' said Elliot, slightly surprised that his garbled explanation had been that clear.

'We'd replace it,' said Virgo, pointing at Hermes's bag.

'Oh . . . yeah,' said Elliot, plunging his hand into the bag, which seemed to go on forever before something met his grasp. 'We'd like to exchange it – for this.'

He pulled his hand from the bag with a proud flourish, expecting the new crown to be met with gasps of delight from the Queen. But upon seeing her politely confused expression and hearing Virgo's groan beside him, he looked more closely at what he had produced from the bag. In return for the priceless Imperial Crown atop Her Majesty's head, Elliot Hooper was now standing in her private parlour, offering the Queen a large rubber chicken.

'Oh, sorry,' he said, thrusting the chicken back in the bag as Virgo shook her silver head and rolled her eyes. He had another rummage around before pulling his hand out again, this time producing the replica crown. 'I meant this.'

This time the Queen gasped on cue and even Elliot couldn't help but admire the intricate detail Hephaestus had put into the crown.

'May I?' asked the Queen.

'Sure,' said Elliot bringing the new crown to her, deciding a small curtsey would be appropriate as he handed it over.

The Queen turned the new Imperial Crown in her hands, highly impressed with the beautiful craftsmanship.

'It's certainly much lighter than this old lump,' she said, pointing to the crown on her head. 'I must admit I've never cared much for it, it's far too heavy.'

'And this one's got the real Cullinan diamond in it,' said Virgo. 'The one that should have been put in originally.'

'So I see,' said the Queen, returning the crown to Elliot. 'It's lovely.'

'Oh, and another thing,' said Elliot, remembering the blacksmith's demonstration the night before. 'Hephaestus, that's the man – well, God really – who made it, thought you might like this.'

Elliot placed the crown on the table in front of the Queen and pressed a large ruby on the side. At his touch, the crown quietly started to rumble, a small wisp of steam twirling from the top for a few moments until the crown made a gentle ping. Elliot lifted the crown to reveal a small golden cup and saucer, which was filled to the brim with a steaming cup of tea.

'The sapphire on the back makes coffee and every turn of the cross on the top will give you a lump of sugar,' he said nervously as the Queen stared at the crown in amazement. 'Do you like it?'

'I think it's quite wonderful, Mr Hooper. But speaking of tea, what on Earth has become of yours? This really is most unlike Jeffers,' she said, insistently ringing her bell again.

'So. Can we swap it for yours?' asked Virgo impatiently, worried that every minute they stayed they risked being thrown out of the palace.

'Well,' said the Queen, 'it's a little difficult . . .'

She was interrupted as a footman, whom Elliot presumed must be the delayed Jeffers, flung the white doors open.

'Ah Jeffers,' said the Queen. 'Would you be so kind as to fetch my guests—'

'Which one is it?' Jeffers growled, looking between the two crowns in the room.

'I beg your pardon?' said the Queen.

'Which one's got the Earth Stone?' shouted Jeffers at the Queen, holding out his hand. 'Give it to me.'

'I can't say I care for your tone, Jeffers,' said the Queen cautiously, rising to her feet. 'Whatever's got into you?'

'I have,' said the footman, his face distorting horribly into the troll-like features of Mammon, as he dissembled into his daemon form. 'Now give me the crown.'

'How did you get here?' said Virgo to the daemon.

'Easy,' said Mammon proudly. 'Your invisibility helmet doesn't work on us daemons. Wasn't that hard to follow a flying horse.'

'What do you want?' asked the Queen, slowly moving in front of the two children.

'I want my stone back,' said Mammon.

'Well you'll have to get through us first,' shouted Virgo, charging at the huge troll. She ran at full speed at the Daemon of Greed, hoping to knock him off his feet. But her small frame was useless against the burly daemon, who picked her up and threw her against the wall like a used tissue.

'Move!' Mammon shouted at the Queen, pushing her aside to get to Elliot, leaving the monarch in a pile of lace petticoats on the floor. 'I'll deal with you in a minute, Queen. First things first.'

Mammon reached one of his enormous hands towards Elliot's neck. Grabbing the nearest thing to hand, Elliot hit the troll with an ornate golden cake stand, but he may as well have attacked the daemon with a banana. Not even flinching at the blow, Mammon grabbed Elliot by the throat and lifted him off the ground. He clasped his iron grip around Elliot's neck and, as the breath was choked from him, Elliot clasped the troll's massive hand and tried to loosen the enormous fingers to get some air. He heard Pegasus's hooves bashing at the window to get inside. But Mammon's grasp was unmovable.

'Thanatos wants you dead. Nothing personal,' he said as he squeezed Elliot's throat, squashing the life breath out of the struggling boy.

'No you don't!' screamed Virgo, running at the troll again, jumping on his back and smashing the Queen's teapot on his head.

Mammon dropped Elliot to the floor with a shriek, holding his burning head in his massive hands, wiping scorching tea from his eyes.

'You're dead!' he shouted when he'd recovered from the shock, walking menacingly towards the window that Elliot and Virgo were struggling to open to reach Pegasus. He reached them both before they could make their escape and towered over them, holding his mighty fists aloft to smash them down on their heads.

'Sorry kids,' he said as he drew himself up to put his full weight behind the death blow, 'this is gonna hurt.'

But before he could deliver it, a heavy object flew across the room and smacked him hard on the back of the head.

'Oi!' he shouted, turning to see what had clobbered him.

'*One doesn't think so, Mammon!*' yelled the furious Queen from across the room, her neat hair pulled out of place from where she had ripped the Imperial Crown from her head and hurled it at the daemon. '*Prepare yourself for a right royal kicking!*'

And with a great wrench, the Queen whipped off her full white dress to reveal a black ninja outfit beneath. Unencumbered by her gown, she leapt up into the air and backflipped across the room, hitting Mammon square in the chest with a flying double-footed kick. Elliot and Virgo just had time to jump out of the way before Mammon came crashing down against the wall, winded from the force of the Queen's attack.

The Queen sprang off her back to her feet with a neat flick, spinning her purple sash around to reveal four ninja stars on the back. She took them in her hands and threw them at the daemon, who defended himself with a priceless vase on a nearby dresser. When all four had been thrown, Mammon retaliated by hurling the chipped vase at the Queen, who smashed it with a yell and a spinning kick on the heel of her court shoe. Mammon ran at the tea-table and threw it blindly at the Queen. But Her Majesty flipped across the room and stood beneath it to catch it, snapping it over her knee and twirling the golden legs threateningly at the daemon.

Elliot and Virgo watched with mouths the size of dinner plates as the Daemon of Greed and the Queen of England circled around the room, neither taking their eyes from the other as they waited to see who would make the first move.

Mammon was the first to strike, with a clumsy lunge that the Queen easily side-stepped, thwacking the daemon on the back with both table legs as he passed. But Mammon recovered more quickly than she expected and immediately lunged again, this time catching the Queen off guard and snatching one of her table legs. A furious duel began, Mammon and the Queen fighting each other with table legs like swords, chips of wood flying everywhere as they thrust and parried around the room.

'Elliot, duck!' cried Virgo as Mammon's table leg came flying towards him, smashing the chair behind him a split second after he dived out of the way. The frantic battle continued, Mammon's brute strength an even match for the Queen's skilled swordsmanship. With an almighty swing, Mammon blasted the table leg from the Queen's hand, forcing her to cartwheel across the carpet to avoid being smashed by Mammon's weapon.

'Mr Hooper,' called the Queen politely, as she ran up the wall and crouched on the top of a glass cabinet. 'Would you be so kind as to pass me the Sword of State please?'

Elliot's head darted around him until he saw an ornate golden sword in a red and gold scabbard at his feet. He picked it up and threw it to the Queen.

'Thank you so much,' she said with a smile, catching the sword mid-air as she performed a flying front somersault from the top of cabinet, mere seconds before Mammon smashed into it.

The two warriors paused for a moment on opposite sides of the room. The Queen unsheathed the Sword of State to reveal a brilliant silver blade underneath. She raised the sword above her head and prepared to charge.

'MAMMON!' the Queen bellowed, her eyes ablaze with fury. 'KISS ONE'S ROYAL BEHIND! AAAR-RGHGHGHGH!'

Her Majesty ran at the terrified daemon, who raised a splinter of a chair leg to defend himself from the murderous monarch, before thinking better of it and running away. The Queen chased the daemon three times around the parlour, holding her sword above her head and roaring her terrifying battle cry. Mammon looked desperately around him for a way to escape the Queen's attack, but with none available, he waited until he reached the window and threw himself headlong at it. Wood and glass shattered everywhere as the enormous troll flew threw the air, smashing the window to a million pieces and dropping instantly out of sight.

Elliot and Virgo rushed to the window to see where the daemon would splat on the floor, but as Mammon fell, he shouted his spells at the ground, which started to wobble like jelly. As the daemon hit the ground, instead of splattering on the concrete beneath, his fall was cushioned by the now soft ground beneath him, which bounced him back into the air, before finally landing him on his feet. Safely on the ground, Mammon dissembled into a fat tourist before scuttling away.

Elliot and Virgo turned back to the demolished room, where the Queen was zipping up her white gown and smoothing the worst of her dishevelled hair as Pegasus finally burst through the smashed window. She picked up the two halves of her broken teapot.

'I never liked this set anyway,' she said as the real Jeffers burst into the room, still in the pink dress, but with a lump the size of an apple on his head.

'Your Majesty!' he cried, taking in the destruction of the sitting room and a large winged horse where the tea-table once stood. 'Are you alright Ma'am?'

'We're fine, thank you Jeffers,' said the Queen calmly. 'But Mr Hooper would like some crumpets and peanut butter. And we might need another table.'

'Yes Ma'am,' said a confused Jeffers as he backed out of the room, rubbing his wounded head and trying not to trip on the hem of his dress.

The Queen walked over to the original Imperial Crown and handed it to Elliot.

'I think you had better take this, Mr Hooper. Clearly it could do great harm in the wrong hands.'

Stunned by what he had just seen, Elliot silently put the crown in Hermes's bag.

'Thank you, Your Majesty,' he said quietly. 'Sorry about the mess.'

'Don't worry about that,' said the Queen. 'Just keep that stone safe.'

'Yes Ma'am,' said Elliot, as Jeffers reappeared with a plate of buttered crumpets and a silver pot of peanut butter.

'Now if you'll excuse me,' said the Queen, 'I must prepare for the ceremony. I can't possibly open Parliament with my hair like this.'

She extended a hand to Elliot and Virgo. 'Goodbye Miss Virgo, goodbye Mr Hooper. I've a feeling we're going to be seeing a lot more of you.'

And with a regal smile, Queen Elizabeth II turned to leave the room, crunching over broken glass and china with every elegant step.

'Your Majesty?' Elliot said admiringly to her retreating figure. 'You rock.'

'One knows,' said the Queen with a wink as she closed the doors on her battle-worn parlour.

The rest of the Queen's day passed as planned, the State Opening of Parliament proceeding without a hitch. Most observers would have noticed nothing extraordinary as the Queen watched serenely over the proceedings, playing her regal role to absolute perfection.

But towards the end of the ceremony, the keenest of eyes not only might have noticed the tiny curl of white steam escaping from the top of the Imperial Crown, but also Her Majesty's contented smile, as she thought of the lovely cup of Earl Grey she was going to enjoy on the carriage ride home.

As Pegasus touched lightly down in Home Farm, Elliot and Virgo jumped triumphantly off his back to the congratulations of the waiting Gods. Elliot clutched the Earth Stone in his palm. He'd done it. He had the answer. He could pay off the money.

'How do I use it?' he asked.

'Tell it what you want,' said Zeus sombrely. 'The Earth Stone will find it for you.'

Elliot tightened his grasp around the huge diamond. He closed his eyes.

'Find me gold,' he commanded and the stone instantly lit up in his palm.

The ground began to tremble and bubble beneath Elliot's feet. A distant rumble became slowly louder and stronger as the Earth Stone glowed brighter in his hand. The quaking Earth started to open up underneath him and Elliot just had time to step aside before the ground spat up a pile of gold at his feet.

'Epic,' whispered Elliot as he gathered handfuls of the precious metal. He stopped and turned to the group of immortals watching him stuff his pockets with gold. He looked at the enchanted jewel in his hand. Imagine what he could do with the power of the stone? Elliot could find gold and jewels anywhere. He and Mum could be rich beyond their wildest dreams. And never have to eat beans again.

'A promise is a promise,' Grandad always said. 'You're only as good as your word.'

Elliot held out the Earth Stone with a sigh.

'Thank you,' he said, giving it to Zeus. 'But this is yours.'

Zeus wrapped his massive hand around Elliot's.

'Good man,' he said with a smile, closing his fingers around the Earth Stone. 'Now go and save your home.'

A week after their luncheon (lunch was for common people) Patricia Porshley-Plum needed to see Josie Hooper again to conclude their business. She had tried every which way to get into Home Farm that week, but she was held back at every attempt by that wretched new fence.

On Monday she tried to climb the fence and erupted in blue boils. On Wednesday, she took a pair of bolt-cutters to the gate and found she could only speak Swahili for the rest of the day. On Thursday she had tried to chainsaw the fence and was rewarded with 24 hours of ear-splitting wind that nearly burnt a hole in her sofa.

But finally on Friday, her moment came. As Elliot and Virgo raced out of the farm for the station, they were so intent on catching their train, they didn't notice that they'd left the high gate open. But Patricia Porshley-Plum never missed a trick.

Around the time Elliot was taking off in his train, Patricia had Josie dressed and in her car. As he battled a daemon in Buckingham Palace, Patricia and Josie were leaving Patricia's solicitors. By the time Elliot returned to Home Farm with the Earth Stone and handed it over to Zeus, Patricia had just got off the phone with her bank manager. And as he ran excitedly back into the farmhouse, he was once again greeted with the worrying sight of his neighbourhood nemesis in the kitchen with his mother.

'Hello honey pot,' she chirped as Elliot came into the kitchen, her eyes as warm as winter. 'Ooh – are you playing pirates?'

'Something like that,' said Elliot suspiciously. 'How did you get in here?'

'Oh we've had the loveliest time, haven't we Josie?' said Patricia, ignoring the question and squeezing Josie's tiny hand.

'Lovely, Elly. We had scones.'

'Sc-oh-nes, dear,' corrected Patricia. 'They're called sc-oh-nes.'

'You look tired, Mum,' Elliot said, his eyes not leaving Patricia's. 'Why don't you go upstairs and run a bath?'

'What a lovely idea, Josie. That way Elly and I can have a little chat.'

Pausing only to give her son a loving squeeze on her way past, Josie headed quietly upstairs to the bathroom.

'Ellykins. I know what's been going on,' said Patricia gravely, as soon as Josie was out of earshot. 'You poor, poor little pickle. What a lot you've had to deal with! You should have asked me for help.'

'We're fine, thank you,' said Elliot, sensing danger from this awful woman.

'Of course you are, Sugar-plum-plum. Or at least you will be now.'

Elliot's blood cooled by several degrees.

'What do you mean?'

'Well . . . Mumsy and I were talking over lunch last week – you know, girl talk – and she told me about your *money worries*,' she whispered, like the dirty words that they were. 'I know about the house.'

'Mum doesn't know about the house,' said Elliot. 'So how could she tell you?'

'Mummies know everything, Pumpkin,' said Patricia, realising she'd given herself away. Not that it mattered now. 'But you don't need to worry about that silly letter any more.'

'What do you mean?' said Elliot suspiciously.

'That horrid ickle bickle letter threatening your home – some people have no shame,' she said with her monkey-bottom pout.

'I don't understand?'

'The money. The twenty thousand pounds. It's gone, paid off, all gone,' trilled Patricia with a voice like a frantic merry-go-round. 'I've paid off your debt in full.'

Elliot couldn't believe it. All this time he thought Patricia was a rotten, interfering harridan. And yet she'd given them this wonderful gift. His gut instincts were never normally wrong. But he'd never been happier to be wrong in all his young life.

'Mrs Porshley-Plum – I don't know how to thank you,' he said.

'Oh no need to worry about that, my little Porkie Pie,' said Patricia. 'Anything to see you and Mumsy happy.'

'That's – that's amazing,' said Elliot.

'Virtue is its own reward,' said Patricia, standing to leave. 'And besides, Mummy has already thanked me in a super special way.'

'Sorry?' said Elliot.

'I'm sure it's for the best anyway – this place must be a lot of work for you.'

'What do you mean?' asked Elliot, his blood temperature starting to dip once more.

'All that cleaning and all those bills to worry about. Not to mention finding some more suitable . . . care for Mumsy.'

'What's for the best?' asked Elliot, practically a popsicle inside as his gold clattered to the floor. 'What have you done?'

'It's good news, Dumpling,' said Patricia, pulling a sheaf of papers from her handbag and tossing them over the kitchen table. 'We've done all the paperwork today. Mummy's sold me your farm.'

Patricia's face lit up like a jack o'lantern as the bottom fell out of Elliot's heart.

'For twenty pounds.'

In a dark, abandoned warehouse much later that night, another difficult conversation was taking place.

'I have failed you, Master,' mumbled Mammon at Thanatos's feet, not daring to look into his ruler's dark face. 'The boy has gone and so has the stone.'

'Well, it was a tricky assignment,' said Thanatos slowly. 'After all, not everyone is capable of killing a defenceless child, then stealing from a pensioner.'

'Absolutely my Lord,' said Mammon, delighted at Thanatos's agreement. 'I mean the Queen is a fearsome fighter.'

'THE QUEEN IS IN HER EIGHTIES!' roared Thanatos at his petrified servant. 'A brainless baboon could have taken that crown!'

'I'm sorry, I'm so sorry,' whimpered the wretched daemon.

'Calm yourself, Mammon,' said Thanatos, his volume returning to normal. 'Clearly I expected too much of you.'

'Yes Master,' said Mammon. 'But I promise that anything else you ask of me, I will do to the best of my ability.'

'Is that so?' asked Thanatos.

'Y-y-yes Master,' blabbered Mammon, the familiar green snot running down his face again.

'Anything at all?' asked Thanatos again.

'Anything you want, Master,' said the daemon, rising to his feet to do his leader's bidding.

'In that case,' considered Thanatos, 'Mammon?'

'Yes My Lord?'

'Die quickly,' said Thanatos, and he thrust his hand over the daemon's heart to suck the pitiful life from the troll's miserable body.

Mammon let out an anguished howl as the souls of all his lifetimes were drawn through Thanatos's cold, thin fingers. Thanatos's eyes lit up with the thrill of the kill, a sick smile on his lips as he watched Mammon's suffering with evil glee.

'Put him down,' said a voice, cutting through the air like a moonbeam.

Thanatos spun around, dropping Mammon on the floor with a wet splat.

'Who's there?' the daemon demanded. 'Reveal yourself.'

The intruder stepped into the darkness.

'How did you find me?' smiled Thanatos admiringly.

'Charon,' said Elliot, illuminated only by a feeble light shining from the street outside. 'It's amazing what he'll do for 8p.'

'I'm rarely surprised, young man,' said Thanatos. 'So I congratulate you on that. But as you can see, I'm a little busy right now.'

'Let him go,' said Elliot.

'Unless I'm very much mistaken, Mammon has tried to

kill you on three separate occasions,' drawled Thanatos. 'You are either very stupid, or very stupid.'

'He was just doing what he had to,' said Elliot. 'Let him go.'

'And why would I do that? He didn't get me my Earth Stone.'

'But I can,' said Elliot. 'Let him go and we can talk.'

Thanatos raised a dark eyebrow while he considered Elliot's proposition.

'Very well,' he said, kicking the snivelling Mammon as he walked over him. 'Start talking.'

'Th- th- thank you!' dribbled Mammon to Elliot as he crawled out of the warehouse, leaving a trail of snotty slime in his wake. 'I will repay this generosity. I swear it on the Styx.'

'Go away you blithering fool,' said Thanatos, kicking him once more for good measure.

Mammon dissembled into a rat and scuttled away into the lonely night.

'You have gone to great lengths to get the Earth Stone before me and now you are simply going to hand it over?' said Thanatos. 'Why?'

'Because I need something from you,' said Elliot.

'Your mother,' Thanatos smiled knowingly. 'You want me to cure your mother.'

'Can you do it?' said Elliot.

'If you're going to steal the Earth Stone, why not keep

it for yourself?' asked Thanatos. 'You could be a very wealthy young man, never work a day in your life.'

'Some things are more important than money,' said Elliot. 'I know that now. Will you do it or not?'

Thanatos stared deep into Elliot's eyes.

'Yes,' he said simply. 'I accept your terms.'

'Swear it,' said Elliot.

'Oh very well,' sighed Thanatos. 'I swear on the Styx – I will cure your mother. When will I get my stone?'

'When I can,' said Elliot.

'Fair enough,' said Thanatos. 'Send Charon for me when you need me. I'll be in the Underworld. Only he can reach me there.'

With a heart of lead, Elliot turned and left for where Charon was waiting for him on the river.

An ugly rasping sound came from Thanatos's body, as the Daemon of Death laughed a twisted laugh.

'You foolish boy,' he laughed. 'You've just invited yourself to your own funeral.'

Chapter Fifteen

A Trip Down Under

After some lengthy debates (and an infinite number of 'Snordlesnots') the Gods decided it was safe for Elliot and Virgo to return to school after their suspension, although they now insisted on accompanying them to and from the school gates every day. As the weeks went by, life at the farm started to settle into a comfortably familiar pattern, with the Gods taking care of Mum and the farm by day and helping Elliot with his studies by night. As the end of term approached, there was still no sign of Thanatos and while the Gods remained on high alert, Elliot alone knew that he was safe while Thanatos waited for him to deliver the Earth Stone.

But with the Earth Stone safe in their possession, the Gods turned their attention to saving Home Farm. The paperwork said that Patricia would complete the sale on December 24th, meaning Elliot and Josie would be homeless on Christmas Eve.

'The harpy-faced hag,' huffed Aphrodite. 'Why, I've a good mind to take her papers and shove them right—'

'Temper will get you nowhere,' said Athene, reading

through the paperwork for the millionth time. 'But this is watertight. She has legally bought the farm. The only thing that can stop the sale is her.'

'Per'aps I should go and negotiate with her,' said Hephaestus, sharpening his axe.

'We can't break mortal laws,' said Virgo. 'However unfair they are.'

'Why can't Elliot just buy it back?' huffed Hermes. 'He only needs twenty pounds. And with the Earth Stone, he could buy King Croesus a condo.'

'It's no good unless this bally Horse's Bum wants to sell it now,' said Zeus. 'And from the sounds of it, she's got plans already. Hang on in there old chap,' he added kindly to a dejected Elliot, who was looking at the glass safe that had the Earth Stone locked inside. 'I'm sure a solution will present itself.'

As they sat around trying to solve his problems, Elliot felt a sickening guilt in his soul at the deception he was planning. But this was his life. And he had to take care of Mum. Elliot had been trying to get his hands on the Earth Stone for weeks, but one of the Gods was always in the shed or with him. He had tried everything to distract them, but they were trying so hard to protect him, they wouldn't leave him alone.

As if things weren't bad enough, the end of term brought the crucial exams Elliot had been dreading, as he knew that Boil would love nothing more than to carry out his threat to the letter and throw Elliot out of Brysmore if he achieved one mark less than the 85% pass mark in every subject.

Exam week came round quickly in December, but after weeks of Athene's tuition, Elliot went into them better prepared than he could ever have imagined. His English exam was a doddle as he recalled the Gods' memorable performance of *Romeo and Juliet*, with Hermes playing the tragic heroine. Latin was a cinch when he had to translate a passage about Perseus, who had dropped in the week before with Hercules, Theseus and Jason, all members of boy band Heroes, and sung a ballad about Medusa called *Heart of Stone*. Even History was a gift, when Elliot had to write an essay about the Roman wars against Carthage, which Athene had re-enacted a few days ago transforming an ant colony into a full-scale Roman battlefield, with a woodlouse taking the role of Hannibal.

The results were to be posted on the school noticeboard on Friday morning, the last day of term. Elliot barely slept a wink on Thursday night. At first he'd felt the exams had gone well, but now he'd had some time to reflect on them, had the French comprehension really been about some talking pigs? And had he actually got Nigeria muddled up with Norfolk in Geography?

Elliot had bigger things to worry about, but by Friday morning Virgo could have put Call Me Graham to shame with her stammering and trembling, banging around the kitchen at breakfast dropping eggs, spreading jam on her

Weetabix and putting three big spoonfuls of salt in her tea.

'For goodness' sake relax,' snapped Elliot, pacing around the kitchen. 'It's all going to be fine. It'll be fine, really fine. Completely fine.'

The Gods came up to the kitchen, looking every bit as nervous as the two students before them.

'How are you feeling?' said Zeus in an attempt at sounding cheery.

'WE'RE FINE!' shouted Virgo angrily from the front room, where she'd gone to consult an encyclopaedia for the fifteenth time. 'Snordlesnot! I knew I'd got that photosynthesis question wrong. That's it, I've failed, it's over.'

'I'm sure you've both done your best,' said Athene, who looked like she hadn't slept, despite the fact she never did.

'Will you all just calm down,' said Aphrodite, perching on the kitchen table and taking a bite of Elliot's toast, the only God to appear entirely calm. 'So you get kicked out of school, big deal. All the best stuff you learn outside school anyway. Don't stress Elly, we'll look after you.'

'That's all he needs,' muttered Athene, who had now taking to pacing around the kitchen behind Virgo as Elliot turned away from the friends he was trying so hard to betray.

'Oh come on, let's get you to school and put you out of your misery,' said Aphrodite, magically summoning her car keys. 'I'll let you drive.'

Elliot had been enjoying this secret part of his daily trip to school down the quiet country lanes, but even he knew that today it would be particularly unwise for a sleepless, worried 13-year-old to get behind the wheel of a car. He threw his school bags into Aphrodite's car, which had been transformed into a luxurious pink 4x4 as a more suitable vehicle for the English winter, and sat in silence as Aphrodite drove them both to the school gates.

'Good luck Virgo, good luck Elly,' she said cheerily as Virgo threw up her breakfast on the side of road. 'I'll see you later. We're proud of you whatever happens.'

Elliot slammed the car door, unable to look at the beautiful Goddess any more.

The two friends trudged towards the school as if they were walking down death row, their nerves keeping them silent as they entered the school through the grand wooden doors. A crowd of pale students gathered around the noticeboard, awaiting their fate with eyes of dread. Torturous evaluations of each individual's performance were the only whispered conversations, with mutterings about maths solutions and physics theories met with disappointed groans as people totted up their errors. Emma and Dominic comforted each other in a corner, each holding a tissue for when the other one looked likely to need it.

The staff door opened with a long, slow creak, spinning every head towards the shaking figure that emerged from it. Call Me Graham walked nervously to the board, apparently surprised to find such a large group of children in his school, and proceeded to staple results sheets for every subject on the board as quickly as he could. With the results up and his nerves shot away, Graham slunk away looking like he might cry. At first, no-one moved, everyone staring at the sheets as if the results would just leap off the page into their eyes. There was a moment's stillness as everyone froze to the spot, not wanting to make the first move towards their doom. But the slightest movement of one foot, or at least the thought that there might have been, was enough to send the entire crowd racing over to the board, the papers now a sea of fingers as everyone frantically searched for their name and results.

Elliot and Virgo hung back, watching people peel away from the crowd with cheers or tears as one by one, each pupil learned their destiny. They waited until the last person had walked away, before looking at each other and walking side-by-side to the board. They looked over every sheet of paper, taking in the information on each one, before turning to each other once more.

'Snordlesnot,' they chimed in unison, unaware of the history teacher sneering at them both from the corner.

Back at the farm, the Gods paced around the cowshed in anxious silence, staring at Hermes's iGod, which Virgo had promised to contact with the phone Aphrodite had smuggled to her, whatever the news might be.

'This is dreadful,' moaned Hermes, who'd been fluttering anxiously from one end of the shed to the other, chewing his nails to the knuckle. 'I haven't been this nervous since the final of *Immortals on Ice*. I can't bear it.'

'He's a clever boy, he'll be fine,' said Aphrodite from the velvet sofa where she was painting her nails. 'Prissy-pants has been stuffing his head with this rubbish for weeks, he'll ace it.'

'I don't know,' said Athene. 'He was a long way behind, if only I'd had more time.'

'You've done everything you can,' said Zeus, looking at the Earth Stone. 'The rest is up to Elliot.'

Hermes's phone beeped a text message, making all the Gods, even Aphrodite gasp. They stood and stared at the phone, no-one daring to read the news the message contained.

'Well go on, for the Heavens' sake!' shrieked Aphrodite to Hermes, all illusion of calm now gone. 'Read it!'

'I can't!' squealed Hermes. 'What if it's bad news?'

'We'll never know unless you read it,' snapped Athene.

'You read it then,' said Hermes childishly.

'Well, I, it's not my – Father, you should read it,' said Athene.

'Not on your Nelly,' said Zeus. 'My nerves can't stand it. Aphy – go on, open the text.'

'But what if my poor Elly's failed?' she wailed. 'I couldn't bear it.'

'Oh give it 'ere,' said Hephaestus, who had come up from the forge and had been feigning his lack of interest in the corner. 'I'll read the bloomin' thing.'

He stormed over to the phone and snatched it up.

'Any chance you could wash your hands before you touch that . . . nope, never mind,' winced Hermes at the sight of the blacksmith's filthy fingers smearing his precious phone.

The tension in the shed rose unbearably as Hephaestus scanned the text.

'Well I'll be,' said Hephaestus, reading the contents of Virgo's message.

'WHAT?!' screamed the other four Gods in perfect harmony.

'The boy done good,' smiled Hephaestus. 'Average of 92% across the board, with 96% in history.'

The Gods exploded into a chorus of whoops and yells, singing and hugging each other at the triumph of their new mortal friend.

'Well this calls for a celebration,' cheered Zeus, as Aphrodite danced around the shed, turning olives into brightly coloured balloons and leaves into streamers. 'Let's go and pick up Elliot in style.'

A short while later, Zeus, Athene and Aphrodite stood outside the shed by the enormous stretch limo created from Aphrodite's car. Zeus was dressed in his bright blue tuxedo with the frilly white shirt, his white hair slicked back on his head. Athene and Aphrodite both wore beautiful long evening dresses, Aphrodite sporting a bright pink strapless number, whilst her sister chose a more modest dark blue satin off-the-shoulder gown. The limo was filled with balloons decorated with Elliot and Virgo's pictures and was laid out inside with a banquet of all their favourite food.

'Hurry up Hermy, we're going to be late,' Aphrodite called inside the shed, as they waited for Hermes and Hephaestus.

Hermes elegantly floated out of the shed in his designer tuxedo, abandoning his usual winged hat for some expensive sunglasses with little gold wings on the side.

'May I present,' he announced in his most dramatic voice, 'your driver for this evening, the grump with a hump, Mr Heph-aes-tus!'

'I am not coming out dressed like this,' huffed a moody voice from inside the shed.

'Oh come on Heffer, you look fab,' pouted Hermes. 'And besides, we've all drunk far too much nectar so you'll have to drive. Come on. Out.'

With a heaving sigh from inside the shed, Hephaestus trudged slowly into the open air. The other Gods bit their lips at the sight of the blacksmith, who had been dressed by Hermes from head to toe in a shiny gold chauffeur's outfit, complete with a gold hat that had 'Congratulations Elliot' written in sequins across its rim.

'Not. One. Word,' he grumbled at the trembling Gods as he assumed his place at the wheel, slamming the door loudly enough to hide the eruption of laughter from his giggling friends outside.

'Good show, old man,' said Zeus as he followed Hermes

and the ladies into the back of the limo. 'To Brysmore. Let's bring our boy home.'

The morning had passed in such a blur that Elliot felt as though he'd barely arrived at Brysmore when the final assembly announced that school was over for another term. His heart was heavier than Mr Boil's backside as he contemplated what he had to do – although he did allow himself a moment of cheer as he passed Mr Boil in the corridor.

'Merry Christmas Sir,' he said with a cheery grin as Boil pushed passed him with a horrible sneer. 'See you next term. Go easy on those mince pies.'

'Get lost, Hooper,' snarled Boil without stopping, furious at losing the chance to be rid of this irksome boy for good and suddenly extremely hungry for a pack of mince pies.

Elliot and Virgo stepped out into the chilly afternoon.

'You did it,' said Virgo, finally over the worst of her wounded pride at being beaten by Elliot in every single exam.

'Never thought I'd be pleased to be coming back to this place,' smiled Elliot. 'But it actually feels good. Not as good as leaving it for four weeks, but pretty good.'

'Yes, this Christmas break will be an excellent chance to get ahead for next term,' said Virgo to Elliot. Elliot said nothing, but felt silently sick at the thought that Virgo probably wouldn't be coming back after he stole the stone.

None of the Gods would. Not after what he was going to do.

'I suppose we can take today off. After the surprise party – oh,' Virgo bit her lip as the words she'd been forbidden to say slipped out of her mouth. 'Snordlesnot – listen, look surprised when they all turn up.'

'They're all coming here?' said Elliot, his mind snapping to attention. Here, at last, was his chance. 'All of them?'

'Yes. No. Urgh – I'm no good at this lying thing,' said Virgo. 'On the Zodiac Council, we never lied. Unless you read anyone's CV.'

'Er – by the way, I forgot,' started Elliot, who was excellent at this lying thing. 'School secretary wants to see you.'

'See me?' questioned Virgo. 'Why?'

'I dunno, something about a special prize or something,' said Elliot to the ground.

'Oh, I see,' said Virgo smugly. 'Well it'll have to wait – they'll be here any moment.'

'I'll stall them,' said Elliot a bit too quickly. 'You go.'

'Well alright then. I suppose it would be rude not to,' said Virgo as she floated through the doors in a cloud of smug. 'See you in a minute.'

'Yeah. See you,' said Elliot as he took the first heavy step back towards the empty cowshed.

Twenty minutes later, Virgo stepped out of the school doors once again, to be greeted by an excited limo-load of immortals, who cheered loudly at her appearance.

'Well that was pointless,' she said irritably. 'So I sat outside the Head's office for ages and when I eventually open the door to see what's going on, Call Me Graham is snoring on his desk next to an empty bowl of egg-nog with a piece of red tinsel tied around his neck. What was all that about? Anyway, who cares – let's party!'

The Gods looked at her blankly.

'Where's Elly?' said Aphrodite, who had been waiting to pull a party popper the size of a champagne bottle.

'He was here, waiting for you – isn't he in there?' said Virgo, her voice tightening with every word.

'No old girl,' said Zeus, his blue eyes clouding over. 'We assumed he was with you.'

'Well, he's not inside,' said Virgo. 'The place is deserted – everyone's locked up and gone home for the holidays.'

'Thanatos,' said Athene, saying what no-one had dared to speak out loud. 'When did you last see him, Virgo?'

'About twenty minutes ago,' said Virgo frantically. 'Oh no, this is all my fault, I should never have left him.'

'Calm yourself,' said Zeus, not looking at all convinced. 'Hermes, fly into the sky, he can't have got far, see what you can see.'

Without a word, Hermes shot up like a rocket, looking out over the horizon in every direction.

'Nothing,' he wailed from up in the air. 'There's no sign of him.'

'He can't just have disappeared,' said Athene. 'Where on Earth can he be?'

Outside Home Farm, Elliot was getting into a different car with a very different passenger.

'Hello Elliot,' said Thanatos, pulling up in what looked like a hearse. 'Charon says you have something for me.'

Elliot looked helplessly out at his home, to the cowshed he had just robbed and to the enormous diamond in his hand.

'Why do I need to get in there?' he said. 'Why can't we just do this here?'

'With your new friends already on their way here?' said Thanatos slowly. 'I don't think either of us wants to be here when that happens, do you? Come with me. You know I can't kill you. More's the pity.'

Elliot couldn't think about the Gods and how they'd feel once they returned. But he could think of Mum and how she'd feel if she were well again. He got into the car and closed the heavy door behind him. The driverless car immediately sped away, slamming Elliot against the seat at the speed of the acceleration.

'Where are you taking me?' he said to a motionless Thanatos, who watched Elliot being thrown around with a smirk.

'You'll see,' said the daemon. 'Just sit back and enjoy the ride.'

Elliot looked helplessly out of the window as the wheels barely touched the grass as it flew across field after field. In the snatched moments between being tossed around the car, Elliot could see nothing ahead of them but the huge river that flowed through the valley near his home. He looked around for any other path the car could take, but the limo was heading straight for the dark water ahead.

'Take a deep breath,' said Thanatos as they reached the riverbank.

Elliot was thrown powerlessly against the floor, cracking his collar bone again and smashing Grandad's watch on the floor as the car accelerated towards the water, taking off from the peak of the bank and flying for a few seconds through the cold air. For a moment, everything was still, the car gently gliding towards the water below. Elliot took the time to scramble back on to his seat and tried to brace himself for the impact, but the car hit the water like a hammer on concrete. Elliot was thrown against the car roof, slamming his head again and sending a sickening spear of pain through his shoulder, leaving him teetering on the brink of consciousness as the car began to slowly sink into the water.

The Earth Stone rolled out of his pocket onto the floor by Thanatos's long feet.

'I rather feel,' Thanatos began as he picked up the Earth Stone and rolled it between his fingers, 'that we got off on the wrong foot, Elliot.'

Elliot said nothing as he desperately tried to stay out of the chasm of unconsciousness.

'Of course, those friends of yours won't have helped,' continued Thanatos. 'I'm sure they've told you all kinds of terrible things about me. They're all true, of course, but I would have preferred to tell you myself. I appreciate that some of my behaviour might have come across as . . . well, murderously enraged, but I'm a death daemon, you see. It rather comes with the territory.'

Elliot turned his stunned gaze to the window, where the murky water formed a solid green wall outside the limo. His battered brain wondered why they hadn't hit the riverbed by now, but the limo simply continued its slow descent into the gloomy depths.

'I must admit,' said Thanatos, 'at first I thought that killing you would be as easy as squashing an earthworm beneath my boot. But when you evaded death for the fourth time, I decided that I should invest some time into researching the boy who refuses to die. You make quite a fascinating study, Elliot. And the more I discover about you, the more I like you.'

'You've got your stone, now you have to cure my Mum,' said Elliot, the pain in his head making his vision blur.

'All in good time, dear boy, all in good time,' said Thanatos snapping his fingers around the stone, before slipping it into his robes.

'You can't kill me, I know that,' said Elliot.

'Yes, sadly, so do I,' said Thanatos. 'So it would seem we are at a bit of a stalemate.'

Elliot returned his gaze to the window, where the view had now changed from the green murk to a swirling mist, which encircled the car in every direction. Elliot peered at the window to take a closer look. He was hypnotised by the mist, which flowed around the car, every so often taking the shape of a human arm, or a foot, or a face. As he felt his breath come back at him as he peered through the glass, a hand suddenly formed out of the mist and slammed against the car window, making Elliot jump back into his seat with fright.

'Welcome to the Underworld,' said Thanatos, gesturing grandly around him. 'Home of the souls of every single person who has ever lived on this miserable Earth, the place where I used to escort the recently deceased – before my contract was so abruptly terminated.'

Elliot looked into the gloomy murk through his fuddled vision.

'Not much to aspire to, is it?' said Thanatos dismissively. 'You spend all your tedious mortal life doing your bit, to end up in this soul soup at the end of it. It's quite pathetic really.'

'What do you want?' said Elliot, suddenly feeling strangely tired, despite the peril of the situation.

'I want you to come and work for me,' said Thanatos. 'You've got tremendous darkness in you. I rather like it. And as I told you before, I'm a powerful friend.'

'Get stuffed,' said Elliot, his eyes swimming like the water outside.

'I thought you might say that,' said Thanatos. 'But I can give you things your God friends cannot. And I think I have something you might want.'

Thanatos waved his long, thin fingers towards the mist, and a figure began to form from the haze. There was something vaguely familiar about the body as it gradually became distinct from the fog around it, but it wasn't until the face became clear that Elliot recognised the man floating before him.

'Grandad,' he whispered, pressing himself against the glass to get a closer look his beloved lost grandfather. Grandad's soul looked exactly as he had done in life and as Elliot's grandfather stood and looked into the limo, his face broke into the happy smile that lived on his lips until the day he died.

'He's yours,' said Thanatos, seeing the longing in Elliot's face.

'What do you mean?' said Elliot, not moving his eyes from his grandfather's. 'You can bring him back to life?'

'I can,' said Thanatos slowly. 'Just don't expect him to do too much heavy lifting. Join with me. I can make you a great man.'

Elliot sat transfixed at the window as he stared at the man who had left such a void in his life since he died on

Easter day. Elliot longed to have Grandad near him again, to hear his voice, to touch his face. A few months ago, he would have given anything for the chance to have Grandad back, even in this ghostly form.

'You're such a good boy, Elliot,' Grandad would tell him all the time. 'Use your life well.'

As he wiped a lone tear from his cheek, Elliot knew what Grandad would have wanted him to do.

'No deal,' said Elliot, his eyes becoming heavier with an unshakable fatigue. 'Besides, Zeus will have figured out what I've done by now. They'll be here any second to kick your—'

'They haven't told you, have they?' said Thanatos with a sneer. 'How interesting.'

'Haven't told me what?'

'About the prophecy?'

'The one that says I can kill you?'

'Not if you want your mother healed. And if you want to know what else the prophecy says.'

'I don't care what it says,' said Elliot sleepily. 'You've got your stone, you need to heal my Mum. After that, you can get stuffed.'

'Oh dear,' sighed Thanatos, dissolving Grandad's form with a click of his fingers, leaving Elliot feeling sick as his grandfather vanished before his eyes. 'Well you can't say I didn't try. I can see we're going to have to do this the hard way.'

The car suddenly thudded to a halt, finally hitting solid

ground after its endless plunge. The hearse melted away to reveal that Elliot and Thanatos were in a vast, dark hall, a large black throne the only thing to furnish the cavernous space, the roof covered with enormous hanging stalactites. They were the ones that hung from the ceiling. Athene taught him that.

'This used to be my home,' sighed Thanatos, looking proudly around at the gloomy hall. 'We had some good times here. Or at least I did. The poor souls I tortured for an eternity might disagree. Each to their own.'

Elliot fell to the floor as the overwhelming exhaustion completely took hold of his body.

'Now, to return to your earlier point,' said Thanatos, walking around his prey as he lay on the floor. 'Your friends will not be here to help you, so you can forget about that. Gods cannot travel to the Underworld and the only one who can – Hades – is this very minute dealing with a particularly nasty fire in his casino. Ironic really, you'd think he of all people would keep a fire extinguisher to hand.'

'I just want you to cure my Mum,' said Elliot.

'And I will,' said Thanatos. 'I swear that your mother will have her mind perfectly restored – just in time for her to realise that her beloved son is dead.'

'You can't kill me,' said Elliot, crawling on the floor for breath.

'No, that is true,' said Thanatos, still circling Elliot's

prostrate body. 'But that doesn't mean you can't die. You see, the Underworld isn't really designed for the living and that tiredness you're feeling right now is the will to live slowly leaving your body. They don't call it resting in peace for nothing.'

Elliot tried to answer, but his tired mouth couldn't form the words.

'It's not a bad way to go, actually,' said Thanatos. 'Trust me, if I had my way, I'd make it much more unpleasant for you. But the second your sorry little life is snuffed out, I shall visit your mother and cure her mind. It should make her grief that much clearer for her.'

Elliot felt rage rise like a fire in his body. It surged through his veins, igniting every muscle in his body. It gave him one last burst of strength as he lunged at Thanatos and grabbed him around his bony middle.

'You lied!' he shouted. 'You swore to me!'

'And I'm keeping every last word of my promise,' said Thanatos, shaking the weakened Elliot off him like a fly as the boy crumpled on the floor again. 'I warned you not to make an enemy of me, Elliot Hooper. Now if you'll excuse me, I'll take a seat over here. I don't want to miss the show.'

As Thanatos positioned himself on the black throne, Elliot lay wilting on the floor, feeling the very life sap out of his veins. He waited for the end to come as half-formed thoughts flitted through his dying mind. He thought of Mr

Boil dancing a jig at his funeral. He thought of Virgo and how she'd love to tell him that she told him so. He couldn't do anything about that.

But there was something he could do.

'Oh do hurry up,' said Thanatos from the other end of the hall. 'I've seen immortals take less time to snuff it.'

Elliot raised his leaden eyes over Thanatos's pale head, to the field of stalactites that clung to the roof above him.

'Drop,' he said in the quietest whisper. He looked to the ceiling, but the stalactites stayed firmly in place.

'What's that?' said Thanatos, standing from his throne. 'You have very few breaths left, I wouldn't waste them on pointless babble.'

'Drop,' he said more firmly, exhausting himself with the effort of speaking.

'Blah, blah, blah – you're as bad as your mother,' sighed Thanatos.

Elliot felt the fury rise up in him again like volcanic lava. The anger radiated from his heart, giving him a surge of power for one last effort.

'I SAID, DROP!' he roared with every last bit of strength he had, holding up the Earth Stone he had 'borrowed' from Thanatos's robes when he grabbed him moments before. The diamond immediately lit up in his palm.

'What the . . . ?' said Thanatos as he searched his empty robes for the stone.

As Thanatos shot up from his chair, an enormous stalactite came loose from the roof with a deafening crack and dropped to the floor, sinking deeply into the ground with its pointed end. It landed directly in front of the death daemon, who snapped his head around at the boy who was supposed to be dead.

'Too little too late,' he snarled, 'you're still going to—'

Another massive rock smashed from the ceiling and stopped him dead, barring Thanatos's way once again. He moved to avoid a third falling on him, but every way he turned, an enormous sharp rock fell from on high to block his way.

'This won't save you,' he screamed at Elliot as another stalactite fell in his path. 'You'll die here anyway.'

But his curses were to no avail – the stalactites kept falling all around him, creating a solid rock prison around the deranged daemon, who raged from within at the mortal who had cheated him out of his Chaos Stone once again.

'I'll get it!' shrieked Thanatos. 'I'll get it, I don't care if it takes me all eternity, I'll get it from you, mortal vermin. I'll get it!'

'Get stuffed,' mumbled Elliot as he commanded the Earth Stone once more, causing a torrent of stalactites to fall from the ceiling, burying the screaming daemon beneath an avalanche of rocks.

Everything in the hall went silent. Elliot took a deep breath. He had done what he could. Even if Thanatos could get out from beneath the tonne of rubble on top of him, the Gods would surely have found Elliot's body by then and taken the stone to safety.

He let out a deep sigh. So this was it. Elliot's leaden eyes took one last look at the lonely grave around him and closed heavily for the final time.

Chapter Sixteen

A Fond Farewell

The doors to the hall exploded open. A huge, black, flame-covered motorbike burst into the room, the sidecar still smoking from its supersonic race beneath the country. It skidded to a halt in front of Elliot's pale body. The driver threw off his helmet and jumped off the bike, falling to his knees at Elliot's side. He felt the boy's neck for a pulse.

'We gotta get him outta here,' shouted Hades to Persephone in the sidecar. 'Move over dollface.'

In one smooth movement, Hades scooped Elliot off the floor and dropped him gently in the sidecar with Persephone before mounting his bike once again.

'Come awn sweet cheeks,' said Persephone softly to Elliot, gently slapping his cheek and rubbing his cold hands. 'Don't you give up now.'

Hades slammed the roof down over the sidecar and revved the roaring engine. With a deafening screech, the bike shot out of the hall on its back wheel, tearing through the Underworld at break-neck speed. A huge spiral path wound upwards towards the River Styx swirling murkily above and Hades charged along it, skidding around the narrow corners, tossing Persephone and Elliot around the sidecar.

'Hey, watch it!' Persephone shouted above the engine's earth-shattering roar. 'Whatcha trying to do? Kill him again?'

But Hades only response was to rev his engine harder and surge even faster towards the Earth's surface, desperate to save the boy who'd defeated a death daemon. As they approached the top of the road, the Styx floated gloomily above them.

'Hold on baby!' shouted Hades to his wife. 'We're goin' for a swim!'

He put his head down and revved the engine hard as he approached the ramp at the end of the spiral hill. The bike charged off the ramp and hurtled towards oblivion, flying upwards into the water above. But such was the bike's speed that it continued to climb even through the water, and as Persephone switched on the wipers in the sidecar, they charged effortlessly up through the river, breaking the surface in moments with an almighty splash.

A soaking wet Hades allowed himself a quick shake, but didn't slow the bike one notch as he charged along the underground bank of the Styx, surging towards a rock wall that stood in front of him. Hades flew towards it, not even bracing himself as the bike hit the wall at full speed. But instead of being smashed to dust, the bike blasted through the rock wall, racing onwards and upwards towards the

Earth. Hades looked into the sidecar at Elliot, who had remained as still as the grave throughout the journey. Persephone was stroking his face tenderly, but seeing her husband's worried gaze, could only meet it with a grim shake of her head.

The bike continued to charge through the rock as though it were made of air, finally exploding through the ground right in front of the cowshed at Home Farm.

'Hey! Out here!' yelled Hades to the Gods within, who rushed outside at the sound of his voice.

'Brother?' said an anxious Zeus to the God who stood before him.

'Elliot!' shouted Virgo seeing his unconscious passenger in the sidecar.

In a mad scramble of arms and hands, the immortals lifted Elliot from Persephone's arms and laid him on the ground.

'He's barely breathing,' said Hades bleakly. 'I don't know how he lasted that long down there. The boy's stronger than Atlas.'

As Hermes flitted about hysterically, Athene started blowing rhythmic breaths into Elliot's mouth as Zeus pumped his chest.

'Come on Elliot,' panted Zeus. 'We need you. Come back to us.'

The other immortals stood motionless around Elliot's body, barely drawing breath as Athene and Zeus tried to bring the boy back to life. They looked on in desperate hope, watching for a flicker of life, a movement, a sound, any sign at all that Elliot was going to pull through. But the pale boy lay lifeless on the floor, not so much as a finger twitch in response to the Gods' desperate efforts to save him. Athene stopped her breaths.

'He's gone,' she said quietly, as Zeus put a heavy hand on her shoulder.

The Gods stood in a solemn circle around Elliot's cold body. They hung their heads as Virgo started to sob into Zeus's side. Unable to stand it any more, a tear-stained Aphrodite forced her way to Elliot's side.

'CALL THAT A KISS OF LIFE!' she screamed wildly, pushing her father and sister out of the way. 'Come on Elly, time to come home!'

And with a tearful sob, Aphrodite lifted Elliot's head from the ground and planted an enormous kiss square on his pale lips. She cradled Elliot to her chest, crying uncontrollably as she rocked him back and forth on her knees.

The Gods hung their heads as Elliot lay limply in Aphrodite's arms. Everything was silent, the still air broken only by Virgo's heaving sobs as she looked helplessly at the body of her friend. Zeus pulled her to him.

'He's at peace,' he said gently to the bereft young girl.

'He's been through enough,' said Athene, biting back the tears that shone from her brown eyes.

'He's a hero,' said Hades, shaking his head at the boy he never got to know.

'He's blushing,' said Persephone, peering intently at the boy in Aphrodite's arms.

Everyone craned their necks to stare at Elliot's face. Persephone was right – the face that had been a sickly shade of grey just moments before was becoming steadily more scarlet, as if it were being filled from the chin with cherryade.

'Elly!' cried Aphrodite. 'Elly, are you there?'

With an almighty gasp, Elliot came spluttering back to life, sitting bolt upright as he took the deep breaths of living air that his body so desperately needed.

'Elliot!' screamed Virgo, freeing herself from Zeus's embrace and hurtling towards her friend, knocking him flying with a diving hug and impulsively kissing him on the cheek with relief.

'I preferred it when she did it,' croaked Elliot, still gasping for air and now rubbing a sore head from Virgo's enthusiastic welcome.

'Elly!' screamed Aphrodite, throwing herself on the ground as well to hug him senseless, smothering his face with grateful kisses.

'Give the boy some air for goodness' sake,' said a relieved Athene, wiping a tear from her eye. 'Oh, what the heck,' she added as she too threw herself at the pile of people on the floor and gave Elliot a delighted squeeze.

'How did you find him?' Zeus asked Hades as they looked at the joyful huddle on the ground.

'Let's just say I know some people, who know some

people, who used to be people,' said Hades, pulling Persephone to him. 'When Thanatos showed up in my old neighbourhood with a mortal, I was always gonna hear about it.'

'I thought you wanted to stay out of it,' said Hermes.

'You kidding me?' said Persephone. 'That creep burned down our casino. This is poisonal now.'

Zeus looked over at Elliot, who had finally been allowed to his feet. He answered Elliot's guilty glance with a reassuring smile. Now was not the time for words. Or at least, not those ones.

'I'm starving,' said Elliot. 'Any chance of some lunch?'

Christmas Eve came around in a flash and although everyone was grateful for Elliot's safe return, the imminent loss of Home Farm weighed heavily on their hearts.

'It's only a house, Elly,' said Aphrodite as the clock ticked towards the midday deadline for Patricia's purchase.

'It's our home,' said Elliot. 'We have nowhere else.'

The Gods looked helplessly at each other as Elliot went to sit next to Josie and explain what was about to happen.

Right on cue at 11.55am, Patricia Porshley-Plum tottered into the farm, still smarting from the smack on her bum that the gate had administered on the way in.

'Happy Chrimbles Cutie-pudding!' shrieked Patricia Porshley-Plum, forcing her way into the house.

'It's not midday,' said Elliot angrily, looking at the grandfather clock. 'It's not yours yet.'

'Details, details my Pookie. Well, well, well – isn't this quite the party?' said Patricia, eyeing up the fuming immortals. 'Aren't you going to introduce me?'

'These are some distant relatives from Greece,' Elliot mumbled quickly.

'Aw, that's lovely dear, just lovely. It's so important to make lovely memories. And this will be a lovely memory of your last Christmas at Home Farm.'

'I don't . . . I can't . . . what . . . ?' started Josie, as Aphrodite put a comforting hand on her shoulder.

'Please,' said Elliot frantically to the Gods. 'Do something . . . anything.'

'We can't break mortal laws,' said Zeus sadly.

'We can break their snotty noses though,' said Aphrodite, her beautiful face screwed up in hatred as she made for Patricia over the other side of the room. Athene held her back.

'I'll handle this,' she said calmly approaching Patricia.

'*You miserable, twisted, odious . . . gorgon fart!*' Athene screamed. 'Why I should take this contract and . . .'

Zeus quickly clamped his hands over Elliot's ears to spare the boy from the torrent of filth that spewed out of Athene's mouth. But from the hand gestures alone, Elliot could gather that whatever Athene was suggesting was going to be extremely energetic, very uncomfortable and Mrs Porshley-Plum was going to be doing it rather a lot for a very long time.

'. . . *until it falls off!*' screamed Athene, taking her first breath for two minutes.

'Charming my dear,' said Patricia, unmoved by Athene's outburst. 'But in three minutes, I will own this farm. And there's nothing you can do about it.'

'You're a monster,' boomed Zeus.

'You're a witch,' hissed Aphrodite.

'You're on the telly,' yelled Hermes, as Patricia's needle nose appeared on the screen.

'What the devil?' huffed Patricia, as Hermes turned the volume on the local news report higher.

'. . . and finally, a lovely Christmas miracle to roast your chestnuts as we cross live to Little Motbury for a special announcement from local businesswoman Patricia Porshley-Plum,' said the newsreader as the screen switched to a press conference outside Patricia's house.

'Wait! That's not me!' cried Patricia as her identical twin started to speak.

'This time of year has caused me to reflect on my selfish and greedy ways,' the onscreen Patricia started. 'I realise that by slavishly pursuing my own wealth, I have hurt the people of this community, people I am in a position to help.'

'Is that slime coming out of her nose?' said Hermes, squinting at Patricia's high definition hooter.

'But, but, but . . .' stammered the Patricia in the room, regretting the second sherry she'd had her butler pour at breakfast.

'And so I've decided to give back to the community from which I've taken so much,' TV Patricia continued.

'I've decided to donate all of my vast wealth to charity.'

'NOOOOOOOOOOO!' screamed Patricia as her mobile phone started to ring.

'And furthermore,' TV Patricia continued, scratching her bottom, 'I'd like to open my house to the poorest members of our community, to become a hostel for those in need of shelter and a place to get back on their feet.'

'WHAT – WHAT – WHAT DO YOU WANT?' she screamed down the phone as the grandfather clock struck midday. 'Bankrupt? No – that's not possible. Of course there are sufficient funds in my account, it's only twenty pounds! What do you mean forfeit the sale? I can't lose Home Farm! I WANT IT!'

Elliot looked more closely at the picture on the TV. At this range, Patricia's nose definitely looked more like a snout. And there was definitely a bit of slime just under her left nostril.

'Finally, I'd like to take this opportunity to apologise to those I've wronged,' said Mammon in his dissembled form. 'I've had reason to reflect on my behaviour lately and never again will I be the greedy idiot I've been my whole life. Now please – come and enjoy my wine cellar – the first 10 inside get a free bottle of '83 Petrus!'

'No – not the Petrus!' screamed Patricia, running for the door as Athene tore up the house sale paperwork. 'Stop – all you disgusting poor people, get your impoverished fingers off my lovely things. Stop! Stop!'

'Wait a minute!' shouted Elliot as Patricia headed for her wine cellar. 'You forgot something.'

He rummaged around in his pocket and pulled out a twenty pound note.

'Here,' he said. 'Now we're even.'

'Aaaaaaaaaargh!' wailed Patricia Porshley-Plum as she raced out of the door and out of Elliot's life.

Because that was the last Elliot ever saw of Patricia Horse's Bum.

Christmas Day was a celebration like none Elliot had seen before. The Christmas dinner was vast and by late afternoon, Elliot and the immortals were flopping around a table the size of a tennis court, piled with enough food to feed a small country.

'I'm stuffed,' groaned Hermes, throwing down the remains of his third piece of Yule log. 'I hope no-one needs me to fly anywhere today. I'd never take off.'

Elliot happily tucked into his third bowl of Christmas pudding, the sling on his arm from his healing collarbone doing nothing to stop him from feeding his enthusiastic appetite.

'Who wants to pull another cracker?' said Aphrodite to a chorus of groans from the group, who were tired of having water sprayed at them or a custard pie thrown at them from the trick crackers she had created. 'Spoilsports,' she pouted, pulling one by herself and being showered in rose-scented pink glitter.

Elliot looked over at Mum, who was happily chatting to Hades about life in the gambling industry. Elliot's mind flashed back to the previous Christmas, when Grandad had been so ill he couldn't make it downstairs for Christmas dinner, so he and Mum sat around his bed with their tiny portions of cold turkey. He wished his Grandad were here to see the cheer around the table, but knew that he'd be happy just to know that he and Mum were safe and being so well looked after.

'Pressie time!' screamed Hermes, flying over to the giant Christmas tree, which was not only surrounded by mountains of presents but also topped with a real fairy. Hermes sifted through the gifts, flying them around the room to their intended recipients until everyone had a pile at least as tall as themselves to open.

As the room filled with grateful coos and aaahs, Elliot set to work on the particularly huge mound of gifts in front of him. Athene had given him an encyclopedia that not only contained every single subject known to man – and a few that weren't – but also projected moving holograms of each subject when you opened the page, much to Aphrodite's delight, who immediately looked up the rudest thing she could think of.

From the love Goddess herself, Elliot received a box of potions to cause all kinds of mischief, from growing excess body hair, to making someone only speak backwards – as well as another wishing pearl that the Goddess had hidden in the box, putting her fingers to her lips with a wink as Elliot quietly slipped it into his pocket.

The gifts went on and on – a designer shirt from Hermes that changed colour to match your outfit, a pen from Zeus that threw thunderbolts with a click of the lid, even his own poker set from Hades, which made sure that he would always get the winning hand.

But his favourite gift came from Hephaestus, who quietly dropped a knotted handkerchief in Elliot's lap as he left the celebrations.

''Appy Christmas,' the blacksmith mumbled as he left the busy farmhouse for the peace and quiet of his forge.

Elliot sensed the blacksmith would rather not see his gift being opened, so waited until he had left before unknotting the handkerchief in his lap. Inside sat his grandfather's watch, restored to perfect working order and now complete with a set of pencil-scrawled instructions about the improvements Hephaestus had made. Elliot wasn't sure he'd ever need a watch that could unlock any combination safe or help him climb the side of buildings, but he was truly touched by Hephaestus's gesture. Virgo leaned over and stole a piece of Christmas cake from Elliot's plate.

'Oi – that's mine!' shouted Elliot.

'Your rules,' smiled Virgo, swallowing it whole. 'Not mine.'

'Do you have a minute?' asked Zeus. 'I think I need to walk off that fourth plate of turkey.'

Elliot strapped his Grandad's watch to his wrist and rose

to leave with Zeus, who took him out of the house and up into the fields, which were still thriving with Demeter's exotic fruit and vegetables. It was slightly odd seeing giant pineapple trees covered in a thin layer of snow, but they appeared to be in rude health in the frosty field.

'How are you, dear boy?' Zeus asked Elliot. 'Really?'

'I'm fine,' said Elliot honestly. 'Don't think I'll be playing tennis anytime soon, but I'm fine.'

'You're a hero, Elliot,' said Zeus. 'I don't know many people who could have resisted Thanatos like you did. You're an exceptional young man, Elliot Hooper.'

'I haven't stopped him though, have I?' said Elliot, voicing the doubt that had been nagging his mind since his return from the Underworld.

'No,' said Zeus softly. 'Unfortunately Thanatos has as many allies as enemies and it won't be long before someone comes to his aid – indeed, I suspect they already have. But don't you underestimate what you did. If you hadn't, Thanatos would have abused the Earth Stone and I dread to think what that would have meant for your fellow mortals. You've saved them all.'

'I'm sorry I betrayed you,' said Elliot, desperate to unburden himself from the guilt he'd been dragging around for weeks. 'I didn't think I had any choice.'

'But you did make a choice. The right one,' smiled Zeus, producing the Earth Stone from his pocket. 'I never thought I'd see this again.'

'What are you going to do with it now?' asked Elliot.

'I was going to ask you the same thing,' said Zeus as he came to a halt, his blue eyes meeting Elliot's.

'What do you mean?' said Elliot as Zeus placed the Earth Stone in his palm. 'Why are you . . . ?'

'Thanatos is afraid of you,' said Zeus, wrapping Elliot's fingers around the stone. 'You're the only person who can keep it safe.'

'Are you sure?' said Elliot, taking the beautiful diamond in his hand. 'Thanks.'

'Don't thank me yet,' said Zeus. 'Guarding the stone won't be easy.'

'You're telling me,' said Elliot. 'The kids at school would nick your gym socks if you left them for a second, it's going to be a nightmare keeping them away from this.'

'Not exactly what I meant,' said Zeus. 'The Chaos Stones don't only manipulate the elements. They can manipulate the person controlling them if you let them. Each stone brings with it a different vice – look at Mammon. The Earth stone promotes greed, the Water Stone – fear, the Air Stone – discord and the Fire Stone – anger. They corrupted a powerful daemon like Thanatos – be careful they don't consume you.'

'So you're saying I could end up like Gollum?' gasped Elliot.

'What? Running your own successful chain of high street jewellers?' said Zeus. 'No, I meant you'd go mad.'

'Right,' said Elliot holding his diamond up to the light.

'This is serious, Elliot,' said Zeus, in a harsher tone than Elliot had heard him use before. 'The stone will do its very best to corrupt you – don't let it. Keep it in this amulet around your neck and only ever use its powers if your life depends on it. Every time you use the power of the stone, it will gain more power over you. Be wise, Elliot. And be careful.'

Elliot took the small golden necklace disdainfully. It was a battered looking thing, a circular pendant divided into four equal parts hanging from the gold chain. Elliot had never been one for jewellery and didn't fancy wearing his diamond around his neck. But he also knew himself well enough to realise that if left to him, this precious stone would be lost or put in the washing machine before the week was through.

He held the Earth Stone to the amulet, wondering how it was going to fit, being at least ten times larger than the space allowed for it in the necklace. But as if hearing his thoughts, as soon as the diamond touched the amulet, it shrank into its place, gleaming brightly as it filled a perfect quarter of the locket.

'We've still got three more stones to find,' said Elliot, tucking the pendant inside his T-shirt.

'Yes we do,' said Zeus. 'And once we've all had a bit of time to get our heads together, we'll start looking for the next one. And the one after that. We'll beat Thanatos in the end, don't you worry.'

Elliot said nothing, but desperately wanted to share Zeus's optimism.

'We'd better get back to the house,' said Zeus. 'Your mother wants to watch the Queen's speech and I must admit so do I. She's a fine looking lady that monarch of yours.'

'Better not let her hear you say that,' said Elliot. 'She'd ninja-kick you into the middle of next week.'

Zeus chortled happily as they set off back to the farm, where everyone had already gathered around the telly on the plush armchairs. Virgo signalled to Elliot to come and sit by her, which he did with a heavy thud.

'Listen,' she said nervously after a short pause. 'There's been something I've been meaning to say to you. Something important.'

Elliot shuddered and gritted his teeth. Something about Christmas brought out the mushy in people and girls were the worst of the lot. He waited to hear Virgo's heartfelt declaration of love and wondered how he was going to let her down gently.

She punched him in his good arm. Hard.

'You are such a gorgon fart,' she said.

'Shut up,' said Elliot.

'You shut up,' said Virgo, the two of them jostling each other for space on the sofa, neither seeing the smile on the other one's face.

'Shhh – it's starting,' said Athene as the Queen took to the screen, wishing her subjects a Merry Christmas.

Elliot listened to Her Majesty's good wishes for the following year with mixed feelings. On the one hand, he had no idea what the next year would bring him. The Gods were a huge help, but he still knew that Mum's health was on a downhill slope. Thanatos wouldn't be happy until the Chaos Stones were his and Elliot was lying dead at his feet. The Gods could only protect him so far and Elliot knew that he was going to have to keep his wits about him if he wanted to be here next Christmas.

But for the first time in a long time, Elliot was also filled with hope. He had spent so much of his life facing an uncertain future that he knew he could handle it. And more importantly, this time he had something he had never had before. He didn't know what the next year might hold for him, but one thing was for sure. Whatever life had in store for him, whatever the future held, for the first time in his life Elliot Hooper knew that from now on, he would face it with his friends.

A knock at the door boomed through the house.

'What the deuce is it now?' said Zeus. 'It's busier than Odysseus's travel agency here today. I'll go.'

Hauling his bulk off the sofa, Zeus padded out of the room into the hallway and round to the front door. The others listened nervously, poised for action as he unlatched the brass latch and pulled the creaking door open.

'Happy Chris—' he started, before the visitor on the other side of the door stunned him into silence.

'Dear Gods!' he stammered eventually, terrified from the hallway. The other Gods leapt to their feet.

'This cannot be! How in all the Heavens did you find me here . . . ?'

THE END

FOR NOW

People I Need To Thank. And Also Want To.

MY FIRST THANKS must go to a writer I only wish I could have met. The works of Roald Dahl enchanted and inspired me as a young thing and they are as wonderful to read as a mother as they were to read as a child. And I will always check my beard for mouldy cornflakes.

To my editor Lucy V Hay, for having eagle eyes and bacon. You have made this so much better and I love/hate you for picking me up on it all.

To my designer Becky Jeffries, thank you for having all the skills that I don't and being better than me at the few that I do.

To my illustrator Mark Beech, for setting the tone on and off the page. You are wonderful and I thank you for your brilliance.

To John O'Farrell and the NewsBiscuit crowd. Thank you for helping me to find my funny. And for laughing in all the right places.

I have the best friends in the world. To you all.

To my beautiful babies, who must share Mummy with

all the people I make up in my head. And my writing career. I love you to the moon and stars. Especially after 7.30am.

To my husband. You said I was a writer the first day we met. So thanks for marrying me anyway. You rock.

And to you, for buying this book. Thank you for supporting The Immortal Chaos Series – check out www.storystew.org for updates on future releases.

If you've enjoyed *Who Let the Gods Out?* please review me on Amazon and Goodreads.

If you haven't, please write to your local MP.

IMMORTAL CHAOS

will return in

2015 AD . . .

SNORDLESNOT!!!

Creative Writing Workshops

with

Mary Evans

What are the ingredients for a great story?

How can we make our stories taste even better?

My fun, interactive and downright daft creative writing workshops will tell you how!

Let Mary Evans come and cook you a Story Stew at your school or event.

Visit www.storystew.org for more details, or drop me a line at

info@storystew.org